Live Ever

Bailey Ball

For Cathy, the brightest star in my sky

Bright Star, Would I were as steadfast as though art –

Not in lone splendour hung aloft the night

And watching, with eternal lids apart,

Like nature's patient, sleepless Erimite,

The moving waters at their priestlike task

Of pure ablution round earth's human shores,

Or gazing on the new soft-fallen mask

Of snow upon the mountains and the moors –

No – yet still steadfast, still unchangeable,

Pillow'd upon my fair love's ripening breast,

To feel forever it's soft fall and swell,

Awake forever in a sweet unrest,

Still, still to hear her tender-taken breath,

And so live ever – or else swoon to death.

~ Sonnet by John Keats Written on a
Blank Page in Shakespeare's Poems, facing 'A
Lover's Complaint'

Part One

"Bright Star, would I were as steadfast as thou art"

~ Sonnet by John Keats
Written on a Blank Page in
Shakespeare's Poems facing *A Lover's Complaint*

If you had asked them a year ago, most people probably would have described me as a bit of a perfectionist. Well, actually that is the understatement of the century. I would agonize over every decision, harboring the certain desire for flawlessness, which when not achieved had the potential to drive me clinically insane. My parents always laughed about it and told all of their friends that they never had to worry about disciplining me because I would punish myself before they even had the opportunity.

I always got perfect grades every term. But, even though it was my absolute favorite subject, poetry had been the one course in which I always got B's, only managing to get an A for the final grade by doing every extra credit assignment. However, there was one semester when I just couldn't pull it off. I remember my teacher handing me my report card; my heart pounding with fear since I knew I was just on the cusp. I opened the envelope and unfolded the piece of paper to see my biggest fear realized. Next to the course listing for Romantic Poetry was what I then considered to be the worst letter in the English language. The B glared back at me. Taunting me. Ruining everything.

I have a vivid memory of coming home that day, taking my report card out of my backpack, crumbling it into a ball, locking it in my lockbox, and chucking it out of my second story bedroom window with as much force as I could humanly muster. My mom, seeing it fly across the kitchen window as she was sweeping the floor, came upstairs to check on me and make sure that everything was okay.

I screamed out that I didn't deserve dinner and that I would be in my bedroom with the lights off until the next morning when I would go back to school and try harder. I cried into my pillow for hours. I wish I were exaggerating.

While all of my friends were out partying, I spent most of my time shelled up in my room studying. But today was the day it was all going to pay off. All of the stress-induced ulcers from school had not been in vain and I was starting a position at Pendleton & Rowe in Washington, D.C.

I would be working as an attorney under the notorious Penelope Pendleton, one of the world's most successful and renowned corporate litigation attorneys and one of the firm's founding partners. As I happily walked down the street towards my new life, I felt like the world was at my fingertips.

I walked through the halls past the rows of cubicles, smiling with butterflies dancing in my stomach. Attorneys were furiously rustling through paperwork, typing, and taking heated phone calls. Finally, I reached a sleek, modern door made of frosted glass with a platinum nameplate next to it engraved with "Penelope Pendleton, Esq." I knocked softly before opening the door and timidly entered the room.

A very well dressed woman screaming into a Bluetooth earpiece greeted me.

"I don't care who the fuck you have to jerk off to get that document Jeff, just get it to me before the end of the day or I'll take your tiny balls into my hand and crush them until they crumble into sand. Now get the fuck off the phone and go do something right for once in your life and do NOT call me back with anything but good news." She slammed the phone down and turned around to face me.

"Who are you and what are you doing in my office?" She snapped.

I was so shocked that I couldn't form words.

She drummed her fingers on her desk and raised her eyebrows in a way that I knew meant I should offer an immediate response.

"Um, Ms. Pendleton, I'm Emma Thorne, I interviewed last week? Your receptionist called me and told me I was offered a position and to report here on Monday. She just sent me back so that you could, assign me my desk and give me my first assignment."

Penelope clutched the middle of her forehead and shook her head. After a deep sigh she said, "That's because she's an incompetent moron."

She turned to her phone and pressed a button buzzing an extension. A timid sounding girl answered, "Yes, Ms. Pendleton?"

"Lily? Would you be a dear and tell Amy that she's fired. Then please post a job listing for a new receptionist. And can someone get me a Goddamn espresso?" She released the button and collapsed into her large leather chair. I'm no expert, but if I had to put money on it I would guess that chair cost at least ten thousand dollars. She started rifling through paperwork as I stood there awkwardly. She looked up and glared up at me with narrowed eyes as she lowered her glasses down her nose.

"And why, may I ask, are you still here?" She said slowly and deliberately.

"Um, I'm sorry ma'am but I don't know where my desk is. I'd be happy to report to it right away and get to work!" I tried to sound alert and eager in hopes of winning her over.

She stared at me for a moment and said, "Well of course you will be assisting me. That's why you're here. Your desk is right outside. If you'd stopped to read the nameplate you would have known that. Now please, be a dear and get out of my office."

She looked back down at the stack of papers and waved her hand to signal that I should leave immediately. After hearing her vivid description of her capability to reduce a man's testicles to tiny particles, I decided I should probably leave, with haste.

I closed the door softly behind me and took a deep breath.

"You shouldn't have just waltzed right in there," I heard a sassy voice declare from behind me. I turned around to see a plain, dark-haired girl with a scowl on her face that looked as though it was probably permanent. She was sitting at one of two desks that faced each other adjacent to the door to Penelope's office.

I paused for a moment and resisted the urge to snap back at her. "Oh, sorry. It's my first day, I didn't know."

I somehow managed a genuine-looking smile and pleasantly said, "I'm Emma, by the way."

She sat down fiercely in her seat without introducing herself. I glanced over at her nameplate. 'Valerie Warren, First Assistant to Ms. Pendleton'. Valerie always sounded like a bitchy name to me. I already had a bad feeling about this.

I spun around to face my own desk. Directions for how to access my computer lay on a printed sheet on my desk. I followed the instructions and logged on before opening my new email account. I already had fifty emails. I glanced up at the clock. It was 7:15 a.m.

––––––––––

I left the office at 8:30 p.m. feeling exhausted. Thankful that at least the workday was over, I made my way to Dupont Circle to meet my two best friends, who had invited me to get some drinks to toast to my first day at the new job.

While I had been a neurotic perfectionist growing up, they, by contrast, were those carefree, yet somehow still extremely successful people that everyone adores and wishes to emulate. My best friend was Scarlett Parker. Scarlett was just one of those effortlessly beautiful people. Her gorgeous, shimmering blonde hair was outdone only by her sparkling emerald eyes, and - of course - her perfect body. As a thriving P.R. representative for a major news network, she got to travel all over the world while the shows were filming and then proceed to plan every swanky premiere once she returned.

While she was actually quite brilliant, I'm sure at least a teensy part of her success was her ability to entrance any man and wrap them tightly around her finger until they followed her every command. But, in spite of it all, she was always a great friend to me. While she had a constant revolving door of admirers, I was always confident that our friendship was a constant in her life.

My other best friend was Tommy Alcott. Tommy's Harvard degree, not to mention the connections of his multi-millionaire father, had gotten him a job working for the Senate that had received over five hundred applicants in the course of one day. He was model-level handsome and one of those naturally charming people that everyone couldn't help but love, including a constant stream of women. While Tommy pretty much always had a "lady friend", (girlfriend being far too strong of a word), he also always made sure to set aside time just for me. In a lot of ways, I was actually closer to him than I was with Scarlett. He even kicked a few girls to the curb when they got too jealous and tried to stop him from seeing me.

The three of us met in sixth grade and had, against all odds, remained incredibly close, even while attending different colleges. As luck would have it, we all reconvened in D.C. They were the two people in the world I could be completely myself around. We never went a week without seeing each other and I always had so much fun with them, laughing hysterically as we reminisced about all of the crazy adventures, inside jokes, and great times we had had growing up.

There was just one teeny, tiny problem. I just happened to be madly, hopelessly, pathetically, soul-crushingly in love with Tommy. I had been ever since I first saw his thick, sandy hair, and gorgeous green eyes, and adorable smile. From then on, it was all over. I was doomed to pine after him forever.

Given his role in fundraising, Tommy was also invited to tons of swanky galas and exclusive parties. He always took me along and proudly introduced me to everyone as his best friend and the 'coolest girl ever'. But, because I had known him forever, I was now unfortunately eternally stuck in the friend-zone. I had become a completely non-sexual entity in his eyes, like a sister, or a goldfish.

After a nerve wrecking, stressful first day at work, I was desperate for a drink and to kick back and relax with them for a while. I walked through the door to the restaurant and saw them sitting at the bar. Scarlett was holding a Manhattan as Tommy clasped a tumbler of scotch. He waved as Scarlett ran up to me enthusiastically.

"So? How was it?" she asked, hugging me tightly.

"Ha, well, let's just put it this way, the first words out of my new boss's mouth were "Who are you and what are you doing in my office?"

"Yikes," Scarlett responded, clenching her teeth. "Well, at least there's no way it was as bad as my first day of work."

I laughed out loud thinking about when the three of us met to hear all about Scarlett's first day at the network. It had been a series of disasters that, I'll put it this way, culminated in her spilling a giant mug of hot coffee all over Anderson Cooper.

"First days are supposed to be terrible Emma," she assured me.

"Yeah, remember mine?" Tommy asked. Scarlett and I both laughed at the thought of Tommy recounting his first day at the Senate when he walked into the supply closet and found a married, quite high profile politician in quite a compromising position with an intern.

Tommy put his arm around me, "Don't sweat it, Thorne," he said, smiling and making my heart melt, "If someone's yelling at you it means they've noticed you. At least she's not ignoring you completely."

He had a point, one that I was really having trouble believing at that moment, but still a valid point nonetheless.

"Well, let's just hope tomorrow when she yells at me, at least she'll know my name."

"That's the spirit," said Tommy, flagging down the bartender, "Now let's get you a drink!"

He ordered me a pomegranate martini, which he knew was my favorite.

"So, what are you going to do once you take the legal world by storm?" Tommy asked, leaning in towards me.

"Hah," I said back, scoffing. "Yeah right. I'll probably be making copies for the entire first year."

"Emma, you are so much more talented than you give yourself credit for," he said, sincerely. "You just need to be confident. I know you have great ideas. Just make sure you pipe up and say something and they'll know how brilliant you really are."

I felt my cheeks flush as I turned beet red again.

Four martinis later the room was practically spinning, but it wasn't enough to stop the nerves about returning to the office the next day – especially with a hangover.

"I think I need to head out guys," I said, admitting defeat.

"No!" lamented Scarlett, "Just one more drink!"

"Really, I can't," I insisted, "but I'll see you guys this weekend!"

"Fine," Scarlett said, rolling her eyes and giving me a hug. Tommy stood up and came over to give me a hug. As he wrapped his arms around me, I breathed in his clean scent. Tommy somehow always smelled exactly how you'd picture one of those perfectly clean-cut Brooks Brothers models smelling. I closed my eyes and inhaled deeply, melting into his chest. Then, he pulled back and put both his hands on my shoulders.

"Tomorrow's another day," he said, flashing me that smirk that always made me swoon, before grabbing Scarlett playfully and yelling "Another round!" to the bartender.

I smiled back at him before snapping back to reality and remembering how early I needed to be awake the next morning.

"Bye guys!" I said, taking advantage of the fact that they were momentarily allowing me to go home without any further argument, "Thanks for the drinks!!"

As I walked home, I tried to stay optimistic, but I was worried I'd made a horrible, horrible mistake starting at that law firm. I hoped that Penelope was just in a really bad mood that day and tomorrow would be much better.

When I got back to my apartment, I got into my comfy P.J.s and snuggled into my bed. With a sigh I picked up the book of John Keats poems from my bedside table.

Despite the hard academic track I'd taken my whole life, it was always poetry where I found the answers I really needed. I've read all of the greats. I adore the breathlessness that overtook me whenever I dove headfirst into William Blake. The powerful emotions I felt when delving into William Wordsworth. The escapism that accompanied drinking up every last work of Percy Bysshe Shelly.

However, no matter how many greats I discovered, my favorite was unquestionably John Keats. I remember feeling changed forever the first time I read his poems. I had gone to the bookstore and bought a cheap copy of the course's required text: *The Complete Poems of John Keats.*

In the years since, the pages had gotten so worn that it was hard to make out some of the words and practically every page was earmarked. But, without that book, I never would have made it through many of the challenges I faced throughout school.

I picked it up and began to read, escaping into the beautiful words of my favorite poet.

Ah, happy, happy boughs! that cannot shed

Your leaves, nor ever bid the Spring adieu;

And, happy melodist, unwearied,

For ever piping songs for ever new;

More happy love! more happy, happy love!

For ever warm and still to be enjoy'd,

For ever panting, and for ever young;

All breathing human passion far above,

I glanced at my alarm clock, which read 2:15am and felt a pang of longing to join the lovers in their freedom from passing time. I thought back to Tommy and how I always wished I could stop time when we're together.

I couldn't help but get caught up in the hopeless fantasy of what it would be like to kiss him, to be with him. I wanted to run my hands through his sandy blonde hair and taste his sweet lips until when I came up for air I would open my eyes to see him smiling back at me.

I closed the book and turned out the light. Today was just a bad day. Everyone had bad days. Tomorrow would be better.

"When I have fears that I may cease to be,

Before my pen has glean'd my teeming brain"

~ *When I Have Fears that I May Cease to Be*
1818

I woke up the next morning to find my fear of a terrible hangover realized. I cursed Scarlett and Tommy as I dragged myself down the street, made my way to the office, and sat down at my desk. I had been sitting in my chair for all of thirty seconds before Penelope burst through the door, marched down the hall and said, "You two, conference room. Now." She streaked down the corridor with incredible speed, never taking her eyes from her iPhone. I paused for a moment in a bit of shock before standing up quickly and started practically jogging down the hall to keep up with her. Valerie led in front, leaving me in her dust.

We entered a huge conference room through beautifully frosted glass panel surrounds. Inside were a gorgeous, shiny black table, state-of-the-art telecoms, five L.C.D. screens, and more fancy chairs.

The room was already filled with lots of people, dressed solely in black, organizing huge stacks of paper in front of them and powering up iPads. Valerie and I took seats toward the back as Penelope seated herself in the grand chair at the head of the table.

"Alright, let's get this over with. I've been going over our productivity records and it's absolutely abysmal. Neanderthals could get research done faster than you people. We need to think efficiency. Someone shock me and actually give me a competent idea for once."

The entire room instantly began furiously typing on iPads in search of answers while Penelope rested her head on her hand, tapping her fingers on the table impatiently.

"Today, people."

The room stayed silent for a few more minutes as everyone kept their eyes glued to their screens. I had an idea, but was too terrified to speak. I glanced around the room nervously to make sure that no one looked as though they were getting ready to pipe up. When I cleared my throat everyone turned and looked at me. I decided I should probably announce my name since it was extremely clear that no one in this room knew who the hell I was.

"Um, hi everyone, I'm Emma Thorne. I just started yesterday as an attorney," I said, shaking.

Penelope was glaring at me.

"One of my professors in law school spoke of the potential benefits of databases that would archive existing case files and provide instant access to details from any past cases using simple key words. The start-up would require a computer programmer, but from there it would only be a matter of inputting data, which could be done in house, perhaps with interns."

Penelope remained silent for a moment before tilting her head to the side and narrowing her eyes. I was terrified of what was about to come next.

She finally opened her mouth and said, "Well, at least one of you has half a brain. Emily was it? Get on that. Anyway on to more of the usual bullshit..."

I actually felt happy, despite being called Emily. Maybe this wouldn't be so terrible after all.

At the end of the meeting Penelope approached me and I smiled broadly expecting a crumb of praise.

"So you'll get that done, Emily?"

"Yes, Miss Pendleton. I'll start hiring interns today. Err, my name is actually..."

"And why would we do that? You're capable of typing, are you not?"

"Oh," I stammered, caught off guard, "Of course, Ms. Pendleton. I'll get started on that right away."

Penelope strode out of the conference room eyes already back on her phone, leaving me shell-shocked and alone in the conference room. I had spent seven years forgoing a social life and studying my ass off to become a lawyer, and instead I had managed to volunteer myself to be a glorified receptionist on my second day? Actually, less than a receptionist, I was going to literally be copying words into a computer, something that required absolutely no brainpower. What had I gotten myself into?

"I think we may class the lawyer in the natural history of monsters."

~ Letter to George and Georgiana Keats
13 March 1819

From the day that Penelope assigned me to the database project, every day was the same. I got up, showered, went to work, and spent all day entering mindless information into the damn computer. Then I would go home, microwave myself some sad frozen meal, drink a glass of wine, and call it a night. Most days I was in the office by 7:00 a.m. and didn't leave until 10:00 or 11:00 at night.

To make matters worse, Valerie had been asked to directly assist Penelope in researching a huge copyright infringement case – which meant she was working late hours with me. Besides the horror of having to put up with her nastiness for over twelve hours a day, she couldn't help but shove in my face how much more interesting her project was. She would always bring up things to intentionally make me jealous like,

"Hey Thorne, have you ever heard of Weinstein v. Fuller? It is absolutely FASCINATING. I'm learning so much. Penelope is going to LOVE this report I'm writing. What number file are you inputting over there?"

She was so pedantic it was almost comical. Using the database I had created and telling me all about cases I practically knew by heart. Plus, she loved asking me about my progress so she could make some passive aggressive comment about my pace.

"Oh, that's great Thorne! Don't worry if you've only done one hundred entries today, I'm sure they were all DREADFULLY long descriptions. Maybe tomorrow will be a more productive day and you'll actually get back on schedule."

It took everything in me to feign pleasantness and not chuck my stapler at her face with as much strength as I could humanly muster.

Normally, by the time the weekend came around, I was either working or so exhausted that I spent the whole time collapsed in bed. I hated myself for suggesting this stupid idea in the first place. But that weekend I was determined to go out, get some fresh air, and have some fun.

As luck would have it, I had seen a listing in the community paper that the local theater was having a filming of Jane Campion's new film, *Bright Star*. The movie was a portrayal of Keats's love affair with Fanny Brawne.

I had been dying to go, but of course work had always gotten in the way. I thought it had already left all of the indie movie theaters, so I was psyched to see it was still playing at the E Street Cinema. I called Tommy to see if he wanted to come with me.

""Hmmm, is this a depressing artsy movies?"

"No!" I insisted, "It's one of the greatest love stories ever!" There was silence on the line "Um... the theater serves alcohol!" I said, hoping to lure him in another way.

"Ok, I'm in."

I smiled. I knew I could always count on him to come with me to these kinds of things, and even though I knew he would probably fall asleep in the movie. It was one of the things I always loved about him; he never acted like he was doing me a favor, or that he would rather be somewhere else. He was always just genuinely happy to see me.

Thirty minutes later, I met him in the lobby. He looked handsome as ever, and butterflies exploded in my stomach when he kissed me on the cheek.

The film was beautiful – it fully captured everything I had always imagined about their young love – their chemistry, their yearning, her longing and his devotion that had inspired so many letters and poems.

I really wished I had the time to devote to reading the couple's love letters. Even though my schedule was crazy and I was always exhausted, I could always manage to squeeze in a short poem before I passed out with the book on my face. But, the letters would take time. I would want to drink in every word. In that moment I vowed to read every one of them. I looked over at Tommy and felt happy for the first time that day.

Once Tommy had dropped me home (he always insisted on walking me right to the door), I opened my copy of Keats's poems, hoping to keep the momentum going and find something to help me escape the fact that I had another week of mindlessly typing on my keyboard ahead of me. I read an excerpt from a letter Keats wrote to Fanny on July 8, 1819:

> *I never knew before, what such a love as you have made me feel, was; I did not believe in it; my Fancy was afraid of it, lest it should burn me up. But if you will fully love me, though there may be some fire, 'twill not be more than we can bear when moistened and bedewed with Pleasures.*

I closed the book and fell asleep thinking of Tommy.

Months passed of hellishly sitting in my cubicle doggedly entering data, my only moments of happiness reserved for time spent with Tommy, Scarlett and Keats. The day I realized that I was finally, freaking finished I was so happy I actually went into the ladies room to allow myself to cry out of sheer relief. I went into Penelope's office to tell her the good news. She smiled at me and said, "Good job, Thorne. Tell Valerie to get started on planning the launch party."

The night of the launch gala arrived. Valerie arranged a huge party for anyone who was anyone in the entire District of Columbia. The party was being held at the Newseum, one of D.C.'s most coveted party venues. It must have cost an absolute fortune to rent. But, Penelope insisted on the Newseum for its representation of the marriage between high-tech and historical methods.

Even though I normally hated these things, I was actually excited for this one. Penelope Pendleton was going to acknowledge me in front of the entire firm and some of D.C.'s most influential people. I'm sure it would only be a brief mention of my name (which, hopefully with a prepared, written speech she would get right this time) but, nevertheless, everyone would know about my hard work and what I achieved. Maybe someone in the crowd would be impressed and recognize me the next time I went on a job interview. Maybe I could finally get out of this hellhole and start doing what I had gone to law school to do – engage in work that mattered.

I had, uncharacteristically, bought an expensive dress with matching shoes and a gorgeous clutch purse. My ensemble cost an amount that was galaxies beyond any outfit I had ever purchased in my life. But I wanted to look pretty, and more importantly, memorable, when Penelope publically recognized me at the gala. I decided on a dress with a modest cut and shimmering silver fabric that the sales woman assured me would make my blue eyes sparkle.

When I entered the Newseum, one of my male co-workers approached me and said, "Wow, Emma, you actually look good tonight! You should dress up more often!" I had no idea how to react to such a backhanded compliment, but I decided I'd take it.

I did a few rounds of fake pleasantries while trying my best not to spill any champagne on my dress. I even refused when the waiter carrying a tray of Peking duck pastries made his way to me. The last thing I needed was a giant hoisin sauce stain on my dress. So, I hadn't eaten anything and kept nursing the same glass of champagne.

While a stain on my dress would have been bad, slurred speech from a liquid dinner would surely be worse. I stood there trying to keep it together until the presentation, chatting with boring people while gradually becoming more anxious.

After another hour, Penelope climbed the stairs to the stage and tapped the microphone to gather everyone's attention. This was it. I was so nervously excited. The waiter brushed by just in time for me to grab a fresh flute of champagne to toast at the end of Penelope's speech.

"Good evening distinguished guests. Welcome to an exciting evening representing great innovation for my company and the legal world at large!"

It was amazing how eloquent she could sound when she put her mind to it. It was strange to hear her get through two whole sentences without a profuse amount of cursing. She looked stunning. She wore a plumb dress with diamond drop earrings and a matching necklace that if I had seen it on one of my colleagues I would have assumed it was cubic zirconia from a fashion-store chain, but on Penelope I knew was real.

I had to admit; I could see why people who didn't have to work with her found her so entrancing. She looked like the embodiment of a strong, independent, brilliant woman who exuded all of the qualities one would expect from someone as successful as she was. I forgot for a minute how much I hated her and took a moment to reconsider everything I could learn from her.

"I want to thank you all for joining us tonight as we introduce an endeavor that will forever change the way we practice law."

A quiet round of applause spread through the large audience. I hadn't expected this much praise, especially an indication that my project would revolutionize the process of law. Penelope went through a visual presentation highlighting the user-friendly input, research, and search pages I had spent the last few months of my life eating, sleeping, and breathing from dawn till dusk.

It looked amazing up on the big screen, and the narrative that Penelope put together made it sound so groundbreaking. I looked around at the influential people around me and they looked so intrigued and impressed. I swelled with pride and took a sip of my champagne to toast myself for all of my hard work.

Penelope wrapped up the presentation by declaring, "I think we can all agree that this will be one of many lasting legacies to come from Pendleton & Rowe." She took off her new glasses and cleared her throat before leaning towards the microphone once again.

"Finally, I must take a moment to ensure that I thank one particular individual for helping me make tonight a reality."

I made sure to stand up straight and put on my humble, yet charming smile and hold my champagne flute as elegantly as humanly possible.

"I need to extend my deepest gratitude to my wonderful first assistant, Valerie Warren, for putting together such a fabulous soiree at such an inspiring venue for us all to experience this exciting innovation together. Please join me in raising a toast to this new venture and to a fabulous evening!"

She took a sip from her glass before handing it to a man behind her and exiting the stage. The music started back up and everyone went back to his or her respective conversations.

Well, son of a bitch.

"Here lies one whose name was writ in water"

~ Text engraved on Keats's Gravestone

Rome, Italy

24 February 1821

The next day, I woke to the sounds of sirens passing by my window. I glanced at the clock; it was already 10:30 a.m. My mind slowly came into focus and I remembered disaster that was last night.

I felt no motivation to get out of bed – all of that work, all of that sacrifice, for nothing. I knew Penelope was an absolute snake, but even I hadn't expect her to do something this deliberately cruel.

I took my pillow and put it over my face, wondering if I could smother myself to death before the survival instinct kicked in and forced me to stop. So, instead I screamed into the pillow before throwing it across the room.

I was just another name written in water; so fleeting that in no time, any indication that I had even existed would be wiped away. I wondered what the point of it all was.

When I came out of the shower, I had a text from Scarlett with the address for the new brunch spot where I was meeting her. I trekked across town quickly and managed to make it on time. The hostess escorted us to an adorably decorated table underneath a beautiful wall sculpture covered in ivy, next to a window looking out onto a picturesque view of downtown D.C. on what was an absolutely perfect day. Scarlett was already there, waiting for me.

"What did I tell you, is this place amazing or what?" Scarlett gushed, standing to give me a kiss on the cheek.

I had to hand it to her; this almost outdid every other glamorous brunch spot we'd been to together over the years.

"It's beautiful Scarlett," I smiled at her again as we both took our seats on the ornately carved chairs. We had barely gotten our napkins into our laps before she plunged right into her ideas for the party, describing the French theme and every detail the two of us needed to focus on to make the party as perfect as she had it pictured in her head.

Finally, after two hours of going over every detail, she cocked her head at me and asked "So, have you talked to Tommy lately?"

I felt my cheeks immediately flush. Damn my stupid, transparent Irish skin.

She rolled her eyes. "Oh, Lord, Emma just freaking tell him you're in love with him or get over it."

She rolled her eyes. I knew she was annoyed that I kept mooning over him and did nothing about it.

"Excuse me, but this kind of stuff is actually difficult for some of us," I said pointedly.

After college, Scarlett's ability to attract powerful, rich, drop dead gorgeous men had only increased with time. Since we'd moved to D.C., Scarlett's beauty and charm had managed to attract the attention of an F.B.I. agent, a British Army Officer, a famous international news correspondent, a celebrity radio D.J., and a Wall Street millionaire - just to name a few.

She waved her hand dismissively again. "Emma, it isn't as impossible as you make it out to be. You think way too much."

If I had a dollar for every time someone said that to me.

She continued, "You just need to be confident. That's all life is! There really isn't any big mystery to it."

"Scarlett, it's not that easy. He has like a hundred women hanging off of his nuts at any given point in time. Now that he's in politics, they are ACTUALLY campaigning for him."

Scarlett rolled her eyes again.

She picked up the check despite my numerous pleas that she let me pay for something and then we got up and headed to the exit.

I smiled and said, "Thanks Scarlett."

Her phone jingled, signaling that she had a text message. When she read it, her face instantly lit up. I recognized that look; it was some guy sending her a dirty text and inviting her to have an afternoon of passion; something she was not likely to pass up.

"Gotta go, feel better!" She scampered off.

We had polished off about six mimosas each during brunch. I had to brace myself before a one on one date with Scarlett, because her seasoned party experience meant that she could definitely drink me under the table. But, since we had also eaten an incredible amount of food, I simply felt blissfully tipsy walking home. It was one of those days when the weather was so perfect that the air just felt like nothing, but every once in a while a warm breeze would gently graze my face. I felt terrible on the walk over here, but now, walking home, I started to think that Scarlett was right. Life was full of possibilities if you were confident enough to grasp them.

I stopped for a moment under a tree and closed my eyes, breathing in the perfect day. My phone buzzed and I saw that Tommy had sent me a text message.

Hey Thorne, Tonight at The Willard, I'm craving their steak frites. Be my date? ;)

My heart swelled as I took in a deep breath and smiled.

"Sweet Hope, ethereal balm upon me shed,

And wave thy silver pinions o'er my head!"

~To Hope

I dug through the back of my closet until I finally found the dress I was looking for. It was about a thousand times more provocative than anything I would even remotely dream of wearing, but Scarlett somehow managed to talk me into it during one of our shopping trips a few years ago. Sometimes Scarlett was so insistent I would just buy the damn thing to shut her up so we could move on from shopping to grabbing lunch.

But tonight I was praising Scarlett's name for making me buy this ridiculously overpriced number. It was a skin-colored dress with a black lace fabric overlay and a plunging neckline that required me having a glass of red wine before even considering showing that much cleavage in public.

I slipped the dress on, closed my eyes, and gave myself a pep talk to gather the courage to glance in the mirror. However, once I reluctantly opened my eyes, I was shocked at how I looked. I never felt so sexy in my life.

I always managed to pick apart something about myself, but the elegant black lace paired with a brand new pair of black stilettos somehow managed to bring out every one of my good features while hiding everything I worried about. Plus, the push-up liner inside made my boobs look phenomenal. Damn that Scarlett. She really was always right when it came to these girly things.

I finished the look off with soft curls and red lip-gloss. I wanted to look my absolute best. I kept desperately fiddling with my hair, applying enough hairspray that if someone lit a match in the room, the entire building would explode. I finally mustered up the courage to head out of my door.

As I walked into the Willard, I tried not to physically drop my jaw when I saw him. He was wearing a perfect navy suit, his blonde hair parted and neatly combed over so he looked like he had walked straight off the cover of G.Q.

As I walked in, he smiled that smile that made me feel better than anything else in the world.

"May I escort you to dinner?" He said bowing humbly, now being deliberately cheesy.

I laughed and said with a smile, "Oh, yeah right. Like any woman would ever turn that down."

He laughed back, straightening up again. "Well then, I hope you're ready for a lovely evening."

With that, I followed him as he put his arm around my shoulders and led me down the hallway towards a night filled with exciting opportunity

As we walked across the lobby towards the restaurant, the sheer beauty of the grand entryway immediately overwhelmed me. The entire corridor was made of brilliant marble adorned with golden accouterments. Gorgeous Corinthian columns towered up to an ornate ceiling with custom moldings. Medallions surrounded the hanging fixtures of each ironwork-adorned chandelier that hung from the middle of each recessed section. Potted plants lined the hall leading up to a magnificent ascending staircase covered with a stunning oriental rug. The shimmering ambiance made me feel as though I had been transported to the luxury and grandeur of the roaring twenties.

As we walked into the restaurant, everything was so beautiful and romantic, I couldn't help myself from slipping into fantasies of Tommy and I returning to this restaurant year after year until finally, one perfect night, he would get on one knee and ask me to marry him.

"Not bad, eh Thorne?" Tommy said with a sideways smile.

I laughed out loud. "Tommy, I have to say, even you have outdone yourself this time, and I never thought that was possible."

He smiled back at me and said, "Well I'm glad you approve."

The maître de led us back to a secluded corner booth that made it feel as though we were the only two people in the restaurant.

"Shall we take a look at the wine list?" he asked, getting straight to the point.

Tommy ordered us a bottle of Chenin Blanc and an appetizer of shrimp wrapped in bacon. As I ate one, it melted in my mouth as I made a noise of ecstasy.

"Well at least now I know what you sound like in bed, Thorne," Tommy said with a smirk.

"Shut up," I said, whacking him from across the table.

He laughed. "Oh relax, I'm just kidding! So what about it? Have you been getting any action these days?"

I couldn't decide if it was a good thing he was asking me, since he was curious and hoping that I wasn't hooking up with anyone else, or if it was a bad thing – a casual question that meant he didn't care if I was seeing someone else. I decided to play it cool.

"Wouldn't you like to know?" I asked with a wink. He narrowed his eyes at me.

"Well, yeah I would actually," he responded, again in a way I couldn't quite read.

"If you must know," I said, rolling my eyes, "The answer is a glaring no. When would I ever have time to have sex these days?"

He laughed.

"Well, I guess that's true," he agreed, "When are you going to tell that woman to fuck off anyway?"

Even though many people had been telling me that lately, it somehow stung more when it was coming from Tommy, like he thought I was weak and couldn't stand up to my boss, even when I was incredibly unhappy. I tried to change the subject.

"What about you, stud?" I asked, "How many ladies are you juggling these days?"

Tommy opened his mouth to say something but just then the waiter arrived with our entrees. I was so annoyed that he had interrupted Tommy's answer that I could have taken my duck l'orange and thrown it at him. Before I could repeat the question, the moment passed and it would have been entirely awkward to bring it back up again.

"So what would you do if you weren't working at that God awful law firm?" Tommy asked, taking a bite of his steak.

I sat silent for a moment as I took time to consider this. I resigned myself to my status quo for so long that I hadn't allowed myself to consider what my dreams actually were. The first thing that came to mind was poetry.

While I never had a desire to write it, I loved studying it. I always felt stupid for thinking such a thing, growing up in a city like D.C. where everyone focused on politics and business. Most people I knew equated the study of the liberal arts as synonymous with poverty, hunger, and weakness. I had never told Tommy how much I had wanted to study poetry because out of anyone, I especially didn't want him thinking I was being ridiculous.

I looked back up at Tommy, his face illuminated by the romantic candlelight. I thought about how badly I wanted the man sitting before me. He was the only person I ever loved, and I loved him so much in that moment that it hurt.

In that instant, I couldn't imagine living my life never having told him how I felt. However, even though my feelings overwhelmed me, my nerves also set in and I became quiet. My face must have fallen slightly because Tommy suddenly looked concerned.

"You okay, Thorne?"

"Yeah," I managed to respond, "I'm fine."

Tommy tilted his head sideways, clearly picking up on the change in my behavior. "Come on, lets get out of here. We can take a stroll and walk off some of this wine."

Tommy picked up the check and I followed him out of the restaurant. We began walking along the picturesque street in front of the Department of Treasury building. Stunning at night, its gorgeous architecture was highlighted by strategic lighting making the building sparkle as the regal form of the Washington Monument rose behind it in the background. I halted mid-stride. Tommy turned around.

"What's wrong, Thorne? You've been so quiet since we left the restaurant."

Looking at him in that perfect setting with the moon gazing over us, my anxiety melted away and I was overcome with calm and I knew that this was the moment. All I could do was hope it worked out and that it would make my life so much better. I took a deep breath and prayed that he felt the same way.

"I love you Tommy," I said, turning towards him as my calm melting into a blend of exhilaration and the return of my nerves as I realized there was no going back. He stared at me for a second as I closed my eyes and took another breath. Well, I was in deep now. Might as well keep going.

"I love you Tommy. I always have. I've been terrified that if I ever told you it would make things weird between us and I never wanted to risk that because you mean more to me than anything else in the world. But, I just needed you to know. I love you."

Realizing I had said, "I love you" three times now, I figured it was time to shut up and stop talking. I stood there for what was the longest moment of my life. It all seemed so surreal and I couldn't believe what I had just done. A dark feeling of foreboding washed over me as I considered the irreversibility of it all.

Tommy was still standing in the same spot. I couldn't read his face at all. I was fixed where I stood and couldn't move. Tommy walked up to me in what felt like slow motion. He took my face delicately into his hands. Then, he drew my lips to his and kissed me, unraveling the many years that had been building up to that one perfect moment.

Tommy broke away and stared into my eyes. After what felt like an eternity, he finally spoke.

"You have no idea how long I've wanted to do that."

With that, he flagged a cab and we rode down the street towards my apartment.

"A thing of Beauty is a joy forever, Its lovliness increases; it will never pass into nothingness."

~ Endymion

I woke the next morning in a bit of a fog. The sun shined through my window, waking me as I opened my eyes and found myself staring at the lamp on my nightstand. I heard someone slowly and steadily breathing behind me. The details of the night came flooding back to me in a wonderful flurry of euphoria. Tommy and me, finally together– I couldn't believe this was actually happening.

I delicately shifted my weight and turned around to make sure I wasn't dreaming. Sure enough, there lay my Tommy sleeping next to me in my bed. I always wondered what Tommy looked like naked. I must say, it did not disappoint.

While many people woke in the morning looking at the very least slightly disheveled, Tommy still looked perfect. He was lying on his side and the sun shone in through the window onto his tattoo, which brought me back to one of my favorite memories.

During the summer before my last year of law school, I decided to fulfill my lifelong dream of traveling throughout Italy. I booked two weeks in Rome so that I would have enough time to explore the city and all of the amazing historical wonders it has to offer.

Tommy had stopped by my apartment one day on the way back from his internship as he often did to have a glass of wine and catch up. Halfway through a story about how he recently broke one of the cardinal rules of his temporary employ and seduced a fellow member of his intern class, he spotted the freshly printed plane ticket that was now stuck to my refrigerator underneath my Art Institute of Chicago magnet.

"What's this?" He asked, pulling the ticket from under the hold of the magnet and reading it before I could stop him. "You're actually going to Rome? Congratulations Thorne! Now you can finally shut up about it!"

I blushed softly. I guess I had mentioned it once or twice over the years.

Tommy smiled and gave me a sideways glance and said, "I'm coming with you."

I laughed and snatched the ticket from his hand. "Alright, alright I know I'm a nerd. No need to keep making fun of me. Let's get back to your story about the up-and-coming whore of the Hill."

He snapped it back from me. "I'm serious! I've always wanted to go to Italy." He held it up and examined the date. "And will you look at that, you will just happen to be in Italy during my week-long break between this "grueling" internship and when my classes start. Do you care if I meet you there?"

Um, did I care? Yeah sure, I really minded being trapped in one of the most romantic cities on earth eating delicious food and seeing some of the world's most amazing historic sites with my best friend who I just happened to be completely in love with.

"I suppose that wouldn't be horrible," I said with a smirk.

"Awesome. Hand me your computer, I need to buy a ticket."

In the elapsed time of just under five minutes, Tommy and I had an international holiday planned together.

I had an entire week to spend on my own, losing myself in the incredible city of Rome and feeling its rich history vibrating at every turn. By the time Tommy got there, I was convinced that what would make me the happiest would be to stay in Rome forever, eating delicious pasta and gelato while sauntering down the Spanish Steps and having Italian men beckon to me, holding out their hands and calling me 'Bella'.

As it happened, apparently being pale and having light brown hair actually made one very exotic in Rome and was a great advantage as I made my way through the city. I saw so many gorgeous Italian men that I almost forgot that Tommy was coming. That is, of course, until I saw him.

We agreed to meet at the Trevi Fountain. I arrived at our set meeting time, but the place was so packed with tourists that I was convinced I would never find him. Then I saw him, casually leaning against the rim of the fountain wearing light khakis, a white linen shirt, and a pair of sunglasses that I'm sure cost just about as much as the price of his plane ticket over here. Even in a crowd of beautiful Italians and tons of tourists, Tommy stood out as the most gorgeous person there. He glanced up and saw me and smiled as I walked over to him.

"Well, well you made it. I thought for sure you would have been swept up by some desperately eager Italian woman by now."

"Yeah right," he responded, "And spend my time with some boring, skinny model that would shun the best food in the entire world? No thanks."

I wasn't quite sure whether to take that as a compliment since he was essentially saying that I was a great partner to eat a ton of food with. But, I knew what he was trying to say and I was so glad to see him that I just smiled. He always had a way to make me feel special.

Tommy smiled back at me and started fishing around in his pocket. His hand re-emerged with two Euro coins. He kept one of them for himself and handed me the other. A jolt of electricity shot through me as our hands met.

"Make a wish, Thorne."

I had a feeling that this experience would be something I could look back on once I fell into the repetitive grind of being a lawyer with absolutely no social life. But I could still hope for a bright and blissful future. So, I turned around, closed my eyes, and threw the coin over my shoulder, wishing that one day I would finally be able to tell Tommy how I felt, he would feel the same way, and we would be happy together forever.

We headed to dinner at a quaint Italian restaurant. As expected, the food was incredible. We spent the whole night stuffing our faces with soft bread, crisp salad, chicken Parmesan, and the best pasta I had ever had in my life. Even though we were both about to explode, we couldn't resist the tiramisu, gelato, and after dinner cordials. Feeling like we were about to die, we decided it was probably for the best that we take a walk.

We walked through the beautiful streets of Rome taking in the sparkling lights that illuminated the gorgeous, ancient city. Tommy put his arm around my shoulders and turned to face me.

"Thorne, this is amazing. I want to remember this forever." He paused for a minute and smirked. "Let's get tattoos."

I burst out laughing.

"Okay, someone may have had a bit too much Amaretto with their dessert."

"I'm serious! Why not? Don't you want to remember this, what it was like before we got so bogged down with responsibilities that we forget what it's like to really have fun? I want something that I can look at in the mirror every morning and remind myself how big the world is. I want to remember that no matter how bad things may get, there is always something beautiful out there."

I smiled and told him I was in. Amid the thriving city nightlife, we easily located a tattoo parlor that was open at 1:00 a.m. and got matching tattoos: a nearly undetectable small cursive word on our left rib cages. We vowed never to share the story of them with anyone. It would be our secret.

Now, lying in bed after our night together, I looked at Tommy's tattoo inscribed on his perfect body, I immediately felt self-conscious about what I must look like. Last night went down in such a whirlwind that I certainly hadn't taken the time to remove my make-up, brush my teeth, or do anything about my hair. I wiped the smudged mascara out from under my eyes and did a quick hair fluff. Tommy shifted, lifted his arms in a stretch, and landed one across my midsection, pulling me in tight. He opened his eyes and smiled.

"Good morning gorgeous," he said, making me swoon even more, which had you asked me thirty seconds before I would have bet the farm I could have never felt happier, but I was proven wrong.

"Morning," I said smiling; trying hard not to breathe what I was worried might be heinous morning breath in his direction.

I was shocked how calm I managed to remain as we lay there laughing about last night and the whole situation. Tommy brushed a lock of hair delicately from my cheek and swept it behind my ear, resting his hand on my neck.

"Why did this take us so long, Thorne?" He asked earnestly.

While I envisioned this scenario about a billion times in my life, I always pictured that I would be the one posing the philosophical questions and asking desperately, repeatedly, whether it was just a fluke or whether it was the start of something real. But, in that moment, Tommy actually seemed like the vulnerable one. I collected myself enough to respond.

"Well it was a little hard to tell you how I felt with all of those other girls hanging off of your nuts all of the time," I said with a laugh.

Tommy scoffed, "Me? What about you with all of those boys chasing you all of the time? How was I supposed to get a word in edge-wise among all of that competition?"

Never in my life would I have imagined that Tommy even thought of me in that way, much less that he had been jealous of other guys I hadn't even noticed over the years.

"What the hell are you talking about?" I couldn't help myself from asking. I genuinely had no idea who these supposed love-struck dudes could have been.

"Come on, Thorne, there's no way you haven't noticed. All of my college friends were obsessed with you. I could have auctioned you off and paid for my entire tuition. Every guy in my office always tells me how hot you are. It's really annoying."

I felt like I had fallen into a warped, parallel universe where nothing made any sense at all. I'd spent so many years agonizing over my feelings for Tommy and being petrified to even hint at the fact that I wanted to be with him. It was a moment that truly proved that you need to go for the things that you care about in life and not obsess so much about every solitary detail and what the consequences might be. Then, Tommy pulled me in closer.

"I'm so glad you said something and that this is all out in the open." He paused for a moment and sighed. "This is the happiest I've ever felt."

He kissed me softly on the lips, and then held my face in his hand for another moment. His phone rang. He picked it up and looked at the caller I.D.

"Sorry, I have to take this," he said, heading into my living room, still naked.

He came back and apologized but said he had to go.

Tommy smiled and kissed me hard on the mouth one more time. He threw his clothes on casually over his perfectly toned body and closed the door behind himself on the way out of my apartment.

I sat there for a moment before the fog finally cleared and my brain returned to a conscious state. Scarlett. I needed to call Scarlett. Immediately. I picked up the phone and dialed her number. My heard pounded harder and harder with every ring she didn't answer. Finally, her familiar voice emerged on the other side of the line.

"Hello?"

"Scar?!" I shrieked, surprised at how high-pitched and ridiculous my voice sounded.

"Emma? Is that you?" She responded, "You sound like a howler monkey for God's sake. What is wrong?"

I cleared my throat. "Sorry, I'm freaking out. Scar, you are never going to believe this. I finally told Tommy."

"Are you serious?" she asked, shocked, "What did he say?"

"He said he feels the same way! Scar, he spent the night last night. You can't even imagine..."

My excitement rose as I took a breath to calm myself slightly. Scarlett broke in.

"Emma, that's so awesome! Listen, I'm so, so sorry, I want to hear all about it, but you caught me at a bad time! Happy hour this week?"

I was really disappointed that I wasn't going to be able to talk to her about it right away, but it was probably for the best because I was still reeling so much that I could hardly finish a sentence.

"Definitely."

"Ok yay!" she said excitedly.

The phone clicked as she hung up. With that, I collapsed on my bed, making sure to relish in this beautiful moment, one that I knew I would remember forever and ever.

"Philosophy will clip an angel's wings"

~ *Lamia*

So, Tommy and I were finally a couple. I was shocked at how seamless the transition was from years of mere friendship into full-fledged relationship status. Everything seemed so natural, like Tommy and I had been together for our entire lives. He filled my senses at every turn and I spent nearly every moment thinking about him.

Even work was going better. Dealing with Penelope was all the more tolerable once I could look forward to seeing Tommy afterwards. Since neither of us had any experience cooking and were terrified we would poison each other if we tried, we went out to dinner almost every night. Tommy's seemingly limitless budget allowed us to try every famous restaurant in the city

Sometimes he would come surprise me at work and take me out for lunch dates. He always looked so handsome. His job dictated that he had to dress in snazzy suits and his expensive ties and shoes always pulled everything together and made him so sexy.

As an added bonus, I could tell that it drove Valerie crazy. Not shockingly, because she was a heinous human being, she had no boyfriend. She always tried to act like it didn't bother her, but I could tell by the way she scowled at us every time he came in that she was filled with envy.

Often times he even brought me flowers. Not just the grocery store pick them up on the way out flowers, but huge, intricate bouquets filled with over two dozen roses arranged by some local florist in Georgetown that I knew cost at least four times the amount of the bouquets one ordered on 1-800-FLOWERS.

One time when I was in the bathroom she even knocked them over and pretended it was an accident. But I just picked them up, put them back in their vase, and re-filled the water, coming back and telling her that it was okay, when the bouquets got that big it was hard to keep them balanced sometimes. She seethed and turned back towards her computer.

When I left the office, I realized that I hadn't talked to my mom in forever. She always said that when she didn't hear from me, she knew not to worry because it just meant I was busy and happy, but that made me feel even more horrible since she was essentially saying that she only heard from me when I was depressed, whining or needed something.

I decided to advantage of the beautiful evening to take a slow stroll and give her a call. She picked up after the first ring.

My mom had a tendency to answer the phone, yet still finish her current conversation with whoever was in the room before she acknowledged the person on the other end of the line. She didn't have caller I.D., so I always thought this was hilarious because it's not like she knew it was just me and I wouldn't mind, she just did it to everyone. It was one of those quirks that endears you and makes you love someone that much more, but also drives you absolutely nuts.

"...Kathy? Kath, I'm sorry I have to go, someone's on the other line. No, it's not the baked ziti recipe. It's the lasagna. No not the one from the picnic, the one you made at book club..."

I sighed as I waited for her to acknowledge me.

"On second thought Kath, I'll just come get it from you. See you in a few! ...Hello?"

"Hey ma!" I said, wondering how much of my life had just been shaved off.

"Emma sweetie! How are you? How's my Tommy?"

Tommy had been around our house so much growing up that my mom already considered him a son and she was thrilled when I first told her we had gotten together.

"He's great," I said, feeling my heart swell. "He brought me flowers again today."

"Aw, he always was such a nice boy. So when are you two going to give me a grandchild?"

"Mom!" I protested. Although it did send me straight into a reeling fantasy of what our children would look like.

"Oh, come on, you know I'm kidding... sort of. Are you seeing him again soon?"

"Yeah, I'm heading to Scarlett's housewarming party now, so I'll see them there."

"It's so great that the three of you are still so close. It's just perfect isn't it? Just like a fairytale. I'm so proud of you honey. Now seriously, get on those grandchildren."

I scoffed to let her know how ridiculous she sounded, feeling happy that she wasn't there to see the uncontrollable grin on my face.

"Now I have to go. Of course, your father waited until the last second to tell me he needed to bring dinner to the poker game. Call me soon though! Give Tommy and Scarlett my love!"

As usual, she hung up without giving me a chance to respond in order to continue her normal routine of running around like a maniac. My grin widened as I walked down the street towards my apartment with pictures of adorable, sandy-haired toddlers filling my head.

———————

Now that she had gotten all of the details down to a tee, Scarlett was finally hosting the French housewarming party at her apartment. Tommy already had plans with some clients from work, but he vowed he would come meet me afterwards. I arrived at Scarlett's building promptly at 8:30 p.m. where the doorman was already waiting outside in anticipation for the night's guests. Scarlett being Scarlett, she somehow managed to charm her way into one of the most exclusive buildings in the city. Last I heard, there was a four year waiting list to even be considered as a resident, and yet Scarlett batted her eyes at a board member enough that she was able to flirt her way right past all of those patiently waiting families and was accommodated immediately. Come to think of it, she probably did a whole lot more than bat her eyes, but I never wanted firm confirmation about these things, so I tended not to ask.

She buzzed me in and told me to have a look around while she finished making mini quiches. Scarlett's 'friend' on the board also somehow managed to secure her the coveted top-floor corner unit with a wraparound porch and a stunning panoramic view of the city from the Capitol Building all the way to the Washington Monument. If you turned around, you could see a beautiful view of the National Cathedral and the Basilica at The Catholic University of America. I thought for a moment and decided that it was definitely not only her smile that she flashed to get her way into this one.

It was a good thing that Scarlett had moved into such a ridiculously large apartment because I'm pretty sure she invited the whole of the D.C. social scene. As much as I considered these things completely ridiculous in the past, I was actually having a great time. The people who I was introduced to included the head event planner for the Smithsonian, the head psychologist for the Department of Veteran's affairs, a lead White House P.R. correspondent, the Executive Director of a think-tank who even after his explaining his job to me for a solid twenty minutes I still had absolutely no idea what he did, and a rather attractive Turkish pop-sensation who was apparently Istanbul's version of Enrique Iglesias.

Just as I was starting to feel completely inferior about all of my life's choices, I felt a hand on my side. I turned to see Tommy standing there, looking as handsome as ever.

"Hey gorgeous," he said, leaning in to give me a kiss, "Sorry I'm late, the guys kept me out on the boat."

I laughed, thinking about the fact that a lot of Tommy's "work" involved playing golf, going to steakhouses, and evidently running around drinking on boats with top-level campaign donors.

"Oh, yeah that sounds really horrible for you," I said sarcastically, noticing the hint of sunburn on his nose and the top of his cheeks, "So, just how many beers have you had then?"

He smiled, "About four."

I snorted, "So, by four you mean ten?" I asked, knowing him and his alcohol tolerance all too well.

"Hey now," he retorted back defensively, "You asked me how many BEERS. I had four beers. And then five mint juleps." He smirked that delicious smile and I thought I was going to melt in his arms. Only Tommy could make binge-drinking look so good.

"You're impossible," I said, not being able to resist a smile.

He laughed and said, "I'm not impossible. I'm challenging. And I know how you love a good challenge," he winked as he picked up a champagne flute and refilled mine before filling his to the brim.

I saw Scarlett come up from behind him and squeeze both of his biceps.

"Ow!" he said, clutching his arms.

He smiled and gave her a hug.

Tommy had brought along one of his coworkers, Simon, who I had met briefly once when I visited Tommy's office and could tell he was quite the 'particular' man. He walked up to Tommy and tapped him on the shoulder.

"Thomas," he said in one of the snootiest voices I'd ever heard, using his full name that no one ever used, "I don't see anything but sparkling wine at this party. I did hope they would have *something* from the champagne region. I'm sorry but I can't drink this, I'll need to go to the store. Care to join me?

Tommy turned to me and rolled his eyes.

"Alright then, come on Si. Be right back babe," he said, kissing me before heading out the door.

I continued to make my rounds and catch up with everyone, waiting for Tommy to return so that I could sneak off with him into Scarlett's guest bedroom. But all of a sudden, the many servings of champagne I had chugged throughout the night caught up with me and I felt woozy on my feet. I wobbled and was starting to fall before I felt someone behind me catch me.

"Whoa there Em!" Scarlett said with a laugh, "Looks like someone might need to lie down for a bit."

"Noooooo," I said back, surprised to hear how slurred my speech was. "I have to wait for Tommy."

She laughed and put her arm around me.

"I'm sure he'll come cuddle with you when he gets back! Come on, let's get you to bed."

She must have carried me to the guest bedroom, but I had absolutely no recollection of it until I woke up hours later. I looked at the clock. It was 3:30 a.m. I glanced down at myself and saw that I was wearing one of Scarlett's t-shirts.

I smiled as I realized she must have dressed me for bed and felt a surge of affection for her, although I was instantly mortified that I might have embarrassed her in front of her friends. I decided to see if she was still awake to check in and make sure I hadn't made a total ass out of myself.

I navigated my way through hallway, wavering slightly before I reached the door to Scarlett's bedroom, which was cracked open. I walked in.

"Ugh Scar. Thanks for taking care of me. Sorry I got so wasted, I hope I didn't do anything stupid. Thanks for dressing by the way. I'm not wearing a bra, so I'm assuming you got a shot of my boobs. My bad."

Looking up, I was instantly embarrassed to realize that Scarlett was currently in her underwear involved in an intimate embrace with an equally undressed man.

"Oh, my God. I'm so sorry Scar! I should have knocked."

I went to avert my eyes when suddenly, the guy's frame shifted slightly into the beam of light shining in from the hallway through the crack in the door. My stomach clenched. The light revealed a small tattoo on his side shortly beneath his armpit.

I recognized it instantly. I loved seeing mine whenever I actually took time to stop to look when I got out of the shower, but there it was, in all of its permanence. Its counterpart was clearly displayed in that small beam of light permeating Scarlett's bedroom, "vita"; the Latin word for "live." Standing there staring at the two of them, it was strange how oddly numb I felt, as Scarlett stood there cross-armed with her face turned away from me while Tommy rubbed his head, looking uncomfortable. I was in such a state of shock that I couldn't believe the scene in front of me. I don't think I took a breath for a solid thirty seconds.

Then, the hurt set in. Wasn't it Scarlett who convinced me to start this whole thing in the first place? Anger boiled up inside of me. My two best friends, ripping each other's clothes off just months after Tommy and I professed our love for each other and finally got together, which had made my dumb ass believe he had actually grown up and would seriously want to be with me.

Tommy opened his mouth as if to say something, but no words came out and he dropped his head and stayed silent. He knew he couldn't charm his way out of this one. I thought about screaming. I wanted to walk up and slap them both in the face and make the dramatic scene that Scarlett most certainly would have made in that same circumstance. But I had nothing left in me, nothing but a broken heart and a desire to get out of that room as soon as humanly possible.

I spun around and left the bedroom without saying anything. Still reeling, I attempted to navigate the hallway to the most direct route to the exit. It seemed like an eternity before I found the front door and was able to descend the elevator and walk out into the crisp night on the D.C. streets.

I got back to my apartment, washed my face, put on my pajamas, and collapsed into bed. I couldn't stop thinking about that image of Scarlett and Tommy, half dressed, sucking on each other's faces. Now that I thought about it, Scarlett didn't seem shocked or remorseful at all. In fact, she had had her lips pursed with an annoyed expression on her face.

I felt rage boil up inside me to the point that I was so livid I thought I would explode. This entire thing had been nothing but a fantasy. It always had been; a false reality that I interpreted as a truth but was nothing but an invention of my own mind.

When my heavy breathing finally subsided, I turned to switch off my lamp and saw my worn copy of *The Complete Works of John Keats* sitting on my nightstand. I picked it up and opened to one of my favorite poems, *Endymion*.

A thing of beauty is a joy for ever:
Its loveliness increases; it will never
Pass into nothingness; but still will keep
A bower quiet for us, and a sleep
Full of sweet dreams, and health, and quiet breathing.
Therefore, on every morrow, are we wreathing
A flowery band to bind us to the earth,
Spite of despondence, of the inhuman dearth

....

We have imagined for the mighty dead;
An endless fountain of immortal drink,
Pouring unto us from the heaven's brink.

The poem spoke of one of his greatest themes: the inevitability of death. He attested that small, slow acts of death occurred with each passing day, and most humans never even stop to consider the vulnerability of our own mortality. While death is inevitable, he felt that with beauty we could live the days that we are given in exquisite splendor.

As I contemplated Keats's musings, I tried to clear my mind of all practicality and think about what would make me truly happy. When it came down to it, I didn't want to waste my life. I didn't want it to pass into nothingness. I wanted to let the shape of beauty move away the pall from any dark spirits. It suddenly became so obvious to me how much more important those things were than stupid, fleeting power.

I had never questioned the power of friendship before tonight. I thought that Tommy and Scarlett would always be my safety net that I could depend on no matter what. Having that notion ripped out from underneath me so harshly had changed just about everything I thought I knew. An odd calm washed over me as I considered this and how quickly things can change; how short our time on earth actually is. And suddenly, in that instant, I knew. I needed a new life.

I took one last hopeful look at my phone for an apology message from Scarlett, a declaration of love from Tommy, and felt a jolt of excitement when I saw a new email notification. I swiped it open feeling sick with nerves and was surprised to see not Scarlett or Tommy's name, but Dr. Olivia Brighton, my old poetry professor.

Hello my dear Emma! Just burning the midnight oil over here with dreadful writer's block trying to meet my deadline for publication. Oh, the perils of academia! As it happens, one of my colleagues from across the pond just forwarded along the details of an internship that would have been perfect for you! Pity it wasn't around when you were applying!

I flashed back to dreadful memories of my own horrendous internship experience. As always, I had forgone glamour for practicality and ended up slaving away at a local Boston law firm for an incredibly lazy man who weighed close to three hundred pounds and smelled like soup. What was advertised as "twenty hours per week conducting research and preparing reports to be utilized by the firm's attorneys" turned out to be about fifty hours a week of me providing free labor that consisted of dusting shelves, lugging moldy files from room to room, and trying to catch my supervisor in his office at a time when he wasn't clipping his toenails while a lingering dollop of a mayo/ketchup combination still resided in the corner of his mouth from his lunch three hours earlier. I shuddered and returned to Dr. Brighton's email.

Nevertheless, the listing reminded me that you might want the contact information for Dr. Edmund Lowell, the director of Keats House. He is a dear friend of mine, such a delightfully charming man. I do think the two of you would have much to talk about! I hope that you have had time to keep your interest in poetry alive; it is such a divine realm! I would love to catch up over coffee when your busy schedule permits! Best wishes! Liv.

The screen was a bit blurry due to the massive amounts of alcohol I had consumed and thus, reading it properly required many attempts. I scrolled down to read the internship description so as to allow myself to relish in the fantasy of what such an experience would have been like.

Keats House Internship

The London Metropolitan Archives seeks an intern to assist in the daily operations of Keats House, the historic house where the poet John Keats lived and wrote from 1818 to 1820. Also known as Wentworth Place, the house is said to be the setting that inspired some of Keats's most memorable poetry.

Situated near Hampstead Heath in North London, Keats House is now a museum dedicated to preserving the history of the house and its influence on the young poet. Keats House has a vast collection of artifacts and documents relating to the poet and provides admission, tours, and conducts many public events and programs including poetry readings, concerts, book talks, writing workshops and teddy bear teas.

I had no idea what a teddy bear tea was, but I liked the sound of it already. I read on.

The Keats House team seeks an enthusiastic individual to join our family and assist in various roles for our wide range of events and activities. Qualities required are a passion for poetry, enthusiasm for sharing poetry with people of all ages, good communication skills, and the ability to thrive working with a team in an exciting environment.

The official announcement actually included the phrase "to join our family". Clearly they do things a bit differently in Britain than they do here in America, where job listings might as well read more like "ability to work long, dull hours without requiring food, water, or fun while resisting the urge to speak to anyone about anything non-work related. Free spirits or those with an imagination need not apply." I continued reading the email.

To apply, please submit a resume and a brief statement of why you feel that Keats House would be a good fit for you to Dr. Edmund Lowell, Keats House Manager, via the email address listed below.

I stared at the computer screen in my drunken stupor, considering the announcement. Nowhere did it say that the applicant still needed to be enrolled in college, nor was there an age requirement for that matter. All that was needed was an "enthusiastic individual". I could be enthusiastic. I happened to be an individual.

I thought back to my time studying with Dr. Brighton, how thrilling it was to drink in the wonderful art of poetry and what an amazing mentor and inspiration she had been.

She gave me so much support and I still looked up to her as a model to which I aspired to live my life. I thought about what she would have done in the same situation and quickly decided that she wouldn't even blink an eye. She would follow her dreams.

John Keats had never even gotten a chance to live a long life. Here I was, with my whole life in front of me, and God knows when it would be taken away. I couldn't just wait around for my dreams to come to me. If I did, I'd spend my entire life putting my happiness off until one day I would cease to be before I ever really lived. There was no beauty in practicality for practicality's sake.

Thinking about it that way, even my practical side wasn't fighting back. I had been very fiscally responsible over the years and I actually managed to save quite a bit of cash. I did some quick calculations in my head and decided that I could afford to travel the world, unpaid, for up to three months. Wait. Forgot to carry the two. Fuck. I could afford it for much longer than that!

Perhaps it was the drunken stupor, but it all seemed like a no-brainer. Fuck it, I decided. I hit the button to compose a new email, attached the most recent copy of my resume, typed a short response as to why I would be a good fit for the internship, signed it sincerely, and hit send. With that, I collapsed face-first, and fully dressed, into my pillow.

"There is nothing stable in the world; uproar's your only music."

~ Letter to his brothers George and Thomas Keats

13 – 19 January 1818

———————

Sunday morning, I woke up to my cell phone buzzing an inch from my face. I struggled to open my eyes as the sun beamed in from the window. My head throbbed viciously and in that moment I never hated anything more than that Godforsaken sunlight for making it a million times worse. I managed to grab my phone and roll over to my other side to avoid at least some of the bright beast's horror.

I picked up my phone and slid the button to unlock the screen expecting a text message from Tommy or Scarlett. I glanced down to the bottom of the screen, no texts but I had a new email.

I vaguely remembered something having to do with my computer that I had an underlying feeling might result in deep feelings of regret and embarrassment.

It all came flooding back to me. Oh my God. Did I apply for an internship? I did a quick check of my sent messages, briefly horrified that I might have sent an email back to Dr. Brighton in my drunken stupor. Luckily, I saw that the only email I sent was to a Dr. Edmund Lowell. With some trepidation that the response was filled with much laughter at my own expense, I double-clicked the message anxiously.

Dear Ms. Thorne,

Thank you very much for your interest in Keats House Museum! We have looked over your resume and were very impressed with your description of your love for Keats. We feel that you would be a perfect fit. I understand that you are currently fully employed by a solicitor and thus, I feel I must notify you that this particular internship comes with no financial compensation.

However, I am confident that if you do choose to become a part of our team, you will be rewarded with much cultural enrichment, an amazing experience, and lots of lifelong friends. We hope that you seriously consider this offer and get back to us in stride! We invite you to begin your internship as soon as you can make arrangements. I can be reached any time via this email address with any questions or concerns.

Many Thanks,

Dr. Edmund Lowell

Manager, Keats House

The logical side of my brain harshly snapped me back into reality. Now that I wasn't under the infectious influence of too much alcohol, I realized how ludicrous the idea was. Quit my job and move to London to take a job that doesn't pay anything not knowing a soul and with no clue where to live? There was no way I could just up and leave everything in D.C. Penelope would destroy me and when I came back to my senses and wanted a paying job back I'd be banished from every law firm in town. If I could just stick it out for another year or so, I'd find a better job that I enjoyed and I'd be on the path that I had so delicately and intricately laid out for myself over the years.

"I must choose between despair and Energy. I choose the latter."

~ Letter to Miss Jeffrey
31 May 1819

I woke up the next morning with the familiar sense of foreboding that accompanied the start of every workweek. I dragged myself out of bed, showered, dressed in a stupor, and sat down to have a quick cup of coffee at my bistro table before heading off to the stark dungeon of my office. I gazed out of my window onto the tree-lined street below and watched the neighborhood slowly start to come alive; people walking their dogs, going for jogs, the occasional girl dressed in last night's dress and high heels doing the token "walk of shame."

I found myself wondering where they were all going for the day and thinking that wherever it was, they were probably looking forward to it far more than I was looking forward to my day. So many people go through life embracing the moment. It seemed like such a shame that dread could consume the greater part of one's life.

I thought back to the email from Dr. Lowell, which got me thinking about John Keats. He had already accomplished so much before his death at age twenty-six, and here I was, two years older than him, feeling as though I had done nothing of value in my life. I wanted to do something that would positively affect people, but instead I was being treated like a cog in a ruthless, soul-sucking machine that did nothing but exploit people. This just wasn't how I pictured my life. I had lost myself in my thoughts for far too long. When I looked up at the clock, I was struck with panic-induced horror at how late it had gotten. I grabbed my bag, dashed out the door, and flagged a cab to the office.

Normally the weekends flew by, but when I entered the office that morning, for some reason it felt like I hadn't been there in forever. I walked swiftly up to my desk, out of breath, and plopped into my chair. As usual, Valerie didn't even break her typing to look up from her computer screen and acknowledge my presence.

Penelope's door flew open and she marched out and stood across from my desk. It scared the absolute shit out of me because Penelope was hardly ever in the office this early in the morning. I raised my hand to my chest in surprise before breathing a sigh of relief after the initial shock wore off.

"Thorne, what are you having a heart attack? Wake up! I need a second set of eyes to look over this. Read it, edit it, and get it back on my desk by noon today so it can be off to the press before deadline." She slammed a file folder on my desk and quickly turned around, slamming the door to her office behind her.

Well, no need for coffee now, since the coronary she had just given me jolted me awake and set my heart racing. I opened the file and saw that the document was a draft of an article to be featured in *The Washington Post.*

New Case File Software Set to Revolutionize Law Research

The Law Offices of Pendleton & Rowe have just developed a groundbreaking database that will forever change the way that attorneys will conduct law research. The world-renowned firm has been developing the software, which was recently unveiled at a gala in Washington D.C.

When asked how she came up with the idea, the firm's leading founder, Penelope Pendleton, described that the idea "just popped into her head one day." Ms. Pendleton's first assistant, Valerie Warren, who worked extensively on the project, described that she "couldn't be happier" to have been integrally involved in such an innovative part of the firm's process.

This method will give Pendleton & Rowe, already one of the world's leading law firms, an even greater advantage over the competition. If competing firms hope to have any chance in the game from now on, they will have to come up with something similar or else perish at the hands of this vastly superior method of investigation.

I sat there in stunned silence for about five minutes before my numbness faded and allowed me to move my arm. I set the article down on my desk. Beyond the obvious fact that this article was a harsh, blatant smack to my face, why in the world would Penelope think it was alright to *show it to me ahead of time and have me edit it* for God's sake? It certainly wasn't as if she was doing me the courtesy of giving me a head's up before the article went to press. She was just that coldhearted and self-centered. I knew she hadn't even done it on purpose. She was just that inhuman.

And Valerie?! Was she kidding? That bitch had not spent one second on that project. I even asked her for help a few times with some very minor details, and she flat-out refused saying she was far too busy, immediately before taking her nail file out of her desk. How did she think it would be ok to say she was an integral part of the process? She obviously didn't even have any concept of what guilt or remorse even felt like. And back to Penelope – why wouldn't she have sent *The Washington Post* to interview me instead of stupid Valerie?

Rage boiled up inside me as I got up, flung open the door to Penelope's office, marched across the room, and forcefully slammed the draft of the article down on her desk. She looked up at me momentarily stunned before her face contorted into an evil look of appall; her eyes narrowing, brow furrowing, lips pursing.

"What do you think you're doing?" she hissed.

If I had even an ounce of uncertainty before, her reaction made me so angry that there was absolutely nothing that would have stopped me at that point.

"No, what the fuck do you think YOU'RE doing Penelope," I snapped back. "Are you kidding me with this? The idea just 'popped into YOUR head'?"

She waved her hand dismissively.

"Oh Emma, get over it. It's MY name out there on that door remember? I don't know who you think you are marching in here like this, but don't forget your place here and how lucky you are. If you have a problem, by all means, leave. A hundred people would apply for your job within the first fifteen minutes of me posting it online. Now get out of my office."

I felt like I was going to scream.

"How could you do this to me? Never mind the fact that it was MY fucking idea, but I've spent MONTHS of my life that I'll never get back slaving over this for you, and you can't give me one line of credit in a newspaper article? And worse, you let Valerie comment on it?"

She rolled her eyes. "Emma, Valerie is my first assistant. The reporter wanted an additional comment and she was the logical choice. Don't take this so personally. Quite frankly, it makes you look weak."

I seethed.

"Well at least I'm not a selfish, narcissistic, soul-sucking monster."

I put my hands in my hair and screamed. Then, I went over to her conference table and swiped all of the files that I had neatly organized for her and delivered in piles for her review so that they scattered all over the floor.

"There. Good luck fucking figuring out how to put that together again."

She put both fists on her desk, using them to slowly raise herself out of her chair and lean over to come at me in that intimidating manner I'm sure she used hundreds of times over the course of her career to bully people into doing exactly what she wanted.

"Emma, I'm warning you. Get out of my office right now and get back to work before I fire your ass for insubordination."

I took a deep breath and said the words I had been dreaming of saying ever since the first day I started that Godforsaken job.

"You know what, don't bother. I quit."

She stared at me, looking horrified. With that, I turned around smiling and walked out of the office, slamming the door behind me. I was surprised to see that a huge crowd had formed in front of the door. All of my coworkers were standing in front of me, their mouths gaping open in shock. In my blind anger, I seem to have forgotten that Penelope had a completely transparent windowed wall to her office and that everyone had just seen the entire thing.

I took a bow as if I had just completed a rousing performance, grabbed my purse, and threw a middle finger up at Valerie without even looking at her as I walked out of the front door, slamming it behind me .It felt fantastic.

"Nothing ever becomes real till experienced – even a proverb is no proverb until your life has illustrated it."

~ Letter to George and Georgiana Keats
14 February to 3 May 1819

I felt instantly liberated as I walked down the street from the building that had felt like a prison to me for so long. It was like a boulder had been lifted off of my chest and I hadn't realized exactly how hard it had been to breathe until it was removed. I felt like skipping down the street. After taking all of that shit, it felt amazing to let go of all of the pent-up rage I had towards that horrible, horrible woman. Why hadn't I done this sooner? So much wasted time. But it didn't matter now. It was all behind me and the entire world was in front of me.

I didn't even realize how far I had walked until I almost passed the entrance to my building. Spinning back around, I walked blissfully into my lobby and up the elevator into my apartment. I plopped down on my bed and took a deep breath; my mind entirely blank for the first time that I could remember. I took time to relish in the moment and feel the joy permeate throughout my body.

Then, as if on cue, the panic settled in. What the hell had I done? What was I thinking? I would probably never be able to get a job as a lawyer again if I was on Penelope Pendleton's shit list. Dammit, see this is what happens to people like me when they think they can get away with the kind of thing that Tommy or Scarlett would do. My anxiety kept building until I was pacing around my room, pulling at my hair, my stomach twisted into knots. I had no idea what to do next. So, I decided to do what any fully-grown, well-educated, self-sufficient woman would do. I called my mommy and daddy.

I normally tried to keep things like this from my parents because I never wanted them to worry about me. They had so much going on in their own lives and they worked so hard to make sure that they gave me so many opportunities. I felt as though if something did go wrong, it was because I made the wrong decision and fucked it up. After all, I had lots of resources at my disposal to make my life a success. Now, I had just taken everything that they worked to provide me with and flushed it down the toilet. I felt terrible. As the outgoing rings continued, I found myself praying that they wouldn't pick up.

"Hello?" my dad's sweet voice answered from the other line.

"Dad?" I said, my voice cracking.

"Oh, hi Emma sweetheart! It's so great to hear from you!" He sounded so jovial at hearing the sound of my voice that I couldn't take it anymore. I burst into tears.

"Honey, are you ok? What's wrong?" I could hear the concern in his voice. I tried desperately to respond, but every time I attempted to form a word, all that came out was an ugly gasp.

My mom picked up the other phone and I told both of them the entire story. I told them about the job, Scarlett, Tommy, everything. It just came pouring out. I just unleashed years of angst in one sitting on my poor, unsuspecting parents. Then, yet again, I started to cry.

My mom's voice sounded on the line.

"Oh dear, Honey, I'm so sorry. I never did like that Tommy."

"Ma, please. You were just gushing the other day about how much you loved him."

She made a 'psh' sound.

"Well, I certainly don't like him now."

I sighed and moved on.

"What about Scarlett?" I asked, "I don't know what I'm going to do without her."

There was silence.

"What?" I asked, flummoxed.

"Well, Emma," said my dad "I can't say I'm surprised. Scarlett never was a very good friend to you. I know you guys have a lot of fun together, but I never did think she was particularly healthy for you. She's sort of a jerk."

I had never in my entire life heard my dad utter one negative word about another human being – and I am not exaggerating. He was the nicest, most positive man in the entire world, almost to the point of caricature. If Steve Martin and Santa Claus had a love child, each bringing their absolute best traits to the table, that love child would be my father. Once he said it, it seemed so blatantly obvious to me. She was a jerk. An asshole.

I snapped back to the conversation at hand, still reeling, but already feeling a lot better. Suddenly, I recalled the huge, glaring, actual adult problem that made the whole Scarlett and Tommy thing seem like a stupid, insignificant teenage soap opera. I had no job. I was unemployed.

"What am I going to do about my job?" I felt like I was going to start sobbing again. "Now Penelope hates me and I'll never get another job at a law firm as long as I live. I'll always be the idiot who walked out on Penelope Pendleton."

My mom snorted.

"No, you'll always be the one who had the balls to stand up to Penelope Pendleton. Hell, you'll probably be flooded with offers from competing firms who would love nothing else but to see her taken down."

I never thought about it like that before, but now that she mentioned it, my mom was probably right. I had been in that microcosm of brainwashing for so long that I forgot that there were a lot of people out there who hated Penelope.

My mom continued, "But, be honest with yourself, Emma, is that what you really want? You just seem so unhappy lately. And, truthfully, I never did see you as a lawyer. You have way too much creativity for that."

I figured she was just trying to make me feel better, but it just made me feel worse.

"Yeah but that's who I am, I'm a lawyer. And I failed. I failed at the one thing I've worked my entire life to achieve."

"Sweetheart, we're so proud of you. Never mind what you think you're supposed to do. What do you *want* to do from here?"

For the first time, or at least the first time while sober, I seriously considered Dr. Lowell's offer for an internship position at Keats House. It still seemed ludicrous, but what the hell, this whole day was insane. Saying it out loud wouldn't make things any weirder and more fucked up than they already were.

"Well, it's stupid. It's totally stupid. But I did get this offer from Keats House, in London. It's for an unpaid internship, but I'd get to spend my time in the house where John Keats lived and worked. I'd actually be sitting where he sat, seeing what he saw when he wrote his poems."

As I described it, I realized how badly I wanted it. I hadn't allowed myself to feel that way up until this point. Then, I remembered why. I continued on, "But it doesn't pay anything and I'd have to find a place to live and pack and figure out what to do with my apartment. It just seems really impractical."

"Oh, psh, well honey you have to go," my mom said so matter-of-factly that it almost made me feel dumb for ever having questioned it. While it was one among so many that was probably the reason for which I was most grateful to have my mother in my life. While I fretted over every solitary detail of decisions, weighing every possible option over and over again so that when I made up my mind I could be confident that I had made the right choice, my mom was completely the opposite.

I greatly admired that about her. She could just discuss something, solve it, and move on with her day. She never brooded over anything and yet she was the strongest, smartest, most creative, caring woman I knew, loved by everyone who met her and the person I respected more than anyone else, next to my dad.

"And honey," my dad chimed in "don't worry about the money. I know you have enough saved to survive without getting paid. And if you ever get into trouble, you always know where to look. We love you, Emma. Life is too short to be anything but happy, and that's all we want for you." And with that, my eyes welled up again. Well, it was about time, I hadn't cried in about five minutes.

I felt so much better after talking to them, my head was finally clear and it was the first time in a while that I felt as though everything made some semblance of sense. I don't know why I had waited so long to talk to them about everything. I should have known better; they always knew exactly what to do.

It dawned on me that if I didn't take this opportunity now, I would never have another chance. Like my mom said, it was simple. I had to go. I entered my apartment and breathed a deep sigh of relief. I seated myself before my laptop, clicked the 'new message' icon and composed a new message to Dr. Lowell.

Dear Dr. Lowell,

Thank you very much for your offer of an internship at Keats House, I would be delighted to join your team! I need to make a few arrangements but I hope to be in London soon.

I will touch base when I get in and settled and I'm looking forward to meeting you!

Best Wishes,

Emma Thorne

I hit the send button, smiling. Then I opened up my web browser and typed in the website for British Airways. I clicked the 'One Way' option and requested a ticket from Dulles International Airport to Heathrow. A flurry of results popped up before me. I scrolled down through the options until a cheap red-eye flight stood out:

IAD (Washington-Dulles) → LHR (London Heathrow); departs August 15th 11:05pm

I entered all of my information before I turned my attention to the bottom of the webpage, which displayed a large, blue button that said 'Confirm Purchase?' I hovered my cursor over the button for a good thirty seconds before taking a deep breath and clicking. And that was that. I had finally taken some control over my life.

"He ne'er is crowned with immortality Who fears to follow where airy voices lead."

~ *Endymion*

The next morning I slept in for the first time since I could remember. It was a peaceful, dreamless sleep that granted me the most solid, uninterrupted rest that I had had in quite some time. The fact that I slept through the night only further reassured me that I had made the right decision. My heart leapt as I sat up in bed. I was moving to London! In the midst of my newfound impulsiveness in booking the plane ticket, I was glad I retained some sense of responsibility and given myself a little bit of time to prepare. I had exactly a week to get myself together and ready to go.

Crap. I needed a place to live. Rather than immediately freak out, as the old me would have done, I took a deep breath, decided to eat some breakfast and clear my head, and then get down to business. At least this time all of my efforts would be going towards something fun, new, and exciting rather than boring, soul sucking, and terrible. I felt so enormously better already.

I whipped up some eggs, made myself some coffee, and set my breakfast in front of my laptop. I looked up the location of Keats House and found that it was in a quaint little neighborhood in North London called Hampstead just off the Northern Line. I did an image search and lots of photos of the town popped up. The neighborhood was gorgeous. There was a cute main street and a beautiful park called Hampstead Heath. The houses and neighborhoods were filled with English townhomes, each residence looking as though it had been a place of dwelling for brilliant, sophisticated tenants. My excitement grew as I pictured myself sitting in one of those picturesque bay windows with a good book and not a care in the world.

I typed in a search for flats to rent in the area. But, when the results popped up, my idealism quickly faded just before it vanished altogether. As I continued to scroll through the rental options, it dawned on me that neighborhoods that lovely and well kept were likely quite desirable and therefore, extremely expensive. Just a tiny room within a house averaged about £1,700 per month, which with the current exchange rate meant about $3,000. There was no way I could afford that, especially now that I had no source of income.

Still, I continued to scroll down to look at the pictures of the beautiful houses to at least imagine what it would be like to live there. Then, a listing advertising a room with a price of £400 caught my eye. I stopped and scrunched my eyebrows together, perplexed. Then, I realized it must be a weekly price. Oh well, moving right along.

But after looking closer, I saw that the price had a "pcm" notation, which I had come to find meant "per calendar month". I clicked the link with curiosity to gather more information. The listing showed an image of a large, gorgeous stone Tudor-style house covered in ivy. The thumbnail indicated that the listing included twelve additional images. The main living area was a large, yet cozy, sitting room with what can only be described as the best parts of an old English cottage complete with walls covered in bookcases, a decorative cast-iron stove, high ceilings, and gorgeous hardwood flooring. While the home itself maintained the air of sixteenth-century English style, the décor was decidedly modern in a way that somehow complimented the charm of the interior.

The images then turned to display a stunning outdoor courtyard that the house wrapped around, leaving a perfect square in the middle complete with lush greenery. Wall baskets contained gorgeous flowers of several varieties and there was an iron table and chair set that looked perfect for enjoying a morning cup of tea or an evening glass of wine.

I could already picture myself there. I could see myself studying poetry in the courtyard during the summertime, a light breeze softly caressing my face as I thumbed through the lines of each masterpiece. I pictured myself cozied up on the couch with a good book next to a roaring fire during the winter.

As I continued to take in the photos, I at last came upon a picture of the room that was for rent. It was an adorable attic loft – the perfect size. Slanted ceilings descended towards mahogany floors with a rustic wool rug half hidden under a four-poster bed.

It made no sense. Why would a room in this flat be less than an eighth of the price of the plain, two hundred square-foot bedrooms with no windows that I had seen so far? It seemed way too good to be true. But if for some miraculous reason it was actually the case, I would never forgive myself if I didn't at least give it a go. I scrolled down to the bottom of the listing, which had a brief message from the owner who was advertising the room for rent.

Twenty-seven-year-old woman seeks a female roommate to occupy one room of a two-bedroom flat in Primrose Hill, Hampstead, North London. Please no smokers.

The very end of the description said. *For inquiries, please contact Tibbie Irving via the email address listed below.* I expected the description to say something about the room only being available on Sundays, or from noon to four or something, but it seemed that this Tibbie Irving really was looking for a full-time roommate at a ludicrously low rate. Curious, I pulled up my mailbox and clicked to compose a new message.

Hello Ms. Irving,

My name is Emma Thorne and I am hoping to find a room to rent in the area. I will be starting a new position at Keats House and will be moving to London from America in one week's time. Your listing appeals to me greatly because of its location near my new workplace. I hope you don't find this rude and I'm sorry to have to ask, but I must inquire about the rent price. I noticed that similar rooms to rent in the area are quite expensive and I just wanted to double check about the asking price. I understand that it's short notice, but if it seems like it might be a good fit for what you are looking for, I'd love to talk with you further about the opportunity!

I thought for a minute and considered attaching a photo of myself to the message so that she could see what I looked like. I thought maybe having an image made it easier to picture who you were talking to, which somehow made electronic conversations more relatable. I decided it was probably a good idea and selected a photo of myself from my trip to Italy so that she could see that I had at least somewhat of a sense of adventure. I continued,

I've attached a photo of myself. Please let me know if you have any further questions. I'm looking forward to speaking with you soon!

Best,

Emma

I read over the message to make sure I sounded sane with a bit of a personality before hitting send. I minimized my email and continued to browse through photos of Hampstead. I was just starting to lose myself in more fantasies when a response message popped up in my inbox that read *From: Tibbie Irving re: Room for Rent.* Surprised by the almost instantaneous response, I paused for a moment before double clicking the icon to reveal the message.

Hello Emma!

Thank you for your inquiry! I love Keats House! Great photo, don't you just love Rome! I would be delighted to have you as a roommate, just let me know when you expect to be in the area and I will ensure that everything is set up for you.

In terms of the price, I inherited the flat not long ago from my grandmother and have been living in it on my own for a little while now, but I've grown a bit lonely and bored and was hoping a flat-mate might shake things up a bit! If the asking price is too high, please let me know and perhaps we can arrange something else! I've attached a photo of myself as well; please forgive the state of my hair! I'll be awaiting your response, hope to hear from you soon!

Many Thanks!

Tibbie

Man, was everyone in England this joyful and enthusiastic? Between Tibbie Irving and Dr. Lowell, I felt as though I had more pleasant interactions while trying to figure out logistics in the past week that I had in my entire tenure as a lawyer.

I double-clicked on the icon to download the photo and was greeted by an image of a petite, sparkly-eyed English girl with beautiful blonde hair that was cropped close to her head with tiny wisps of loosely curled locks sticking out from behind her ears.

She was dressed in a navy blue dress covered with a pattern of small white flowers, accented by a red rope belt, a long, cream-colored cardigan, black leggings, and brown boots. She was leaning back on both of her hands on a wooden dock-fence with sun-lit water shimmering behind her in the background, the breeze gently ruffling her hair. Her mouth was open in one of those smiles that someone captures as one is laughing with pure joy. She looked so carefree and fun. I know it was only one photo, but I instantly got a very good feeling and could picture us being great friends.

Part Two

"I can be a raven no more"

~ Letter to Fanny Brawne
Shanklin, Isle of Wight
15 July 1819

I woke up the morning of August 15th feeling light and elated. Up until that point, while I had been furiously preparing for my journey, I think that a part of me didn't truly believe I was going. But once I walked over to my computer, checked into the flight, and printed out my boarding pass, I let myself get really excited for the first time since booking the ticket. I stared at the piece of paper with my boarding time and seat number, taking pride in my uncharacteristic impulsiveness and the control I had finally taken into my own hands. I took a deep breath and smiled as I folded the sheet and tucked it into the front pocket of my passport cover.

I gathered all of my belongings, which were now neatly packed into the two allotted suitcases that the airline allowed for international flights, along with my one handbag that I would be carrying on the plane with me. It was bizarre to have reduced my entire life into a small pile of bags, but the minimalism was oddly freeing. I made sure to schedule an airport shuttle for a time that would provide me with what would probably be an unnecessary amount of time at the airport before my flight. Right on time, the shuttle called my cell phone to let me know it had arrived and was now waiting outside of my building.

As I opened the front door to exit, I turned around to take one last look at my life in D.C. I had expected to experience feelings of nostalgia when the time came to leave, but in truth the barren apartment looked so unlike what it resembled when I lived there that it was hardly difficult at all to turn around and close the door behind me, leaving everything I had known for my entire adult life so far.

As we traveled down the street that I loved, I did feel a bit contemplative as I took in all of the landmarks I had passed on my walks to and from work. D.C. had been such a learning experience for me and I stopped to drink in its significance in my life. I had always been one to picture things a certain way, map out very specific plans, and forge exact paths that I thought would lead me in a particular direction. But I was realizing that the paths we think we are following for a one reason or another might be there to guide us somewhere else entirely; a place that we never would have thought of as a destination on the original trajectory we set out to conquer.

The plane ride passed quicker than I had anticipated. Before I knew it, the flight attendant's voice projected over the loudspeaker requesting that we turn our tray tables up and return our seats to their upright position. I was shuffled out of the plane and onto the hangar before I could make any sort of ceremony about it. I followed the fast-paced herd down the various hallways until I reached baggage claim.

After I collected my luggage, I made my way to the desk that sold passes to the tube. I walked up timidly.

"Hello?" I said gently in an attempt to rouse the station manager away from his reading.

A small, wrinkled man with kind eyes looked up at me from behind the pages of his book and gave me a charming smile. "Lovely accent my dear, just come from America?"

Great, I had been in the country no less than thirty seconds and I was already standing out as a foreigner. I smiled back and said "Um, yes." I returned my focus back on my goal of obtaining my tube pass without looking like a complete tourist, "One one-way ticket from Heathrow to Zone 3 and then one one-week Oyster Card for zones 1-3 please," I said with an air of confidence, prepared for any colloquialism he might throw at me. I was quite confident that I had studied up well on my Britishisms.

The man smiled, revealing an adorable grin missing certain teeth, "Well, you sure know your onions! Jolly good!"

Knew my onions? Okay, I did not know that one.

He punched a bunch of information into a computer before swiping a transport card and placing it into a bi-fold plastic holder with the London tube symbol emblazoned on the front. He handed it over and said, "There you are my dear, safe travels!" before tipping his hat in my direction.

In what seemed to be the airport's way of idiot-proofing the transportation system for the many varieties of people from several different backgrounds who flew through Heathrow, the platform for the tube was immediately next to the arrivals terminal. I climbed aboard, stowed my bags, and took a seat.

The train sputtered to a start and began its way down the track towards Central London. With each stop, passengers kept boarding until the car was quite full. The more people who boarded the train, the more out of place I felt.

For starters, I seemed to be completely underdressed. All of the Londoners on the train seemed to be put together so well. I had on my standard flight outfit of yoga pants, a zip-up hoodie, and flip-flops. I stuck out like a sore thumb.

It all seemed very exotic to me, but I suddenly got very nervous. What if I didn't fit in here? What if I annoyed people? What if Tibbie didn't like me once she got to know me, or maybe she was completely different than she sounded in her emails?

She seemed to be a completely lovely person, but I had heard many a horror story of roommates who seemed sane at first, but slowly denigrated into a complete psychos.

I charted the journey at around one hour, but it seemed to pass so quickly that I was shocked when I heard the speaker announce that the Northern Line train was pulling into Hampstead. The doors opened and I found myself in the quaint station. I extended the handle on my suitcase and walked towards the elevator, passing beautiful walls adorned with cream and dark-red tile work that lead to a domed ceiling. I passed the words "Heath Street" sprawled across one wall in the same rustic red and cream-tone tiles. The whole station looked untouched by time, as though it had been plucked from the turn of the century when the underground was first constructed. I proceeded to the elevator and was whisked up to the street level.

When the elevator doors slid open, I was met with a charming main street that cascaded down a hill and ultimately veered to the left where it vanished out of view. The street was lined with a series of identical row houses, no higher than four stories. They were made of brick and adorned with ornamental almond-colored window fittings that framed charming wooden muntins housing beautiful glass panes. Chimneys lined the tops of each respective roof, nestled behind façade peaks. The bottom row featured delightful shops, cafes, and restaurants. As I walked down the street, my nervousness subsided and I thought about the fact that I had an entire adventure ahead of me.

I continued meandering the twisted, winding roads of Hampstead, which, while beautiful, were confusing as hell to a first timer. Plus, I kept getting distracted by the serene atmosphere of the neighborhood and all of the gigantic houses and gardens, each of which was more beautiful than the last. I began seeing signs for Primrose Hill and knew that I had arrived in the correct area. After a bit more meandering, I came upon King Henry's Road. I turned left, struggling with my luggage. I stopped on the corner and glanced briefly at the sheet of paper on which I had written the details of the address. I looked up and realized that I was standing right in front of the house where I would be living for the foreseeable future.

When I came to my senses, I took a moment to glance up and take in the house in front of me. It was beautiful. The ivy-covered stone front was even more breathtaking in person. I tried to settle my nerves, for while everything I was feeling was exhilarating, I really wanted to calm myself before meeting Tibbie for the first time.

I closed my eyes and took one more deep breath, opened them once again, and slowly made my way up to the arched red door, taking hold of the circular iron doorknocker. I paused for a moment before picking up the heavy metal device and letting it fall, repeating the action three times.

Almost immediately, the door swung open and I was met with the bubbly young girl I had seen in the photo. Her hair had grown slightly since the picture was taken, but it was still a short, glistening blonde style that suited her face really well. She wore a silk scarf decorated with red roses draped around a loose-fitting, ivory-colored sweater on top of tight-legged jeans and socks, somehow managing to look quite relaxed and yet very stylish at the same time. Her brown eyes sparkled as she offered me a welcoming smile.

"You must be Emma!" She said excitedly as she leaned forward and gave me a quick, sincere hug, "Please do come in!"

She picked up one of the bags that I had temporarily placed on the floor.

"Oh, you don't have to do that!" I protested, feeling guilty since she was so tiny she was about the size of the suitcase itself.

"Nonsense," she said in a way that was kind and lighthearted, yet left no room for argument. "Come, come!"

I walked across the threshold of the house and looked up at what was to be my new home. The ground floor was beautiful, the afternoon sunshine poured in at all angles. The beautifully polished mahogany floors stretched across the cozy living room with a large, plush couch, two arm chairs, and a gorgeous antique table.

"Let me show you around a bit!" Tibbie said cheerfully as she set my bag down next to the door.

She grabbed ahold of my hand and led me to the right of the kitchen. A striking sunroom backed up to the sitting area, delicately decorated in calming light blues and bright, sunny yellows. Comfy daybeds surrounded by glittering trinkets and gorgeous, fresh flowers sat in front of the paneled glass wall that lined the entire room. The windows overlooked the back courtyard, which Tibbie guided me towards as the starting point of the tour.

The courtyard was comprised of stone floor and more ivy-covered walls. Various plants and flowers filled the whole area, displayed in pots, flowerbeds, and on the walls in metal baskets. A decorative iron table stood in the middle surrounded by four iron chairs with broad, intricately molded ornamental seat-backs and plush, deep red seat cushions that matched the surrounding red roses. The back wall featured a fountain that trickled water into a pool enhanced with beautiful vines and delicate lily pads.

"This here is the courtyard. It's where I spend most of my time when the weather cooperates. However, when it doesn't there's always the sunroom! That's why Gran had it put in. She couldn't bear to let a little rain keep her from her favorite part of the house, so she made it so that she could come read out here without getting wet!" Tibbie said, her smile fading slightly at the mention of her grandmother.

"I can show you around the rest of the house in a few, but I'd imagine you want to rest your feet for a bit. Let's have a sit. How was your trip? Let me get you a cup of tea."

Before I could answer or attempt to save her the trouble of having to serve me, she scampered off into the kitchen to start the kettle. As Tibbie prepared the tea, I took another glance around. The cottage itself was so rustic and classic, yet Tibbie's décor made it bright and contemporary. The artwork was all subtle shots of city scenes with no people, just cool, architectural angles and street pathways, each with their own unique filter that made them quite intriguing. Brightly colored pillows and rugs accented an otherwise black and white scheme. A sparkly crystal chandelier hung above a bay-style window in a place where I never would have thought to place it and yet, it fit right in. I noticed an iron spiral staircase in the corner that must have led to the upper level. I assumed Tibbie would show me the rest of the house later, but honestly I was glad that she had suggested I sit for a moment. I hadn't realized just how jet-lagged I was.

I turned to glance over at Tibbie to see if she needed help, but she looked fully engrossed in arranging the tea tray. She moved gracefully to compile all of the components. As she made her turns, I took note of the kitchen. Black cabinets hung with windows showing off artsy mugs, exquisite wine glasses, and black and pink dishes. They sat above a white quartzite countertop speckled with gray and black stone fragments interspersed between glittering crystalline flecks. The counter was lined with state-of-the-art appliances, an expensive looking coffee machine, a fully stocked spice rack, and lots of other fun tools. Everything was so tasteful. I was very impressed with Tibbie's style.

She returned with a tray filled with a teapot and two cups with saucers, a matching cream spout and sugar bowl, tiny sandwiches, and delicious-looking shortbread cookies. She poured us each a cup and plopped down on the couch next to me.

"Please, dig in, you must be starving!" She said, helping herself to two cubes of sugar. "I'm so glad you're here!"

I smiled back at her.

"I'm glad to be here too," I said, "Thank you so much for the wonderful hospitality! Your place is gorgeous."

She beamed, "It's our place, silly! But, I'm so glad you like it. I've been doing a great deal of redecorating lately. Needed a change. It's good to hear I haven't mucked the place up entirely!"

She took a sip of her tea and placed one of the shortbread cookies on a napkin, raising it to rest on her knee. "So you're working at Keats House, are you? I love it there! Where did you study poetry?"

I chuckled, almost spitting tea everywhere, having just raised the delicate teacup to my lips. I coughed and wiped my mouth with a napkin.

"Oh, no I didn't study poetry, I'm actually a lawyer by training. About as opposite end of the spectrum as you can get, I suppose."

"Oh!" Tibbie said with surprise, "Well that's quite the change! How did you end up here?"

For a moment, I contemplated how in-depth to answer her question. If I told my whole sob story right away, she might think me a lunatic. However for some reason, I was so comfortable around her already. While I hadn't known her that long, I'd say I felt more at-ease with Tibbie than I ever had around Scarlett. Surprising myself, I immediately opened up to Tibbie and delved right into the entire story – Tommy, Scarlett, Penelope, the whole bit.

"Oh, that's awful. I'm so sorry Emma!" Tibbie said with sympathy in her eyes. She slowly reached across the couch and gently placed her hand on top of mine. "But, I'm very glad it brought you here! Don't you worry about them. They sound like they're not worth your time anyway!"

I smiled back at her, feeling guilty that I had monopolized the entire conversation.

"Anyway enough of my drama, tell me a little about you!" I said, placing my empty teacup on the table and turning my body towards Tibbie.

"Oh!" She said enthusiastically. She was so funny; it was as if everything I said or asked her excited her more and more. I had never met anyone quite so bubbly, yet in a way that was genuine and endearing rather than overcompensating and nauseating.

"Well, where to start! I grew up here, in this house. My parents died when I was quite young and I was raised by my grandmother."

"I'm sorry," I said.

"Oh, it's quite alright," she responded, "I actually don't remember them. They died in a car crash when I was just one year old. I had a wonderful life here, I've been very fortunate."

She paused for a moment and I was unsure whether to bring up the subject of her grandmother. It was clear that something was bothering her, but I didn't want to take my own ease around her for granted and assume that she felt the same way about me. After all, we only met about an hour ago and I didn't want to overstep my boundaries. Just as I was mulling over the options in my head, Tibbie broke into soft sobs.

Her sudden change in disposition startled me and it was a moment before I could compose myself enough to react. I lifted myself from the couch and moved over to her slowly, placing my hand on top of hers.

"Are you alright?"

She pulled a napkin from the tea tray with her other hand and put it to each of her glistening eyes.

"I'm so sorry," she said gently between breaths, "I'm just really glad you're here. It's been so lonely since my grandmother died. I miss her so much. I've been so sad and as soon as I feel as though I'm starting to get a bit better, I want to ring her up and tell her how much better I'm doing, and then I realize that she's not here anymore. Isn't that silly?"

I knew exactly how she felt. It was the same way I felt when my own grandmother passed away. I felt so terrible after that happened and my subconscious kept picking up the phone to call her since she always made me feel better. Then, I would inevitably remember the terrible truth and become all the sadder because of it. I squeezed her hand harder.

"That's not silly at all," I said sincerely.

Tibbie straightened up and composed herself a little, wiping each eye and giving her nose a quick, soft blow.

"Anyway, it's just been hard in this empty house without her. I keep waiting for her to come around the corner and ask me about my day. It will be so nice to have someone to talk to again."

I smiled back at her and said, "Why don't we change the subject? What about you, what do you do for a living?"

"I'm sort of a conservator," she said, still sniffling but her smile was returning, "It's a bit of a funny job, I make casts of bones."

I was both fascinated and very confused at the same time.

She smiled, "That's not the first time I've gotten that look, trust me. I studied science at university and specialized in evolutionary biology, but I was sort of a sculptor on the side. I had a professor who was very encouraging and I gave her a sculpture I made for her as a thank you for everything she'd done for me. She told me that she had an idea and that there was a friend of hers that she wanted me to meet.

Turns out she had a colleague who specialized in molding and casting dinosaur bones so that paleontologists can study them without having to alter or destroy the original specimens.

Every once in a while I work on ancient pottery as well. I don't work full time though, I'm a contractor for The Natural History Museum in South Kensington. I go in when they need me for a particular project."

She seemed so passionate about her work. I wondered what that must be like to love your job so much that you couldn't wait for your next assignment.

"That's amazing," I said, fascinated. "If you don't mind me asking, where did you go to school?"

"Cambridge," she said casually while she picked up another piece of shortbread, as if it wasn't one of the best schools in the world.

We talked for hours, filling each other in on our lives. I learned about her passion for gardening, which explained the beautiful courtyard. She told me that her love for sculpture was a result of her grandmother's adoration for the art and her constant striving to find the perfect pieces to compliment her garden. She started sculpting so she could give her grandmother the statues that she dreamt up but was never able to find.

In addition to her art, she was clearly smart and worked hard at school, but it seemed that she still managed to have a lot of fun growing up. She returned to her grandmother's home upon starting her job right after university and lived here in Hampstead ever since. Her financial freedom and job flexibility allowed her to travel all over the world. Her life sounded so fun; so fulfilling. I felt like I could learn a great deal from her.

I had no idea how long we had been talking until I suddenly felt exhausted. I looked at the clock and realized it was 9:00 p.m. Tibbie must have seen me yawning because she said, "Well look at the time! You must be positively knackered after your long trip. Let's get you to your room!"

We had gotten so wrapped up in talking that Tibbie hadn't finished the house tour. But, the fatigue hit me full on and for now, I had to admit that all I really wanted to do was head straight to my new room and collapse face first in a bed. Tibbie crossed the living area to the corner by the kitchen that held the gorgeous spiral staircase. I followed her as she ascended.

I heard Tibbie say, "Sorry it's not much room, you're welcome to keep things in other areas of the house if you need to!"

I glanced upward. The room was simply darling. The four-poster bed sat in the corner of the cozy attic bedroom that I had seen in the listing, but the photos didn't give justice to the warm, welcoming feel of the room. Tibbie had changed the bedding to a pristine, plush duvet with two of the fluffiest looking pillows I had ever seen.

The slanted roof reached to a peak at the center, enveloping the entire room in a comfortable embrace. A beautiful black and white fluffy rug adorned the floor, leading up to an antique desk that doubled as a vanity. I walked gently across the room, placed my bag down next to the nightstand and sat on the bed.

"It's perfect Tibbie," I said, my eyes now tearing up for the first time. It was probably just the exhaustion, but I could no longer hold back my emotions.

"Oh, dear I'm sorry! I didn't mean to upset you!" Tibbie said clasping her hands at her mouth.

"Don't feel bad Tibbie," I said, "I'm just happy. I'm really glad I'm here."

She smiled softly and dropped her hands gently by her sides.

"Well sweet dreams then! Do let me know if you need anything. My room is the one straight across from the living area." She turned on her heels and headed through the hole in the floor and down the spiral staircase.

I collapsed in my bed and stared at the ceiling, smiling. I wanted to make sure I took care to drink in this moment and recognize everything it meant about my life and my opportunities.

Then, I stood up slowly and walked across the room to sit down at the desk. It was decorated with numerous trinkets that looked as though they originated from around the world – no doubt souvenirs from Tibbie's many trips throughout Europe, Africa and Asia. I lightly touched a multi-colored ceramic lion that looked as though it traveled from somewhere in the Far East. Next to it was a beautiful custom glass perfume vial that I imagined came from somewhere romantic like Paris or Milan. I knew that in time, Tibbie could tell me all of the stories, but for now I was happy to imagine her picking them up through her many adventures in her exciting and fulfilling life.

I looked beyond my own reflection and caught a glimpse of the beautiful courtyard in the background. I turned around and took in the sight of the garden at night. The flowers weren't as bold as they were in the daytime, but they had a soft shimmer. The lights danced gently on the surface of the water that flowed from the fountain. The perfect breeze blew in through the window and I paused for a moment, closing my eyes to let the air rush gently past my face.

My thoughts went back to all of the great times I had with Scarlett and Tommy and how much I wished things were different and that they were here. Even though they had hurt me, they had been such a huge part of my life for so long that I didn't know what I was going to do without them. My eyes welled up with tears before I broke down into soft sobs, trying to keep quiet so Tibbie wouldn't hear me. I cried for a good five minutes before my head started hurting and I decided it was time to go to sleep.

After a moment, I turned to pick up my carry-on bag, tossed it on the bed and started unpacking, taking out my toothbrush and other things I had thrown in for the journey. I went to the bathroom to brush my teeth and get ready for bed. When I came back and went to climb under the covers, all I could picture was Tommy and I cuddling after our first night together. I really wished he were there with me. Even though I was really upset about Scarlett, I was absolutely heartbroken about Tommy. I had loved him for so long and poof, now I knew that we would never happen. I didn't know what would make me happy anymore.

I spotted my worn copy of Keats's poems. I thought about all of the places I had taken that book and how it had ended up here, so close to where Keats had actually written what was inside of it. I opened it to see the words I had inscribed on the inside of the front cover back when I first got it, one of my favorite lines.

Thou wast not born for death, immortal Bird

I closed the book and set it down on the nightstand next to me. I remembered something Dr. Brighton said once about that poem, *Ode to a Nightingale.* She said that the poem spoke of transience and mortality; that the nightingale Keats writes of experiences death but doesn't really die since it lives on through its song, which is a fate humans cannot expect.

Pleasure can't last forever and death is an inevitable part of life. But, the nightingale's song is happy. Its voice urges the narrator not to dwell on the inevitability of death but to instead embrace the beauty and possibilities of life and forget the sorrows of the world.

I realized that Keats had written that poem under a plum tree in a house not a mile away from where I was at that moment. I thought back to where I was when I wrote that inscription in the front of that book and considered where I was now. Maybe I should stop dwelling on the past and instead focus on the future.

"Heard melodies are sweet, but those unheard are sweeter"

~ *Ode on a Grecian Urn*

I awoke the next morning to a slightly crisp breeze grazing my cheek. I felt the rising sun resting gently on my eyelids and shifted slightly to free my arm, which must have been directly underneath my side for quite some time because there was very little blood still flowing through it. It would appear that the jetlag paired with what was undoubtedly the most comfortable bed I'd ever slept in resulted in me hardly moving throughout the entire night.

I sat up slowly and stretched my arms towards the ceiling before opening my eyes. The room took on an entirely different feeling in the day, transforming from the enchanting, twinkling nook from the night before into a charmingly bright and inspiring dormer by day. I glanced out of my window. The flowers from the garden rose to meet the sun, the entire courtyard cascading with various colors. It was a perfect day.

My nose was met with the delicious aromas of coffee and crackling bacon. I heard Tibbie rummaging around the kitchen and realized that she must have been up for quite some time cooking breakfast. As much as I wanted to continue to enjoy the moment in the comfy bed, I figured it was probably time to get up and go give her a hand.

However, by the time I actually pulled myself together enough to descend the stairs, it appeared as if there was nothing left for me to do. The table was covered with a delicate white lace tablecloth upon which rested a light blue and white polka dot dining and tea set. A freshly plucked pink rose from the garden rested in a narrow vase at the center of the table, surrounded by a blue pitcher of orange juice and a small tray with sugar, cream, and small spoons. It was a nice alternative to my usual breakfast, which mostly consisted of burnt, butter-less toast. Tibbie turned around to greet me.

"Morning!" She said cheerfully, crossing the kitchen to pick up a teacup. She scampered lightly towards me across the kitchen floor in her white socks, wearing a cotton pajama set that was black adorned with tiny white flowers. "I normally drink tea, but I know how you Americans love your coffee!"

I grinned and took the cup handle between my fingers, cradling the saucer with my other hand. "You're very kind. Thank you Tibbie. I wish you hadn't gone to so much trouble."

"Oh nonsense," Tibbie said with what I was gathering to be her signature playfully dismissive wave of the hand, "Happy to do it! Now how do you take your eggs?"

Tibbie finished cooking us breakfast and joined me at the table with toast, bacon, and two plates of eggs over medium. She smiled, taking her flatware into each hand and cutting the egg into pieces. The two of us talked non-stop as we dined, filling each other in on more details of our lives, interests, stories of woe, and just about everything else. She was so easy to talk to. I again had lost track of time until she glanced at her watch and sighed lightly.

"I'm so sorry I must abandon you today. I've been called to work, a Byzantine vase has been delivered with water damage and they need me to do a quick fix before it goes on display at the exhibition opening next week. Sorry, I know it's Saturday, I planned on showing you around a bit, but unfortunately agents of deterioration never take a holiday!"

I really just couldn't get over how cool her job was and how adorably dorky and passionate she was when she spoke about it.

"No worries!" I said.

"Do make yourself comfortable, I'm just going to get myself together!"

She scampered off to her bedroom in her usual jovial fashion and left me to myself in the beautiful kitchen. I did the dishes to repay her for putting together such a wonderful breakfast, refilled my coffee, and wandered into the sunroom. I plopped on the sofa and lost myself in thought, staring out into the courtyard garden.

After what seemed like only a moment, Tibbie returned wearing tight black leggings, a black and white striped shirt, a red scarf, and a black beret. I was realizing (and envying) her uncanny ability to jump from classic, to chic, to edgy, at will. She threw on a black trench coat and picked up her satchel.

"What are you doing tonight?" She asked.

I hadn't considered it. Being as I had exactly one friend in this city, I assumed I'd be doing what ever Tibbie was doing.

"I haven't the slightest idea," I responded honestly.

"Well, my friend Beatrice is returning to town. She travels for work quite a bit, so since she'll be here we thought we'd show you around Central London and go for dinner and some drinks if you're up for it! Or if you're too tired and want to stay in, that's fine too!"

I thought it was so considerate of her to already include me in her plans. I had to admit that while this was all very exciting, it was a bit intimidating. I didn't have the slightest idea where to start in this city. I was very grateful to have a comrade and a tour guide.

"That sounds wonderful!" I said sincerely.

Tibbie smiled widely and said "Fabulous! I'll return no later than six, please call if you have any questions!" She turned to leave and was halfway out the door before turning around. "Oh! Your key! I almost forgot, silly me."

She rushed across the room and pulled out an old rustic key adorned with a bright red ribbon knotted in a bow on one end.

"There you are! That should get you in and out. Have a lovely day! See you this evening!"

She ran off, closing the door swiftly behind her. Once she was gone, I glanced around at the beautiful place I now called home. I had a clean slate, a fresh start. I could do anything I wanted. I only knew one person within a three thousand mile radius. I had nothing to do today. It was an amazing feeling

I got myself put together and picked up my bag. I had no idea where to go or what to do, so I figured I would just head to the center stop on the tube map. I walked up the hill to Hampstead station. The sky was a bright blue and the trees that lined the streets were just beginning to turn the warm, pastoral hues of late summer. People dressed in light sweaters, scarves, and boots. Many sat at café tables reading the morning news and sipping tea.

I reached the station and descended the elevator, heading onto the Northern Line train. I glanced at the map and decided to alight at Leicester Square, which seemed to be right in the middle. Upon exiting the train, I was struck by how much more bustling this station was than Hampstead. Londoners wove about the busy station corridors hustling off to work.

Something about it just seemed different from D.C. It might have just been since everything was new and exciting to me as a foreigner, but everyone somehow seemed statelier; more put together. D.C. certainly had its share of people who walked with the confident conviction of living and working in the most powerful city in America. But, D.C. seemed so pedantic by comparison. Here in London, it was as though people here knew their talents and privileges but didn't feel the need to go strutting them around like proud peacocks.

Since I had nowhere in particular to be, I decided to just walk and see where I ended up. I kept walking and walking until I found myself in a beautiful courtyard. The center displayed a large fountain surrounded by ornate benches that sat beneath a circle of trees. The leaves on the trees had already started to turn to rich gold, reds, and browns. Various visitors sat beneath them sipping coffee or sketching, taking mid-morning breaks from whatever responsibilities filled their days. Breathtaking buildings with ornate archways complete with sculptural embellishments encased the square. I sat down on a bench, taking everything in.

I was struck with the notion that I should probably find a map. But then I remembered that I had nowhere to rush off to. I noticed a sign that said "Russell Square". Underneath was a list of local attractions with arrows pointing in various directions. I got up and walked over slowly. I smiled. Less than a quarter of a mile away was number one on my to-do list. The British Museum.

I followed the signs and soon found myself standing in front of the museum I dreamt about visiting since I could remember. The outside looked a lot like my favorite building in D.C., The National Archives, with an ornate pediment held up by a row of grand Corinthian columns displaying striking, Grecian-style architecture. I could make out the sculptor's representations of the steps of humanity's development, from man learning the basics, to expanding his knowledge, and finally the pinnacle figure of the educated man on the far right. I walked slowly across the courtyard to the entrance past contentedly lounging tourists and lines of eager school groups.

I opened the door and passed the threshold, entering the museum. Distracted, I clumsily followed the incoming crowd, making sure I wasn't encroaching on anyone else's path. When I finally looked up, I was completely stunned. I found myself standing in the middle of the museum's famous inner rotunda.

While I had seen about a thousand images of the grand inner space, nothing could do justice to seeing it in real life. Magnificent cross-struts of strong, steel beams secured hundreds of triangular, tessellated glass panels that rained shimmering rays of the sun's light onto the museum's visitors. It was breathtaking. I stood there, staring, for at least five minutes before being able to shake myself back into some semblance of reality. While I could have sat in that courtyard all day, completely content to do nothing but stare at the architecture and people-watch, I reminded myself that I was surrounded by some of the most magnificent artifacts in the world and it would likely behoove me to take at least one step forward.

I spent the whole day taking in the wonders of thousands of years of human genius and creativity. It occurred to me how long it had been since I was fully able to take my time and really enjoy a museum, drinking in cultural riches and reminding myself what great achievements people are capable of when they have talent and time. I browsed hundreds of artifacts depicting epic tales and heroes that I remembered vividly from my favorite history courses in high school and college.

I caught a glimpse of a woman who looked to be a museum employee walking briskly across the gallery. She strode with such a purposeful air, looking composed and collected in her suit with an I.D. badge hanging around her neck that likely granted her access to places that few people would ever be fortunate enough to experience. She had been deemed trustworthy enough to protect some of the world's most valuable pieces of the past. I felt an instant admiration for her. She just looked so smart. It was a nice reminder that there were opportunities to make an impact in your career and still feel inspired rather than trudge along in a contemptuously competitive environment, working merely to survive as your dreams died a little more each day.

I strolled around the museum for a few more hours, taking my time to digest everything at my own pace. As I stood there in that magnificent place I had always dreamt of visiting, I couldn't help but think of Tommy. He always pretended to make fun of me for being a nerd and liking museums but then would make sure to forward me emails about upcoming exhibitions at D.C. museums so that we could go together. Some of my favorite memories with him had been the two of us meandering through galleries, taking in fascinating history and brilliant art. I wished that everything was different and that he was with me in this amazing museum so we could take in the experience together.

When I got sad about Tommy, my knee jerk reaction was that I wanted to call Scarlett so that she could make me feel better. Whenever anything bad happened, Scarlett had always been there to listen to me and help me pick up the pieces. I felt like I didn't know how to do it without her. But, then the vivid image of my so-called friends with their hands all over each other returned and I remembered that things were never going to be the same. I sighed and glanced at my watch.

I realized the museum would be closing in forty-five minutes. In spite of myself, I had to admit that I really, really wanted to visit the glorious gift shop I had seen on my way in. I felt like I earned it, I did learn a lot after all. I made my way there, browsing through all of the cool (and overpriced) mugs, totes, scarves, books and trinkets that the shop had to offer. Then, I felt my phone vibrate in my bag. Since Tibbie was the only one who had my phone number so far, I knew it was her calling to tell me she was home and check in about plans for that night. Figuring she was probably a bit worn out from work, I thought I'd answer in a way that would hopefully re-spark her zeal for the evening.

"Hey girl heyyyy! Ready for tonight? I can't wait to spend all night hearing British boys speak to me in that sexy accent..."

However, rather than Tibbie's sweet, rapid tone, I was instead startled when I was met with a very professional, yet gentle, male voice.

"Ms. Thorne?" he asked, sounding confused. "This is Dr. Lowell calling from Keats House. I do hope you found your way to London safely and soundly!"

I doubled back, embarrassed. Shit. Tibbie wasn't the only one with my number. It now came flooding back to me; the horrifying realization that I had also sent it to Keats House in an email so that they could call me to firm up logistics after my arrival. I scrambled to think of some way to redeem myself without looking like a complete idiot. After a brief pause, I managed to clear my throat and responded.

"Oh! Hello Dr. Lowell, my apologies, I thought you were... someone else."

Smooth. I could feel my face reddening. I quickly exited the gift shop, trotted down the stairs, and exited the museum so as to not disturb the other visitors.

On the other end of the line, Dr. Lowell gave a jolly laugh.

"So it would seem! Not to worry, Ms. Thorne. I admire your enthusiasm!"

Phew. I liked him already. While he had only spoken two sentences to me so far, his tone suggested he was intelligent, yet humble. And apparently not completely horrified by my verbal clumsiness – which was good, since that was pretty much my natural tendency. If I made that mistake with Penelope she would have made it a point to publicly berate me at the first opportunity possible.

He continued, "I was just checking in to see about your starting date. No rush, I want to make sure you get yourself settled in, but I just wanted to ensure that I had the proper paperwork in order for you and your workstation prepared by the time you arrive. I wouldn't want you to have to fuss with all of that nonsense yourself."

I had my own workstation? He was bringing the paperwork to me, rather than forcing me to fend for myself before getting my ass handed to me by human resources when I didn't turn in a form that I had no idea existed?

"We'd love to welcome you as early as Monday, but please dear, don't feel rushed. Take your time if you need to settle in!"

"Monday would be great, sir!" I responded enthusiastically.

Dr. Lowell laughed as he responded, "Please, do not feel the need to call me sir. It makes me feel pompous and rusty. If you need help finding your way, don't hesitate to give me a call. Enjoy the rest of your weekend! I look forward to meeting you Ms. Thorne!"

"I look forward to meeting you too!" I said with a smile. Then I realized I should probably mirror his informality. "And please, call me Emma!"

Dr. Lowell gave another cheerful laugh. "Right. See you soon, Emma!"

With that, the phone clicked to signal the end of the call and yet another detail of my new life snapped perfectly into place.

"A man's life of any worth is a continual allegory –
and very few eyes can see the mystery of life."

~ Letter to George and Georgiana Keats
14 February – 3 May 1819

———————

I walked home after work still relishing in the grandeur of the museum. When I entered our flat, I was greeted by the sight of Tibbie sitting cross-legged on the sofa sipping a glass of white wine. Suddenly, I realized she wasn't alone. Sitting across from her was a gorgeous, tall brunette girl wearing a white dress – which I could never, ever pull off – and stunning, black designer heels. Her legs were crossed delicately at the ankles as she sat across from Tibbie sipping wine from her own glass.

"Emma!" Tibbie shouted with her usual ebullient fervor, "So happy you're back!" She stood up and turned to the girl, holding out her hand in acknowledgement. "Emma, this is my best friend Beatrice Mulligan. Beatrice, meet my new roommate, Emma Thorne."

Beatrice stood, smiling and walked across the room to greet me, holding out her hand.

"So nice to meet you Emma. Thank you for taking care of my best girl here!"

I stood for a moment stunned by how poised and gorgeous she was. I snapped back to reality and raised my hand to meet hers.

"So nice to meet you Beatrice!" I said enthusiastically.

"I love your shoes!" I said, panicking and saying the first thing that came to my mind.

"Thank you!" She said enthusiastically, "I love your bag!"

I glanced downward. I was wearing a small, pink bag that my mom had given me before Tommy and I went on our trip to Italy. She bought it for me because she said the strap was long enough that I could wear it across my body and keep it in front of me so that I could protect my things from pickpockets. It was old and practically falling apart, so I didn't know if she was lying to be polite or if it fit some sort of British hipster-chic mold that I wasn't aware of.

"Thank you!"

Tibbie ran into the kitchen and grabbed another wine glass, quickly pouring me my own portion before sitting down and tapping a couch cushion, signaling for me to come join them. I sat down between them. It felt great to rest my feet after a long day of standing in the museum.

"So, how do you two know each other?" I asked.

"Beatrice and I were flat mates at Cambridge," Emma said excitedly.

Great. One genius wasn't enough. Now I'd probably really sound like a real moron.

"We both studied evolutionary biology, so we spent pretty much every waking moment together at university between our coursework and living together. To be honest, I'm surprised she hasn't tried to chuck me out of a window by now."

Beatrice chuckled. "Well, as if that weren't enough," she said jokingly, "Now we work together. She just can't seem to get enough of me."

"So you work with dinosaur bones?" I inquired.

"No, I'm not bloody artistic enough for that," she said, "Tibbie is the one with all of the talent in that department. I work in the division of research within the museum. Microbiology. What can I say, I just love the little buggers."

"Lucky Beatrice here gets to travel all over the world conducting research to write her fancy journals and boggle minds at seminars," Tibbie said smiling.

My brain started to reel in its struggle to rectify this stunningly beautiful, fashionable, confidently mannered woman with her role as a brilliantly innovative scientist who was a world master in a subject that sent me running in tears from a lecture hall my junior year of college.

"It's not quite as glamorous as it seems," said Beatrice. I was fairly certain her demure British nature was humbling her from admitting how amazingly exciting it really was.

"Plus, it's the only thing that keeps me from Tibbie here."

Tibbie grinned and refilled their wine glasses. "Beatrice is getting ready to leave for Geneva on Monday to go to the World Health Organization headquarters, so I made her promise that she'd come out with us tonight so you two could meet each other. We thought we could go head into Central London and grab some dinner and then go out to a nightclub, if that sounds alright with you?"

"Sounds great!"

"We thought we'd give you a proper welcome," Beatrice added. "The Central London clubs are a bit cheesy but they do represent a good example of the young British experience. Plus, they're crawling with randy boys. It's been far too long since my last shag and in those clubs, it's like fishing with dynamite."

"Beatrice!" Tibbie said, cutting her off.

Beatrice waved her hand dismissively. "Oh, psh, Tibbie stop being such a prude. It wouldn't kill you to tickle a knob once in a while. Before you know it you'll be so shriveled up like a dried fig that even Jude Law won't want to get into your knickers."

I worked to adjust to the fact that these hilariously profane words were coming out of the mouth of a girl named "Beatrice." I laughed as Tibbie hit Beatrice in the arm before getting up to retrieve another bottle of wine from the kitchen. Beatrice scooted closer to me on the couch and leaned in, placing her hand lightly on my knee.

"Before she gets back, I just wanted to let you know that I'm so glad you're here with Tibbie. I feel ghastly every time I have to leave her during the hard time she's been having. She was so lonely, the poor thing. Her grandmother meant everything to her. Anyway, it's nice to know that someone's here to keep her company. She really likes you. She was just telling me how great you are."

I was so glad she said that. When I first heard how close they were, I was afraid that it might be one of those catty situations where she saw me as competition between her and Tibbie and instantly hated me. But, I could tell that Beatrice was too self-assured for that. She was just genuinely happy that I could be there for her best friend.

We chatted for a bit while we finished our next round of wine. Then Tibbie said, "Well ladies we had better get a move on! I made us dinner reservations for 8:30."

We made our way to the tube station and took the train into Central London, emerging at the Covent Garden station. Tibbie had made us reservations at a Greek restaurant at the top of the square. We checked in with the hostess and settled in at a cozy high-top table in the back. We ordered a bottle of wine and a huge spread of food. I was wondering how our poor waitress was ever going to fit all of those plates on the tiny bistro-style table, but to my surprise, everything was served tapas-style on a tiered serving platter.

It seemed like Britain had a solution for everything. America was just so different. Everything needed to be so big, so much better than everything else. The constant competition just kept everyone on edge all of the time and so eager to tear down anything and anyone that posed even the slightest threat. I glanced around at the other tables and saw people who just looked so relaxed, so comfortable in who they were.

I heard all about Tibbie and Beatrice's travels. It sounded like they had been practically all over the world together, vising countries in Europe, Asia, Africa, South America, and North America. Since Beatrice's job required her to travel so much, Tibbie took advantage of her own flexible schedule and tagged along with Beatrice on a lot of her business trips. Then, since people in the U.K. get five weeks of vacation minimum, plus Beatrice was so in demand that she was able to negotiate her way all the way up to ten weeks off, they were often able to stay long after Beatrice's work duties were taken care of. They got to tour and relax in some of the most beautiful cities on earth.

In keeping with her candor from earlier that evening, Beatrice detailed her exploits with various men across the globe. She was hilarious. All of her stories were these crazy experiences that would never happen to most people. Even though she slept around a lot, for some reason she didn't come across as slutty. I think it was just because she was so smart and had her life together in every other area, so her fun-loving outlook on life and freedom with men was just a reflection of how confident and independent she was. I was pretty sure that while she liked to mess around, she would never go after a guy she thought you were interested in. Unlike some former childhood best friends I might mention.

"I probably should have warned you about Beatrice's bluntness when it comes to these things," Tibbie said smiling.

"No, trust me, I think it's great," I said. "It's about time someone gave these stupid boys a taste of their own medicine."

Beatrice raised her glass. "Here's to that!"

We paid our bill and left the Greek restaurant, stuffed to the gills with delicious food and wine. We walked across the square towards the center of Covent Garden where I saw a tremendous line coming from an otherwise innocuous looking stairwell leading to what appeared to be an underground basement. I realized that this was the wait for the club. It wrapped around the block. We would probably be waiting for at least an hour.

Except, to my surprise, Beatrice and Tibbie walked straight ahead to the entrance to the stairwell rather than turning right to make their way to the back of the dreadful line. Beatrice walked up to the bouncer and gave him a smile before giving him a quick kiss on the cheek and he escorted the three of us in, much to the chagrin of the people stuck in the long queue.

Tibbie turned around to explain. "She knows just about every bouncer in town. I used to feel really bad about cutting in line past all of these poor people, but now I just kind of go with it."

We headed over to the bar where Beatrice bought us a round of gin and tonics. Not two minutes passed before we were approached by a group of three British boys. I had a feeling Beatrice's come-hither look may have had something to do with it. One of the boys was quite handsome, bright green eyes and black hair. He was tall with one of those sideways smirks. He walked right up to me and leaned in, placing his hand on the bar right next to where I was standing.

"Hi there," he said confidently. I still definitely had not gotten over the novelty of a man speaking to me in a British accent.

"Why hello," I responded, shocking myself with how sultry I sounded.

The guy paused for a moment before a smile slowly spread across his face. "You're American," he said in a satisfied manner, "Even better. I'm James."

"Emma," I said, taking a sip of my drink, "Very nice to meet you, James." I tilted my head down and glanced at him upwards, lifting my eyebrows before narrowing my eyes in a flirtatious manner. Where the hell was this coming from? All of a sudden these things were coming naturally to me. It was like I had this sexy version of myself that had been in hibernation up until it was unleashed by cheap gin and the soft touch of a Thomas Pink button-down shirt on my forearm. Sensing my impending success, Beatrice and Tibbie grinned at me from behind James's back before turning to busy themselves with the remaining two guys, giving the two of us some privacy.

I quickly came to realize how valuable having a foreign accent could be. I thought American accents were quite crass and terrible compared to the rest of the world, but it turns out, they're quite exotic and inviting to British men. After some quick and idle chatter, James and I headed out onto the crowded dance floor where things escalated quickly. Before I knew it we were grinding, groping, and making out. Lost in the moment, I completely failed to consider how graphic we were being in front of that many people but it hardly mattered anyway. I was sure that in the dark, packed club where everyone was drunk and full of lust, few people are actually paying attention to anyone else around them.

We pulled away from each other, practically panting. "Want to get out of here?" he said, raising his eyebrows. I smiled, taking his hand as he turned eagerly towards the exit.

What the hell was I doing? I never in my life had a random hook up after a night at the bar, much less in a foreign country where I had no idea how to even get around. I would probably end up hacked up in an abandoned alley, never to be seen or heard from again. I was still my neurotic self after all, but while the thoughts did briefly cross my mind, I hardly cared. It was like this care-free British version of me emerged and I was unexpectedly filled with the kind of confidence I desperately wished I had when I was eating Swedish meatballs by myself in a corner at a fundraiser gala while Scarlett chatted up rich, gorgeous men as if it were the easiest thing in the world. I decided what the hell. Who in their late twenties hadn't had a one-night stand for God's sake? I might feel completely gross and trashy tomorrow, but screw it, he was hot and I was turned on from dry-humping on the dance floor for the past half an hour.

Thinking I should at least tell Beatrice and Tibbie before I ran off with this strange guy and they thought I had been kidnapped and murdered, I glanced around trying to locate them among the huge crowd. Beatrice was already sitting on one of James's friend's laps, fully ensconced in his mouth while his hand rubbed up and down her thigh.

Meanwhile, Tibbie was, true to form, taking a bit more of an innocent approach and smiling sweetly at the third guy while swirling her straw around in what I was pretty sure was the same gin and tonic drink she was given at the beginning of the night. I found it so funny that they were best friends. They were so different yet they somehow seemed to complement each other perfectly.

Beatrice emerged from her 'snogging' and did a quick glance around the room. She saw me standing there as James tugged my arm towards the door. She hit Tibbie on the leg.

Tibbie looked at her confused for a moment before she pointed in my direction and Tibbie turned her head towards me, realization dawning on her face. She smiled at me, waving me off to encourage me as Beatrice winked while alternating her fingers in a sultry wave. I smiled back before taking James's hand and following him out the door.

We emerged into Covent Garden, which took on an even more magical air at night, street lights glittering as a gentle breeze blew through the mild air. It was still relatively early for the downtown clubs so we were able to get a taxi quickly. James opened the door for me as I scooted across the back seat to make room for him as he followed me in.

"Green Park, please," he instructed the driver.

He slid across the seat towards me, taking my hand. I rested my head on his shoulder as he stroked his thumb across the top the top of my grip. I didn't say anything on the ride there. I was too taken back by the sights of London at night.

We passed beautiful building after breathtaking monument, all highlighted by twinkling lights. After a little while, the driver turned onto the main road that bordered the gorgeous park.

We pulled into a curved driveway in front of a red building with white-rimmed windows adorned with ornamental plaster protected by swirled iron balconies. James paid the cab driver and we ascended the red velvet carpeted staircase into the main lobby. Painted portraits of various past royals and politicians hung salon-style underneath a golden ceiling.

I followed him up the winding staircase to the third floor. We walked about half way down the decorative carpet to a room on the left. James unlocked the door, unveiling a massive flat complete with a chandelier in the middle of the room and a giant mahogany bed next to a matching wardrobe. I walked across the room to gaze out of the window, pulling the curtains back to reveal a gorgeous view of the park and the cobblestone streets. I turned back around to see James removing his watch and placing it on the nightstand before unbuttoning the cuffs of his dress shirt.

After some quick, idle chatter; it didn't take long before we got straight to the point. I have to admit, I half expected British men to be very formal and methodical in the sack, taking on a systematic rhythm and climaxing silently before following it up with something like, "Ah, yes, there we are. Job well done."

But I was way off. It was incredible. James was such a gentleman about things. It was all so romantic, gentle, and passionate. Not like the few guys I hooked up with since college who basically ripped my clothes off awkwardly and did their thing before rolling over and falling fast asleep, snoring.

Afterwards, talking to James was a piece of cake. Everything seemed so much more natural. The entire time our bodies were entwined as we held hands, rubbed our feet together, stroked each other's arms and gave soft kisses on each other's shoulders. We talked and laughed for hours until my eyes were so heavy I couldn't hold them open anymore and they slowly shut.

He gently kissed my eyelid and said "Goodnight, darling." He placed his forehead against mine, settling in for the night as I quickly drifted off into a sweet and satisfied sleep.

"The only means of strengthening one's intellect is to make up one's mind about nothing – to let the mind be a thoroughfare for all thoughts. Not a select party."

~ Letter to George and Georgiana Keats

24 September 1819

———————

The next morning I woke up to the sight of delicate morning rays beaming in through intricately embroidered, radiant, golden curtains. I stretched and rolled over to my other side to see a British man lying beside me. The events of the previous night started slowly coming back to me. James must have felt me stir because he rubbed his eyes and stretched his arms up over his head. He placed his hand gently on my cheek before pulling my face closer and kissing me.

Suddenly, I started to feel a bit dirty. Last night, after quickly gulping down more than one (okay more than four) drinks at the club, I think I was so inspired by Beatrice's devil-may-care attitude that I wanted to be more like her. But in the light of day, I realized that I really wasn't. I turned towards the window and James pulled me closer, hugging me from behind. As I gazed out onto the morning sky, I thought back to that morning after I was with Tommy, before I found out all of the horrible things that were happening behind my back. I had been so happy in that moment, so content with the intimacy I felt after spending the night with him. But, now I just felt uncomfortably and nervous. I wanted to get out of there as soon as humanly possible.

I glanced at my watch, it was rounding noon. "Well, I'd better get going," I said.

"So soon?" he said with disappointment, "I thought we could order breakfast in bed. Then work up an appetite while we wait for it to be delivered."

He started kissing the back of my shoulder in the same spot where Tommy had kissed me that morning. When Tommy had done it, it felt so wonderful. Now, all it did was remind me of him and I felt the sadness and longing returning

"Um, no actually I have to meet my friends, we are supposed to go shopping today," I said, thinking of the first excuse I could come up with.

"Oh, alright," he said frowning. I could tell he really wasn't heartbroken though, just disappointed that we weren't going to get in another round, that apparently would have taken less time than it would have taken for a hotel employee to toast some croissants and ascend seven floors. I had a feeling he would be just fine and that he would be right back on the prowl the following weekend.

Once I was dressed and collected all of my belongings, James threw a towel around his waist and walked me over to the door. He kissed me one last time. I turned back at him as I crossed the threshold of the exit and gave him a forced smile. He smirked back at me before closing the door. I didn't ask for his number and he didn't ask for mine.

I took my time as I walked towards the tube station. I felt my phone buzz in my pocket. Given that there were only two people in London who had my number and I doubted that Dr. Lowell was texting me in the middle of a Sunday afternoon, I had the distinct feeling that it was Tibbie.

Hi there! Hope you had a good time ;)
Stayed at Beatrice's place last night. If you've
freed up, we'll be heading to lunch in about a
half an hour – The Woodsman right by Hyde
Park Corner. Come join!

I smiled at the prospect of a huge order of fish and chips.

I found my way to the pub, immediately seeing Tibbie waving at me enthusiastically from a booth in the back. I sat down and the two of them grinned at me knowingly.

"Well then? Was he as good as he looked?" Beatrice asked with a smirk.

I decided to try to play it cool and at least come across like I was a confident woman who relished in one-night stands like Beatrice.

"Hah! I knew it!" Beatrice said. "He was tall with big hands, always a good sign. How many times did you manage to get it in?"

"Beatrice!" Tibbie said with a gasp. "You can't just ask people that."

I smiled. "Let's just say I'm quite famished. How about you guys? Any luck with the friends?"

Beatrice waved her hand dismissively. "Nah, nothing worth my time, really. I could tell he would be terrible in bed. He had really awkward hand gestures, licked his lips a lot. And soon enough, you'll learn that it would take about five dates and three bouquets of flowers before Tibbie would even kiss a bloke using her tongue."

Tibbie furrowed her eyebrows. "That's not true!"

I laughed and said, "Oh well. Beatrice, your guy was quite cute though. He looked like Joseph Gordon-Levitt from *Inception* in that vest."

"He was not wearing a vest!" Beatrice shouted at me defensively. I turned to her, confused, and furrowed my brow.

"He was so," I insisted, "How drunk *were* you?"

"Emma, he was NOT wearing a vest!"

She was so insistent that I thought I might be going crazy. I would have sworn he was wearing a vest. I had a few drinks, but I specifically remember when I was leaving and she was sitting on his lap. I recalled thinking how adorable he looked in it. I knew I wasn't wrong.

We went back and forth for a few minutes before Beatrice held out her hand.

"Hang on," she said before a quick pause, "What do you think a vest is?"

"You know, a vest! The thing that guys put over dress shirts but under jackets, with the little pockets you can put a pocket watch in or whatever. I know he wasn't wearing the traditional jacket, but that 40's gangster look is in these days, just look at Justin Timberlake!" I was finding it hard to believe that she was so appalled by the notion. Then, Beatrice and Tibbie broke into fits of laughter.

"What?" I asked, puzzled, "What is it?"

I had to wait a moment before their giggles died down but Beatrice eventually wiped the tears of laughter out of her eyes and was able to respond.

"That's a waistcoat!" she snickered, "I had no idea you Americans called it a vest!

I laughed, relieved that I hadn't offended her after all.

"Oh, thank God, I thought I was going crazy! What do you guys think a vest is then?"

"It's sort of an undershirt," Tibbie chimed in, "You know, like the tight white kind men wear under their dress shirts."

"Ohhhhh, you mean a wife-beater!" I said, realization dawning on me. This just sent Tibbie and Beatrice into more bouts of hysterics.

"Well, I've certainly never heard that term before," Beatrice admitted, "But I'm glad that settles that!"

I laughed until I became horrified.

"Oh my God, Beatrice, you thought I was saying you were dancing with a guy who was wearing his underwear in the middle of Central London? Thank God you said something! That's so embarrassing!"

I suddenly felt incredibly self-conscious. Even though English culture was sort of similar to American, it didn't occur to me that there could be small differences that would mean so much. This one luckily turned out to be funny and was something that could be laughed off, but what if I said something that really insulted someone because I was completely ignorant about what something means over here? What if I had been hurting people's feelings already and didn't know it?

I sat there, semi-distracted, until we decided that it was probably for the best that we head home. We took the tube back to Hampstead and stumbled through the front door. I said good night to Tibbie and turned to climb the stairs to my room. She tapped me on the shoulder and handed me a bottle of water.

"Here you are love! You might want to drink that before you drift off, water always helps avoid a dreadful hangover and that wouldn't be fun on your first day of work!"

I turned and took the water from her. My insecurities from earlier melted away and I became filled with happiness that I was in this amazing place with two great new people in my life. I stepped forward to give her a huge hug, the warmth of the multitude of drinks rolling over me.

"Thank you Tibbie! I'm so glad I'm here. You guys are such fun."

She smiled back drunkenly. "Pleasure dearest! Now go get some sleep! You have an early morning tomorrow!"

I climbed the stairs and crawled into bed feeling very happy.

"We read fine things but never feel them to the full until we have gone the same steps as the author."

~ Letter to John Hamilton Reynolds
3 May 1818

I got out of bed on Monday morning a half an hour before my alarm clock went off. Despite my alcohol-assisted euphoria from the night before, my good ol' reliable neuroses seemed to have won out. I was so worried that I was going to do something to make myself look like an idiot on my first day of work at Keats house that my anxious brain had only let me get two hours of sleep.

What was British office decorum like? Maybe they had some weird customary taboo about borrowing another person's stapler or something? Yep, that is *actually* what my brain came up with to worry about at 3:00 a.m. rather than getting a good night's sleep: stapler etiquette.

I took a shower and spent the next hour trying to pick out the perfect outfit. I settled on a knee-length black skirt, a white camisole, and a purple cardigan with low heels. Boring old classics can't go wrong with that, right? Although, with my luck I was sure I'd have a heel fall off by the time I got there.

I checked the map about a billion times to make sure I was 100% sure of where I was going. Even though the map said it was only 0.7 miles from my flat, I was convinced I was somehow going to take a wrong turn and end up horribly late. After I finally felt confident that there was no way in hell even I could mess it up at that point, I grabbed my bag and headed outside. The leaves were beautiful shades of green and a crisp breeze blew through the air, but the sun shone warm on my face. I walked up the street lined with English cottages and row houses adorned with petite flowers and I felt my anxiety slowly melt away.

I started up the hill towards Keats Grove. I took the turn and up the street. Just when I began to worry that I had gone completely in the wrong direction, I saw the distinctive fence that I had seen in all of my Google searches.

It was a solid, green metal fence that hid the house completely. It blended right in with the neighborhood around it where every house was completely shielded, not unlike the homes of the Hollywood hills. I couldn't help but wonder what bajillionaires and famous people resided behind those fences.

I walked up to the metal fence and pushed the button on the intercom, which immediately buzzed me in. I slid the heavy door open and walked over its threshold and was met face to face with the house's famous garden. The famous mulberry tree shaded a peaceful bench in the far corner of the lawn.

The house looked just how I imagined it from the pictures, a Regency Era home painted pristine white with seven windows lined up neatly in two rows. Three chimneys rose from the house's slightly slanted roof. Wrought-iron balconies protected the two arched windows on the ground floor, which bookended a beautiful green entry door. I walked up to the door timidly, took a deep breath, and knocked. Almost instantly, a short, pretty girl greeted me with wavy brown hair trimmed into a neat chin-length haircut. She looked very stylish in a vintage mod dress, purple tights, and 20s-era styled heels.

"You must be Emma!" she said, smiling. She shook my hand, clasping both hands around mine warmly. "I'm Violet. Please, do come in!"

I followed her across the threshold of the house and was met with a quaint foyer split by a staircase and a hallway.

"Let me take you on a brief tour and then I'll show you to the office!"

Violet led me left into a bright room with gorgeous windows, an ornate fireplace, and beautiful early nineteenth-century couches, armchairs, and bureaus.

"This here is the parlor," she said with a smile, "This is where our visitors enter, get their tickets and information, and can pick up some souvenirs. All of us get a chance to sit at the register and interact with the public. They're all lovely for the most part!"

I glanced around at all of the charming trinkets in the gift shop and desperately hoped that staff got some sort of discount.

From there, Violet showed me around the rest of the house. It was so beautiful with lovely wallpaper, lavish carpets, and giant windows that let the bright sun shine in. There were two bedrooms, where John Keats and Fanny Brawne had shared a wall.

It was here that Keats met the love of his life – the elegant yet indefatigable Fanny– when the Brawne family moved into the other side of Wentworth Place in Hampstead where Keats lived with his friend and fellow poet, Charles Brown.

Over the summer, his romance with Fanny blossomed as the two met often among the idyllic scenery of the house's garden. It was in this house that Keats wrote his most influential works under the spell of Fanny Brawne's beauty and the love that continued to grow between them.

Keats abandoned much of the melancholy of his earlier works and moved on to lovelorn manifestations such as "Ode to a Nightingale," where he describes his adulation as powerful and addicting as a drug.

Fanny's room had mannequins adorned with ornate dresses to showcase her experience as a seamstress. The kitchen and servant quarters in the basement were adorable with an impressive coal stove and authentic era copper cookware.

Finally, Violet took me to the Chester Room, the drawing room that the actress Eliza Jane Chester added to the house when she bought it in 1838. The room had deep crimson walls with a matching patterned carpet, rich velvet drapes and another ornately carved fireplace.

Violet raised her hand casually towards the room, "This is where we host our events and public programs. We do a lot of weddings here."

Well, good Lord, I could see why. I wanted to move into this room and spend the rest of my days in a plush, oversized armchair pompously sipping gin and tonics as I listened to jazz music and cavorted with high society.

"Well that about sums it up, let me bring you up to meet Dr. Lowell!" She escorted me back up the stairs to the wing we hadn't yet explored. She opened a door to reveal a slightly plump, jolly man with kind eyes shining behind round glasses. He looked exactly as I pictured him from his voice on the phone.

"Emma my dear!" he said as he stood up excitedly, "So nice to meet you darling! I'm glad you've traveled safely to us. I hope Violet has been taking good care of you so far."

He emerged from behind his desk and approached me, gently grabbing my two arms as he leaned in to give me two quick kisses on each cheek.

"Oh yes, she's been wonderful!" I said, nodding towards Violet as she smiled back at me.

"I don't know what I'd do without her," Dr. Lowell continued, "It's just the two of us here you know, but with Violet I never feel shorthanded. We are quite glad to have you here though, my dear. I know Violet will certainly appreciate some help!"

He gave her a quick, affectionate pat on the shoulder before pulling his overcoat off the back of his chair. "Well I have to run on a quick errand, but it's about time for tea, so why don't you ladies take a break and then we'll go over some things when I get back! Thank you again for helping us Emma, we're very excited you're here!"

I'd been here for a total of forty-five minutes and it was already time for a break. I could get used to this.

Violet brought me to a cozy corner room with a small table and some tiny kitchen appliances. She filled a kettle and placed it on a range. We chatted over tea and fresh pastries. She was so laid back and easy to talk to, it was obvious we were going to have a great time working together.

I learned a lot about her past and how she arrived at Keats House. She studied romantic poetry at Kings College before getting her master's degree in Museum Studies from University College London. I envied her as she answered my questions about her coursework, wishing I could go back in time and spend my college days learning all about the romantic poets, their influences, and their legacies. It must have been so fulfilling, unlike my horrendous law coursework.

As it turned out, her unique style was no coincidence. In her spare time she sewed her own clothes from her own unique patterns. She even sold her work to a local boutique and sometimes worked there on the weekends. It was one of the things that drew her to Keats House in the first place. She had been fascinated by Fanny Brawne's life and style as a seamstress. Violet lived in a loft flat in the area with her boyfriend Daniel and spent a lot of her time creating her own designs, decorating wine glasses and dinnerware, making mosaic vases, and even painting her own canvases to hang on the walls. She showed me some photos of her flat.

"You should come for a wine night with me and Daniel soon!" She said genuinely.

"I would love that!" I responded, so happy that we were hitting it off so well already.

After tea was finished, she led me down the narrow hallway to the closed door directly across from Dr. Lowell's office. The door opened to a charming converted bedroom with two small desks, each of which had its own small vase of fresh flowers.

"I thought it needed a bit of color! Anyway, this here is your desk. Luckily, I'm straight across the room so I'll be here to answer any questions! I normally come in around 9:00 or 9:30 in the morning and Dr. Lowell closes up the house at 4:30 p.m."

People here actually went home BEFORE 5:00 p.m. Back in D.C. that would have been about the halfway point of my day.

"Now I've made a list of small, fun projects to get you started. Have a seat and I'll be right over!"

I sat down at my little Regency era style desk (a stark contrast from my dumpster chair at Pendleton & Rowe) and gazed out onto the garden.

After we settled in, Violet showed me where the collections were stored and introduced me to the computer program used to input all of the information about each piece.

"Emma, I wanted to talk to you about a potential research project. We really need someone to go through Keats's original letters that we have in storage, organize them, write summaries, and store them in the proper acid-free folders. They've been so woefully neglected! I'm hoping that if everything is in order and easily accessible that we can start a blog that posts tid-bits of their love affair through quotes of the letters, which I'm hoping will draw more people to the house. It's something I've wanted to do forever but I've just been so swamped with public programs! Before you came, it was just the two of us and we were so overwhelmed. It would be a lot of work though; do you think it's something you might be interested in?"

I instantly got excited. I'd always been able to take a few minutes to read Keats's odes since they were so short that I could squeeze them into my hectic life, but I had always wanted to read the love letters he and Fanny exchanged while they were away from each other more closely. I read a short one once and it was so beautiful, I had ached to read more.

"That sounds perfect!" I said enthusiastically.

Violet breathed a sigh of relief. "Thank you so much Emma, this is a huge favor!"

I was eager to get started immediately. I wanted to know as much as possible about the romance that had so intrigued me and been such a big part of why I moved here in the first place. Violet led me into the room where the letters were currently laid flat and scattered in drawers.

"The first thing I need you to do is just put them in order. All you'd have to do is look at the dates at the top. Sorry, I know it's a bit tedious!"

"Oh trust me, I don't mind at all," I assured her.

I sat down to get to work. The first thing I did was put everything into chronological order so that I could see their romance bloom from start to finish. I had read that Keats had met Fanny in the midst of great personal turmoil (something I could currently sympathize with, although my problems weren't quite as bad as his).

His mother had just died of tuberculosis and his brother George was quite sick with the disease. Plus, he had no money. He couldn't quite devote his time to his feelings towards Fanny. She intrigued him and she was a welcomed distraction, but that was it at the very beginning. That first day, I only got through the early letters, but I could hardly wait to read more about how their relationship grew over time. I couldn't believe this was actually my job.

"Give me books, French wine, fruit, fine weather and a little music played out of doors by somebody I do not know."

~ Letter to Fanny Keats
Winchester
28 August 1819

———————

I spent the remainder of my first week getting settled in, shown around, and introduced to all of the wonderful programs, events, and tours that the house offered. Everything seemed so wonderful, so happy and enlightening. It was a reminder that life can be euphoric and uplifting, and jobs didn't have to be depressing and make one so forlorn they lose themselves.

The following Saturday, the house was hosting a young piano prodigy who had written a concerto inspired by Keats's poetry. I was eager to see it, as I've always loved classical music, and was curious about how the beauty of Keats's poems could nurture young talent. Plus, I just loved being at Keats House. It made me feel so light, so content.

I hadn't gotten a chance to continue my project on the letters, so I got to my desk early in hopes that the environment would be inspirational. There were a lot of letters to sift through and I wanted to get started right away so I could report back to Violet and show her how seriously I was taking it. I sat down at my computer, logged in, and pulled up a blank word document. I stared at the screen for five minutes, drumming my fingers and trying to decide where to start. Finally, I lifted my fingers and started typing.

Twenty-three-year-old John Keats met eighteen-year-old Fanny Brawne in the autumn of 1818. The thirty-seven love letters and notes Keats wrote to Fanny bear compelling witness to their romance...

After that, I had nothing. I sifted through the copies I had made of the original letters earlier in the week so I would have them on hand but wouldn't have to handle the delicate originals. After about an hour of looking for themes and a way to begin, I finally gave up and went to help Violet set up in the garden.

The garden had already been prepped for the performance. Elegant white chairs with golden cushions were neatly positioned in lines with sparkly white ribbons connecting each row from behind. The house's historic piano had been moved from Chester drawing room onto a white stage underneath a trellis in the garden lined with ivy. A few visitors were beginning to trickle in and take advantage of a table that was set up with a tea service complete with finger sandwiches and various cakes and tarts. I walked up to Violet and smiled a sideways grin apologetically.

"Sorry I'm late Violet, I was upstairs working on my project. I didn't expect everything to be set up already! I was hoping I'd be able to help."

She immediately greeted me with a huge hug. "Oh, nonsense Emma. Today is your day off and I'm just happy you're joining. Thank you for helping us get the word out, we have more R.S.V.P.s for this event than any of our public programs in years!"

Keats enthusiasts continued to pour into the garden, helping themselves to the snacks and glasses of lemonade before taking their seats in front of the lovely outdoor stage. I took my seat next to Violet. Dr. Lowell stood up and took to the microphone to address the large crowd.

"Today, we are quite pleased to have with us an inspiring up-and-coming pianist whose talent is matched only by his creativity. We are honored that he has agreed to perform songs from his thesis project at the Royal Academy of Music, all of which were inspired by the words and legacy of the one and only John Keats. Please join me in welcoming today's distinguished guest, Anders Enfield!"

Anders waved to the crowd before sitting down at the piano bench. He took a moment to close his eyes, stretching out his fingers and rolling his neck in preparation. Then, he placed his fingers gently on the keys and began to play.

The concerto was exquisite, capturing the essence of Keats's romantic themes with delicate notes evoking images of starry skies, nightingales, and pining hearts. I was blown away by how talented this boy was at just twenty years old. It was obvious that those twelve hours a day of practice paid off, but I could tell that he had a natural talent that could be matched by very few.

After Anders finished, I walked up and shook his hand, thanking him for appearing and giving the Keats House audience such a wonderful treat. He thanked me humbly for the opportunity and said that any time we'd like to have him back, he'd be happy to oblige. For such a phenomenal musician, he was surprisingly modest. I assured him that I'd be in touch. He turned around and disappeared into the crowd, off to enjoy the reception and the certain praise with which all of the attendees were sure to shower him.

I scanned the crowd and found Violet neatly arranging a stack of Anders's C.D.s on a table in the garden. She leaned one against the pile to display the album entitled *The Threshold of the Morn,* a reference to one of Keats's lesser-known poems, "Apollo and the Graces". She continued organizing the small table of ephemera as I turned back to the crowd and glanced around, happy to see that everyone seemed to be enjoying themselves. I walked across the garden to give her a hand.

"He's amazing!" I said enthusiastically, glad that the performance went off without a hitch and I could breathe a sigh of relief at not having embarrassed my mentors on my first attempt at assisting with a public program.

"That was wonderful," Violet, agreed, "I have a feeling we're going to sell quite a few of these!" She spun back to the check-in table and continued putting everything into perfect order.

My gaze reached the end of the garden. Suddenly, my eyes fell upon a tall, very handsome guy standing off on his own in the corner with a glass of champagne, surveying the garden. Perhaps I was love-drunk from being exposed to romantic piano music all afternoon, but I was immediately stricken. He looked about my age with brown hair that matched his gorgeous brown eyes. He wore a tailored black sport coat atop a white dress shirt with the top button casually unfastened, making him look effortlessly, debonair. He looked like the perfect combination of a Proust-reading art enthusiast and a Burberry model.

I couldn't help but stare at him as he strode across the lawn leisurely, while I prayed the entire time that he wouldn't look up to see me gawking. I felt a tap on my shoulder and realized Violet had been trying to summon my attention. I regained my composure slightly, turning to face her.

"You alright there, Emma?" She said with a hint of concern, "I've called your name three times now. Is everything ok?"

I cleared my throat, shaking it off.

"Yes! Fine! Sorry Violet. How can I help?"

"I was asking if you could bring some of these albums up to Anders to see if he'd be nice enough to sign them. Would you mind? I think it might help us with the sales."

She handed me a stack of discs. I took them from her absentmindedly, trying very hard to resist the temptation to turn around and ogle awkwardly some more. Somehow gathering the wherewithal to form a sentence, I collected my courage and decided to ask Violet if she knew him.

"Hey, Violet," I said nervously, in spite of myself, "Do you happen to know that guy over there?" I pointed him out with a delicate head nod to avoid drawing attention to the fact that I was talking about him.

She whipped around hastily, drawing the exact kind of attention I had been trying to avoid. Luckily, his back was turned at the time.

"Ohhhh, him," she said knowingly, "That's Andrew Bradford, believe it or not. He's one of our members."

She smirked slightly and handed me more discs.

"He's... quite handsome, isn't he?" I tried to say casually.

"Oh, yes he's lovely," said Violet, with a hint of longing. Had I not met her cute, charming boyfriend and seen how in love they were, I would have sworn she had a major crush on him. But, I couldn't say I would blame her.

"He's actually quite nice too, surprisingly."

"Why is that surprising?" I asked.

Violet looked confused at first, until I think it dawned on her that I wasn't exactly from around here.

"Well, he's the only son of the Bradford family, one of the oldest and wealthiest noble families in the U.K. His father is a Duke. I think that's why he keeps to himself most of the time, likes to keep a low profile. We've actually had a few paparazzi trying to get some snaps of him before at events. Dr. Lowell went after them though. I think they're a bit afraid to come back here. Dr. Lowell's a sweet man, but you wouldn't want to mess around with him when he means business."

So, basically, I just fell for the most eligible bachelor in the U.K. Fabulous.

"He's here most weekends," Violet said when I didn't respond. "Andrew really loves Keats, studied British Literature at Oxford."

Great. Now he was even more perfect. This was turning into a tragedy.

"He frequents our public programs. I'm fairly certain that his presence accounts for at least half of our female visitors. But, I'd still like to think Keats has at least something to do with it."

A woman walked up to the table and Violet turned to tend to her new customer. Meanwhile, I couldn't help myself from wanting to stare at Andrew Bradford. Casually, I brushed my hair behind my ear and darted my eyes to the left to steal a glance. To my enormous surprise, I found him looking directly at me. Startled, I quickly darted my eyes away. From then on, I resisted any temptation to look in his direction, determined to be "cooler" than all of those other girls who constantly gawked at him. Although, I'm sure you could likely feel my nervousness in the air from five feet away.

I somehow managed to distract myself by helping Violet breakdown all of the tables and putting away the leftover refreshments. By the next time I allowed myself to do a full survey of the garden, he was gone. At around 4:30, Violet thanked me profusely and gave me a huge hug and told me to get out of there because it was Saturday and I should be having fun. I assured her that I had indeed been having fun with her at the house and that I was definitely planning on helping out with more events in the future.

As I started my stroll home, I couldn't stop thinking about Andrew. While I hardly even exchanged a glance with him, there was just something about him I couldn't quite put my finger on. I'm sure it was just good old fashioned primal attraction, but it was a unique feeling I'd never had before. I realized how ludicrous and desperate I sounded in my head, like one of those damn young adult novels where the girl is instantly captivated by the intriguing, handsome stranger and slowly denigrates into a blithering hot mess who can't even imagine life without him. I vividly remember reading one of those for book club once and actually feeling feminism taking a decade-long step backwards. As I reached out to turn my key to open the front door, I decided to shake it off and focus on what Tibbie and Beatrice had in store for the night.

I opened the door to see Tibbie and Beatrice already indulging in a round of red wine.

"Emma! Come join us!" Tibbie said enthusiastically. She patted the spot next to her on the couch and poured a glass of wine.

"Thanks Tib. Hey, so what do you guys feel like doing tonight?" I asked, hoping to go out and be served with some distractions to divert my attention from Andrew Bradford.

"Well," Tibbie said smiling, "I think I have a good suggestion. The museum is having an after-hours event this evening for adults only. They'll have food, drinks, and a live jazz band. Plus, we'd get to have an exclusive sneak preview of the new exhibition. It's all about the nature of sex and how different species mate."

Beatrice raised her glass in agreement. "Sexual nature, eh? Should get all of those lovely young lads in the mood for when we're ready to head out. I vote yes."

We quickly got ready. I settled on a simple black cocktail dress, hot pink shoes and a silver clutch. I did a quick spin in the mirror, quite pleased with how I looked. All of the walking around London gave me some exercise and while I didn't own a scale, I was pretty sure I managed to lose some weight since I arrived – despite my frequent indulgences in British chocolate. Of course I was knocked down a peg once I came downstairs and saw Beatrice looking amazing in a sultry, purple plunging number and Tibbie looking adorable in a brightly colored mod-style dress that I could never pull off. Nevertheless, I was still quite happy with myself.

Rather than bother with the tube, Tibbie insisted on paying for the expensive cab ride to South Kensington. After a long and beautiful drive soaking up the sights of London at night, the cabbie pulled over to signal that we had arrived at our destination. I climbed out of the cab, making sure that my dress stayed in the appropriate areas so as not to give any passersby an unwelcomed show.

The museum was a gorgeous, ornate stone building with embellished windows that lined up on either side to intersect two climbing turrets that surrounded a large arched entryway. We entered through the high, heavy iron doors into an open interior hall reminiscent of the grand architecture of impressive nineteenth-century train station terminals.

Decorative iron crossbeams hugged each interior arch periodically interrupted a tall, dramatic coffered ceiling. I was immediately greeted by the skeleton of a huge dinosaur whose label informed me was a *Wyoming diplodocus*. Tibbie ran up and tapped me on the arm.

"Emma, meet George!" she said excitedly. "Ok, so he doesn't have a real name, but that's what I call him. He's a to-scale plaster model. I helped cast a lot of his parts! He's so friendly, isn't he?"

He actually did look kind of friendly. Not a word I thought I'd ever use to describe a dinosaur skeleton, but there you go. I took a photo of Tibbie in her adorable outfit with her hands thrown out at her side and her head turned up, pretending to kiss George the dinosaur.

We made our way over to the center of the amazing atrium, of course going directly to the bar. We ordered some specialty cocktails based on the exhibition's theme – the Ravishing Raspberry – and moved more towards the side of the room to have a better angle for scoping out the situation. Beatrice instantly began making eyes at a tall, handsome guy in the corner who looked as though he just stepped out of the halls of Parliament. There were a ton of cute, young guys there. Apparently, we had stumbled upon a great venue with an ample selection of able-bodied men. We vowed to return to these events more often. Tibbie then informed us that we couldn't bring our drinks into the exhibition for risk of damaging the artifacts and specimens. We quickly knocked back our cocktails and made our way to the gallery.

The exhibition was fascinating. I had no idea how complex sex really was. There were all sorts of courtship rituals and seduction methods that were so perplexing. For instance, I learned that female duck vaginas are so complicated and convoluted that they can actually block the sperm of unwanted males and save the semen from their desired companions to fertilize themselves. Did you know that a male octopus's penis literally breaks off during mating and grows back the following season? Because I didn't. Apparently snail genatalia are on their necks. And my favorite fact: a barnacle has a penis thirty times his body length.

The end of the gallery concluded with a discussion about the complexity of human reproduction and its non-conventional elements that drive sexual attraction. Basically, it focused on how fucking complicated sex becomes when emotions get involved.

I managed to distract myself all night by glancing around at all of the gorgeous, eligible bachelors around me, but when I was confronted with explicit images of humans having sex, I was immediately aroused by the thought of Andrew in that adorable outfit, modestly radiating sexiness as he moved his way calmly and collectedly through the Keats House garden.

I thought for sure that Beatrice was going to go home with the gorgeous budding politician she had been eye-fucking all night, but in the end she surprised me by coming up to Tibbie and I and asking if we'd like to stay at her flat for the evening.

"I don't know about you, but I'm completely knackered," she said in a way that made me think that she really wasn't but was saying it for our advantage so we'd have somewhere in the area to crash for the night. "Why don't you come to mine and we'll have a night cap and some dessert?"

Tibbie and I smiled at each other before she responded, "We'd love to."

It was a relatively short walk back to Beatrice's flat. Until I hit the night air, it hadn't hit me just how drunk I was. Tibbie and Beatrice must have felt the same way because as soon as we walked through the door to Beatrice's apartment, Tibbie stumbled over to the pantry and took out a bag of popcorn kernels. I plopped into a chair as Beatrice started munching on some biscuits from the cabinet.

"You alright Em?" Tibbie said as she began to make a batch of popcorn on the stove, "You seem a bit quiet."

I had a bit of a propensity to shut down and cease talking whenever I had too much to drink. I think my body knew me well enough to know that if I did open my mouth, I'd likely say something stupid and make a fool out of myself. But this time, I had something on my mind. Despite my better efforts, my brain kept wandering back to that damn Andrew Bradford with the sun reflecting off of his coiffed hair. Ordinarily I would have probably been super shy and changed the subject, but I had a feeling Beatrice might have some good, and likely quite forthcoming, advice.

"I can't stop thinking about this guy who came to the program at Keats House today," I blurted out.

Beatrice looked up and in her drunken state, dropped the biscuit she was eating. She waltzed over to the table. She smirked at me and leaned in.

"Go on then, let us have it."

"He was so unbelievably gorgeous," I recounted.

Tibbie attempted to pour the popcorn from the pot into a bowl, spilling about half of it on the floor in the process. She walked over and plunked the bowl on the table, taking the seat across from me.

"Did you talk to him? What's he like?" she asked excitedly.

"No I didn't talk to him!" I said as if it was the most ridiculous suggestion on the planet, which it might as well have been.

"Well why not, you idiot?" Beatrice asked frankly.

Seriously what the hell was wrong with me? I couldn't have picked one of the other four million men living in London?

"Apparently, he's one of the most desired bachelors in Europe."

Tibbie and Beatrice shouted at the same time, "Who?"

"Oh, I don't know he's probably not that famous. His name is Radford. No. Bradford. Andrew Bradford," my drunken ass finally managed to put together.

Tibbie and Beatrice's jaws dropped as they snapped to look at each other and then back to me.

"Andrew Bradford?" Beatrice gasped, "Are you fucking serious? You actually SAW Andrew Bradford today. In the flesh?" She asked skeptically.

Tibbie looked stunned. "Are you absolutely positive it was him?"

I doubled back a bit, shocked. The way they were acting made it seem like he was more famous than William and Harry.

"Yeah, it was definitely him, Violet says he's a big Keats fan and comes there sometimes on the weekends. Why, is he really a big deal?"

Beatrice guffawed.

"Have you even picked up a newspaper or magazine since you've been here?"

She walked over to her nightstand and picked up an issue of *OK! Magazine*. She returned to the table and plopped it in front of me. The headline read *Love Reunited? Andrew Bradford and Amelie L'Amour Spotted Having Coffee Together in Paris Café*. There he was right on the cover, sitting at a bistro table in front of a charming French restaurant across from an extremely elegant girl with a chin-length haircut laced with soft, brown waves.

"I'm so jealous you saw him in person!" Tibbie chimed in, "Is he every bit as gorgeous as he looks in pictures?"

Beatrice picked up the magazine again and stared at its cover, shaking her head. "I can't believe you're going to shag Andrew Bradford. You lucky, lucky slag."

"No I'm not," I said, my heart dropping, "He clearly has a girlfriend." It occurred to me that she was probably super famous and coveted as well. "Who is she?" I inquired.

"She's a French socialite," Beatrice explained, "Might was well be royalty though since her family has so much old money they pretty much run half of France. She works in European high fashion, so there are always pictures of her all over the Internet of her at fancy runway shows. Everyone thinks she's all perfect and glamorous. But she's always seemed so uppity and vile to me. For some reason it seems like everyone else is obsessed with her. Probably just because she's French."

Not to mention stunning. Looking at the photo, I felt instantly inferior by comparison.

"How did they meet?"

Tibbie chimed in. "They went to Oxford together. There's this famous story that they met in a literature class, so it's been reported as a fairy tale romance from there. Everyone was quite crushed when they broke up last year."

"But this says they're dating again," I said, disappointedly.

"There's always gossip that they're back together," Tibbie explained, "But then the next day it says they're broken up.

"It's such a saga," Beatrice said exhaustedly.

"What does he do?" I asked curiously.

"He mostly works for charities and does pretty much everything pro bono. He's a huge philanthropist, advocates for a lot of good causes. Doesn't need the money, that's for bloody sure."

Beatrice and I looked at each other and raised our eyebrows. That was the first time I'd ever heard Tibbie curse.

"Anyway, back to Amelie," Beatrice continued, "Can you please get on with it and break them up for good so that I don't have to hear about it anymore?"

"Um, yeah right. That would require talking to him."

"Oh just talk to him for fuck's sake, what's the worst that could happen?" Beatrice said with a wave of her hand.

My mind immediately thought of about a thousand things that could go wrong. There was no way I was talking to him, but staring at him was good enough.

"For myself I know not how to express my devotion to so fair a form: I want a brighter word than bright, a fairer word than fair. I almost wish we were butterflies that liv'd but three summer days – three such days with you I could fill with more delight than fifty common years could ever contain."

~ Letter to Fanny Brawne
Shanklin, Isle of Wight
3 July 1819

On Wednesday mornings, Keats House hosted a book club. It was mostly stuff about poets, but overall it was a way to give the house more exposure. Violet told me that this was her favorite program, and I was certainly having a lot of fun helping her with it. It was an eclectic group of people young and old, college students to retired senior citizens, and everyone always had fascinating perspectives.

We always started the day by heading to a bakery at the top of the hill and picking up their famous croissants. To be honest, I think they were probably one of the main reasons that people showed up for the poetry club at all. They melted in your mouth and tasted like heaven – I swear I could eat about five of them and still be desperate for more.

We ordered three dozen and paid the cashier. Violet headed to the end of the counter to pick up a stack of napkins. I was struggling a bit to stay awake, so I decided to indulge in an iced latte. I had just taken the lid off to pour in some cream when I spun around and slammed right into a poor, unsuspecting guy who doubled back as my cup smashed into his chest and the liquid doused his very expensive looking shirt and blazer. My mouth dropped, horrified as I scrambled to find some napkins.

"Oh my God, I am so, so, so sorry! I didn't see you!"

I spun around from the counter to grab a fist fill of napkins to lap up the mess. As I lunged frantically trying to soak up the coffee before it stained the poor guy's posh looking outfit, I looked up and found myself face-to-face with Andrew Bradford. I froze in my tracks. Shocked, my grip loosened and the napkins fluttered down to the floor. He paused for a moment before offering a friendly smirk.

"Don't worry, it was my fault. I wasn't looking where I was going."

Still frozen, I focused all of my energy on making sure that my mouth didn't gape open. I realized that I had just made matters worse by dropping the napkins and making an even bigger mess.

Snapping back to reality, I bent over to pick up the napkins and lap up the mess. However, just as I leaned down, Andrew simultaneously ducked to clean the mess and our heads slammed together. I fell back on my ass, my legs sprawling awkwardly into the air.

I lay there for a moment, desperately hoping that it hadn't looked as mortifying as it felt. I finally concluded that it was probably even worse than I thought. Yep, leave it to me. I had just successfully done the exact worst thing one could do in front of a hot, sexy, famous heartthrob.

Swallowing my pride, I struggled to sit up. Then, I saw a masculine hand reaching out to assist me. I looked up and found myself staring straight into Andrew Bradford's chocolate brown eyes. Even with their dark hue, they somehow sparkled. He gazed back into mine. After what felt like an eternity, I reached out and took his hand. As he pulled me up, I felt a rush of excitement ripple throughout my entire body.

"Thanks," I said, smiling back at him dumbly. Then, horrified, I remembered that I had just soaked the entire front of him with coffee.

"Oh God! Your shirt! I'm so sorry!! Here, please, let me help."

I squatted down frantically and picked up the napkins, now sprawled all over the floor. I stood up and instinctively started pressing the napkins across his shirt in a likely futile attempt to soak it up before it set in. As I dabbed the sprawling stains, I felt his rock hard chest before moving my way down to his lean, tight abs. I lingered on his stomach and felt the lines of his six-pack as my body clenched with magnetism. Then, realizing what I was doing, I snapped back and turned away frantically, pretending to search for a trash can as an excuse to collect myself.

I felt a strong, yet gentle hand rest on my shoulder. I twirled around and almost fell over again before harnessing my balance, regaining my composure, and looking back up. He took the drenched napkins from my grip, his hands grazing mine and sending goose bumps down my spine.

"The rubbish bin is over there," he said, grinning before turning around and depositing the napkins into the bin. While his back was turned, I took the opportunity to fluff my hair and pull my shirt back down into position. He walked back to where I was standing and gave me another heart-melting smile.

I saw that my attempts to salvage his perfectly tailored designer outfit were in vain and that he was still doused with dark liquid. As he approached, he took off his blazer, revealing the button-down dress shirt beneath. As he reached to pull off the second sleeve, I could see the taut musculature of his arm rippling against the crisp, white fabric.

Somehow shaking off my primal instinct to jump him right then and there, I was about to apologize again when he asked,

"Haven't I seen you at Keats House?"

Shocked that he recognized me, I attempted to calm myself before responding.

"Um, yes! Yes you did! I was there. I actually work there." I stumbled. I hated myself.

Despite my life-ruining awkwardness, he smiled.

"So you're from America?" he asked upon hearing my accent, sounding intrigued. "Whereabouts?"

"Washington, D.C." I said timidly.

"I've visited America a few times on business, it's quite lovely. I'm Andrew, by the way," he said, extending his hand.

"Emma," I said shakily, holding out a limp hand in response. He gently gripped my hand and shook it in greeting, sending another current of chills throughout every inch of my body.

There was a long pause. I got worried that this was becoming idle chat and since I couldn't think of anything interesting to say and he would soon become terribly bored and run off. But, it turns out, I was wrong.

"So, Emma. Would you like to go to dinner sometime?" he asked bluntly, taking me completely surprise. Not only was his tousled John Mayer-esque hair enough to make any woman melt, but that posh, British accent was just plain unfair. I swooned thinking about sitting down to a fancy dinner, seeing him all dressed up sitting across from me, radiating that power swag that always made me melt, one of the things I always loved about Tommy.

Tommy. The thought of power swag sent my brain right back to Tommy. I flashed back to him standing in his underwear, betraying me. Then, reality started to set in. When it came down to it, weren't all hot, powerful guys like Tommy? Out for themselves with the world at their disposal and tons of women ready to drop everything to be with them, leading girls on to get one thing before they moved on to the next one? I just couldn't take another hit like the one I had when I saw Tommy hooking up with Scarlett. I just wasn't ready. Then, I realized that an embarrassingly long period of time had past and that since Andrew had asked me a very direct question that I probably should have answered him by now.

"Um... well... the thing is..." I stammered. I couldn't believe myself standing there about to turn down a guy who millions of women would kill for one drink with.

"So, is that a no?" he asked.

"No! Not no. I mean that's not what I meant. No..."

He smirked, leaning in closer.

"So, that's a firm no?" he asked, although he still sounded quite confident.

"No!" I said desperately. Jesus, just stop saying no, I thought. I flashed back to my fantasy of him sitting across from me at the restaurant. Suddenly, it all started to seem like a great idea.

"So, does that mean no you don't want do or no you don't mean no?" he said, smiling a gorgeous grin. He was so charming. It just wasn't fair. Finally I thought what the hell, at least it would be a fun fling.

"I mean yes. I'd love to."

"Great," he said, turning to grab a napkin. He took out a pen and jotted down some digits.

"Here's my number," he said, his hand brushing against mine as he handed me the napkin. "Talk to you soon."

As he turned and exited the restaurant, several women followed his path, gawking at him shamelessly before twisting back and staring at me in shock.

Violet approached me from the other side of the cafe, her mouth hanging open in the same look as every other female presence in the room.

"Was that what I think it was?" she asked, in shock, "Did you just get Andrew Bradford's number?"

"Yes," I responded, feeling stunned. "I guess I did."

"You could sell that for about a million pounds you know," she said, grinning.

The next day, I gave Andrew a call. It was so refreshing that he had given me his number instead of asking me for mine. That way I didn't have to do the whole staring at my phone pathetically for three days routine, the way it always had gone down with American guys in D.C. After debating with myself for about an hour, I decided to call him rather than text. I was originally afraid it would seem so old fashioned in this day and age, but I came to the conclusion that it would be more personal and show him how much I wanted to see him again.

My heart pounded as I dialed his number. Worried that my voice would crack or sound horse, I cleared my throat loudly. Just as the action was at the peak of its disgustingness, he simultaneously answered the phone.

"Hello?"

Ugh. Talk about awkward. I sounded like some sort of classless elephant.

"Um, sorry. I had something in my throat. It's Emma by the way!"

We arranged a date for the following Friday. I wrote down the name and the address and made a mental note to look it up way ahead of time and figure out how long it would take me to get there so I wouldn't be late.

Friday came before I knew it, and of course I was an absolute wreck. I hated all of my clothes, my hair wasn't cooperating, and I just could not get my make-up right. I kept picturing that damn photo of Amelie L'Amour in her perfect outfit with her immaculate hair and impossibly fashionable shoes. Here I was, in my discount wear that I bought at some bargain outlet about four years ago.

Tibbie was trying desperately to help me and calm me down, but I was just way too nervous.

"He's just a person!" she kept insisting, "You didn't even know who he was until less than a week ago. Just pretend he's an ordinary guy."

"That's easy for you to say!" I said, harsher than I meant to. "I'm sorry Tibbie, I'm just a mess right now."

To my great relief, she giggled.

"Oh Emma, I know. Don't worry, we'll figure this out."

As it turns out, Tibbie was really good at hair and make-up. She looked so effortlessly adorable all of the time, so I just figured that look came to her naturally, but it turns out she was a whiz with a curling iron. She somehow got my hair to fall into a perfect wavy style.

Then, even though I had never seen her with more than a sparse dose of eyeliner, she somehow managed to do my makeup so that my skin looked flawless and my lips were the perfect shade of pink. Plus, she gave me smoky-eyes that looked straight off the cover of *Vogue*. Beatrice came over with two bottles of wine and a selection of options from her designer wardrobe. She was quite close to my size, so it was nice to have a new selection of viable options. I settled on a little black dress with a plunging neckline and a lacy back.

After two glasses of wine, I was finally calming down a bit until I glanced up at the clock. It read 7:12 p.m. I was due to meet Andrew in Central London in less than an hour, so I popped up in a panic, grabbing my jacket to run out the door. I turned around desperately to Beatrice and Tibbie trying to compose myself. Luckily, Beatrice read my mind, waltzed over, and put both of her hands on my shoulders.

"Alright love, you can do this. Just remember to wrap it up. He's a famous millionaire after all. Wouldn't be surprised if he's been around the block a wee bit."

Not the most soothing of advice.

Tibbie stepped in, "Just be you! There's nothing not to love about you," she said with a sparkle in her eye. Part of me wanted to go through the laundry list of things that were wrong with me, but she sounded so genuine that for a moment, I believed her. It was just enough to get me through the door and to the tube station before I started panicking again.

Andrew picked a nice French restaurant by Bond Street. If nothing else, I was excited about the meal itself because I loved French food. My mouth started watering on the way to the tube station.

I was abruptly struck with anxiety over what was appropriate to order on the first date. Should I just order a salad or some lean fish and steamed vegetables? I had been out of the game for so long that I had no idea how it worked anymore.

Before I knew it, I was approaching the entrance to the restaurant. I could see him through the set of double doors waiting for me in the vestibule by the host stand. He looked so handsome in a burgundy tie and a black suit jacket. I took a deep breath and walked through the door.

He looked up and gave me an endearing, sideways smile before simply saying, "You look lovely. Shall we?"

The maître de ushered us through the restaurant in an attentive manner that made me feel as though Andrew was a frequent patron who tipped generously. We arrived at a table towards the back. I slid across my end of the booth carefully in an attempt to avoid flashing everyone or pressing too hard against the bench and exposing the cellulite on my thighs. I managed to sidle in without exposing myself, mentally claiming a small victory. The maître de handed us the menus before saying, "Enjoy" with a gentle bow and walking back to his post. Andrew looked across the table and smiled at me.

"I'm not sure what sort of food you like, but they have the most exquisite duck a l'orange. Of course it's almost all pure fat, but I say life isn't worth living without delicious food."

My absolute favorite. Well, looks like I didn't have to worry about watching my calorie intake around him after all.

"That sounds wonderful," I said, "I'll have that."

When the waiter returned, Andrew ordered us the chef's recommended bottle of wine (that I'm sure I didn't even want to know the cost of), some mushroom tartlets for an hors d'oeuvre, and two orders of the duck. He handed the menus back to the waiter and turned his attention back to me.

"So, Emma," he asked, "What brings you to London?"

While I'm sure he figured this was a benign question, it led to an internal struggle where I evaluated just how much to reveal to him on this first date.

"Well," I said, clearing my throat, "I was lucky enough to get the opportunity to work at the house, and I love John Keats, so it seemed like a good fit. Plus, I've always wanted to live in London."

Again, I hated myself. I sounded so trite and stupid. I resolved to redeem myself but my heart was pounding so hard and my brain was racing so fast that I hardly even knew what I was saying anymore. Realizing he was speaking again, I snapped my attention back in his direction.

"Did you work in an historic house back home in D.C.?" He asked in response.

I laughed and took a sip of my wine. "No, no. I was actually a lawyer."

"Wow, I never would have guess that one," he said, surprised. "I'm glad you decided to keep your soul instead!"

I laughed. I went on to tell the entire woe-is-me story about how I'd finally stormed into her office, thrown her papers off her desk, told everyone off, and finally made a dramatic exit. Then, I realized how long I must have been talking. I had just been complaining and profusely cursing for the past ten minutes, not even letting him get a word in edgewise. My cheeks flushed, hot with embarrassment.

But, Andrew laughed and said, "That must have felt fantastic."

"So, what do you do?" I asked, feigning ignorance. Once Tibbie and Beatrice had told me about him, I shamelessly spent about an hour Googling him and studying up on his projects so I'd be better educated about the organizations he represented when he talked about them. Tibbie and Beatrice weren't kidding when they said he was philanthropic. He had worked pro-bono for anti-violence organizations, Amnesty International, for the underprivileged, animal rights, pretty much for any type of charity you could imagine.

"I get to work for some really great causes. I'm so lucky, it's the least I could do to help some other people," he said, humbly, before taking another bite of his duck.

I smiled with admiration. Then, I decided that maybe it was time to change the subject.

"So, when did you start getting into Keats?" I asked, buttering a piece of bread.

"Well, I always loved him, but it wasn't until I got to devote time to studying his poems at university that I truly decided he was my favorite."

"I wish I had gotten to study him that closely," I said, thinking of my coursework and lamenting how absolutely soulless law really was.

"So what's your favorite poem?" I asked, eager to keep the Keats dialogue going.

"It's hard to pick, there are so many that I love. But, I have to say that my favorite is his last. It just seems to be the peak of his love for Fanny Brawne. I know it's sad since it is his final one, but I feel like that makes it even more special. That's probably why it lives so long in perpetuity – it's all the more precious because of its legacy of being so bittersweet."

My jaw almost dropped. He was describing the exact thought that I'd had hundreds of times when I read and was so affected by the poem. Fearing he would think I was exaggerating if I disclosed just how similar I thought, I simply smiled and said,

"I couldn't agree more."

The waiter returned with our hors meals. I cut into my duck and brought the fork to my mouth, taking care to do so in the proper British manner where the fork is flipped downward. It melted in my mouth as I struggled not to salivate everywhere.

The wine kicked in and I was feeling sexier and more confident. I fingered the stem of my glass lightly and leaned in closer. Even though I already pretty much knew everything about him from the tabloids, I wanted to appear at least a little bit aloof. Plus, I was interested to hear everything from his perspective. I had a feeling all of those gossip magazines tended to throw things out of proportion. Hopefully if I laid the groundwork, it would leave an opening for me to find out more about him and Amelie.

"Where did you go to school?" I asked, even though I already knew the answer from my conversation with Tibbie and Beatrice.

"Oxford," he said casually, as if not wanting to sound pompous and pedantic, "I studied British Literature, specialized in romantic poetry. That's why I love Keats House, it gives me an excuse to pause and take some time to get back to it for a little while."

"Why romantic poetry?" I asked, wondering why that's what he chose to study. For someone who was so wealthy with so many connections and privileges, I was sure a college degree was a mere formality. He could certainly have picked any subject he wanted.

"I think it is the idea of the unpredictability of nature. It goes against all of the rationalism we're supposed to follow. It just gave me the means to consider things in my own way, I guess."

"I know what you mean," I responded, "I can't tell you how many times escaping into poems helped me escape the dull, uncreative life of being a lawyer."

From then on, he continued asking me a lot of questions. He asked about my family, what I'd been up to since I'd been in London, if I'd had a chance to travel abroad yet, where I thought I might want to go next, what programs were coming up at Keats House. I tried answering as briefly as possible before turning the conversation back towards him and trying desperately to learn more about him. But, every time I asked him a question about himself, he somehow masterly redirected the conversation back to me. It was extremely flattering and frustrating at the same time since I was learning absolutely nothing about him and was practically dying from desperate curiosity, and his mysteriousness was driving me crazy and making me more and more intrigued.

Andrew asked the waiter for our check. I offered to split the bill and was enormously relieved when he insisted on picking up the entire thing himself. I'm sure even half of that bill would have been the equivalent to about two months of my rent.

Upon leaving, Andrew hailed us a cab to escort me home. It turned out he also lived in Hampstead, only about a twenty-minute walk from my place, in what I'm sure was one of the palatial mansions I'd passed during my walks through the neighborhood. We kept chatting effortlessly in the cab, laughing and smiling at one another. I was shocked how much we had in common, considering we came from completely different worlds. As the ride went on, I slid across the back seat to get closer to him and he put his arm around me as he rested his hand lightly on my thigh. My head fit perfectly against his chest in that sweet spot between his shoulder and his neck.

Before I knew it, we were pulling up in front of my place. He got out of the cab and leaned in to help me out.

"I had a really great time," he said smiling.

I beamed back, "Me too! Thank you so much for dinner."

Despite my inebriation, I still maintained enough clarity to remember the girl etiquette that you must never sleep with a guy on a first date when you want to see him again, even though literally every fiber of my being was desperate for him. I tried to think of puppies and sandcastles and all of the other stuff they tell you to think of when you're trying to talk yourself down from being randy.

He grabbed me softly by the waist and kissed me. I inhaled deeply with longing. He smelled incredible, musky with a hint of sandalwood. It was so different from Tommy's clean cologne that I always loved, but I preferred this more, much, much more. My entire mind and body got completely lost in him in a way I had never experienced before.

We pulled away and he swept a piece of my hair that had gone haywire behind my ear.

"I hope to see you again soon, Emma."

I was incapable of speech, so I simply smiled back. He started walking back to the car, but then turned around to give me one last glance. I gave a small wave, still frozen solid where I stood. I stayed there for more than five minutes after the cab pulled away, trying to digest everything that just happened. Finally, I managed to make my way back to my front door.

I walked through the door in a haze intending to amble right up to my bed when I heard an excited voice come from the couch that scared the absolute shit out of me.

"How did it go?" I recognized Tibbie's voice ask excitedly.

I grabbed my chest, gasping and flung my gaze over to the couch to see Tibbie and Beatrice snuggled on the couch, a bowl of popcorn between them, watching a movie.

"Holy shit, I saw it was dark and thought you were already in bed," I said, feeling my heart race as I continued to clutch my chest.

Beatrice piped up. "Um, and go to bed without knowing the verdict? Not bloody likely. Well, go on then, don't keep us waiting!"

"It was... awesome," was all I could manage to say.

"Do you think you'll see him again?" Tibbie asked excitedly.

"I really hope so," I was struck with a sudden feeling of euphoria at the thought. "Guess we'll just have to see! Anyways, you guys, I'm a bit tired. I think I'll head upstairs and see you in the morning."

"Don't strum it too hard up there thinking about him," Beatrice quipped. Tibbie smacked her on the shoulder.

"I'll do my best," I said laughing it off, but really secretly wondering if I'd be able to control myself.

"I am certain of nothing but the holiness of the Heart's affections and the truth of the Imagination."

~ Letter to Benjamin Bailey

22 November 1817

Three days later, my stupid brain was still in hyper-drive, bouncing back and forth trying to decide whether to call Andrew Bradford or not. In a way, I knew I would have to be a complete moron not to. He was so sweet and smart and GORGEOUS. But, every time I let my mind slip into the bliss of his seeming perfection and what it would be like to be with him, my brain snapped back to the vision of Scarlett and Tommy standing there nearly naked and I felt my heart shatter all over again. There was no way I'd survive another disappointment like that, and boys were all the same. Well, to be fair they weren't all wealthy, famous, high-society, Goddamn super-models. But, still.

The Natural History Museum was getting ready to open a new exhibition on evolution during the Triassic period, so Tibbie had been working so much I'd hardly gotten a chance to talk to her since my date. I was secretly elated because I was happy to avoid a conversation that revealed the deepest chasms of my neurotic craziness. But, I heard her stirring in her room and knew that there was no avoiding it for long. A few minutes later, she came scampering out in a pair of matching pink and white striped pajamas.

"Morning!" she said with her usual unfathomable level of enthusiasm. I had never met a bigger morning person in my entire life.

"Good morning!" I replied, my anxiety melting as I realized how happy I was to see her after her not being around for so long.

She had barely put the kettle on when there was a knock at the door. I walked up to answer it and was met with Beatrice holding a purple cardboard box topped with a fancy white bow.

"Good morning ladies," she said as she crossed the threshold into the living room, somehow looking completely coiffed and gorgeous already.

"I stopped by that snobby bakery and got those cupcakes everyone's been raving about. Cost a bloody fortune, but I couldn't resist. Hope you're hungry!"

She put down the box, opened it to retrieve a German chocolate cupcake, and sat down on the couch, crossing her legs.

"So, Emma, how is Andrew Bradford's penis doing?"

"BEATRICE!" Tibbie scolded.

"Oh, relax, I'm only kidding. Come have your plain vanilla cupcake then."

Tibbie rushed over excitedly and scooped up a cupcake (she actually picked vanilla). She came back to the couch and delivered me a coconut, which she knew was my favorite.

"Seriously though, how are things with you and Mr. Fancy? I've been positively dying to know more."

"He's fine," I said, saved by the whistle of the kettle. I got up and walked over to the counter, pouring steaming hot water into the three teacups Tibbie had set out on the tray along with a plate of shortbread biscuits.

"Fine?" Beatrice said sounding appalled.

"Um, yeah, good I mean."

I picked up the tray to bring it over to the coffee table. When I looked up, Beatrice's lips were pursed and her eyes narrowed.

"Oh, for fuck's sake, what did the idiot do?"

"Nothing!" I said, scrambling, "He's, you know, he's just busy that's all."

Tibbie furrowed her brow as Beatrice tilted her head.

"Ok, fine," I said, setting the tray down and rubbing my hands over my face. I exhaled as I collapsed onto the couch. "I haven't... exactly... called him again yet..." I said, the volume of my voice trailing off at the end of the sentence in the hopes that Beatrice and Tibbie would miss it and miraculously move on to another topic.

Instead, I heard a simultaneous scream of horror.

"WHAT?!"

"Are you serious?!" Beatrice continued appalled. "Hang on. He hasn't very well called you either, now has he? Bloody wanker. He can take his..."

"Whoa, whoa, whoa," I said, raising my hands and trying to spare us all from whatever graphic description Beatrice was about to grace us with. "He can't call me. He doesn't have my number."

Tibbie looked like she was about to cry.

"So you just... haven't called him..." Beatrice said, flabbergasted. "What in the bloody hell is the matter with you?! Give me that thing," she said, reaching across the table to grab my cell phone that was resting at the corner. She started scrolling furiously through my contact list.

"DON'T!" I said, panicked, snatching it from her grasp.

"Alright, alright! Don't get your knickers in a twist about it."

"Sorry," I said, realizing how brash I must have seemed.

"Why haven't you called him?" Tibbie asked, flummoxed.

I struggled to put into words my unique brand of maniacal psychoses.

"I thought you had a great time?"

"Yeah, you could barely contain your erection when you got back here," Beatrice pointed out. I was extremely confused at her reference, but I was pretty sure she had a point nonetheless.

"I did have a great time," I admitted, sighing and trying to think of a way I could explain it so they would understand.

"Then what's the bloody problem you twit?" Beatrice asked, not taking any time to mince words, as usual.

I buried my head in my hands.

"I know, I know," I said, muffled, from behind my palms, "What is wrong with me?"

"I don't know," Tibbie responded, shaking her head back and forth.

"Look, I know it sounds crazy. I really liked him, I did. He was sweet and smart and funny. I had a great time."

"Then what's the problem?" Beatrice asked in outrage.

"Nothing!" I said defensively, "It's just, I don't know. It's never going to go anywhere is it? I might as well spare myself the trouble."

"Oh, will you listen to yourself," Beatrice said, verbally smacking me from across the room. "You're smart, gorgeous, funny, and most importantly, not psychotic. Do you have any idea how hard that is to come by these days? Bloody lucky he is. If he doesn't realize it, he's a twat."

She took another big bite of her cupcake. I was shocked that Beatrice thought those things about me. I admired her so much that it was a pleasant surprise to think that she even considered me in that way. She said it so matter-of-factly that I thought maybe I really was being an enormous idiot.

I was still trying to sort through my thoughts enough to respond to her when the doorbell rang.

"I'll get it!" I shouted with relief, glad to have an excuse to exit the conversation. I trotted across the room and flung open the door, expecting to see the postman holding the package my mom had alerted me that she had sent earlier that week. Instead, I saw Andrew Bradford. I froze.

"Hi there," he said, giving me a gorgeous smile.

"Um... hi..." I finally managed.

After a horribly awkward amount of time had passed, he took his hands out of his pockets and asked, "May I come in?"

"Oh! Yeah! Sorry," I said, my brain still scrambling to catch up to what was happening. I turned and motioned for him to cross the threshold into the living area. When I looked up, I saw Tibbie and Beatrice, their eyes wide and their mouths hanging open. Tibbie was holding a teacup, her arm frozen halfway in her attempt to reach it to her mouth. Beatrice had paused with a piece of cupcake to her mouth.

"How did you know where I lived?" I asked, bewildered.

He grinned.

"I dropped you off the other night, remember?"

"Oh! Right…" I stammered. Idiot. Trying to change the subject, I remembered that Tibbie and Beatrice were behind me on the couch and that I should introduce them.

"Andrew this is my roommate Tibbie and my good friend Beatrice. Guys, this is Andrew."

Beatrice dropped the piece of cake she was holding, her mouth still gaping open and her eyes still fixed on Andrew. I realized that they probably needed some time to get used to it and that maybe we should go somewhere else before Andrew got totally freaked out.

"Do you want to go for a walk?" he asked, reading my thoughts.

"Absolutely," I said, "See you guys later!"

Beatrice and Tibbie finally managed a weak wave as we walked through the front door and I shut the door behind us.

Andrew and I turned to walk up the street towards the heath.

"You never called me," he said, getting straight to the point.

While I had been anticipating this conversation, I still hadn't come up with an acceptable explanation. I certainly didn't want to delve right into the whole Tommy story and come across like a pathetic idiot.

"I'm sorry, I've just been really busy," I said, coming up with the first trite excuse that came into my head.

He turned and gave me a smile that let me know that he knew that I was lying. But, instead of looking hurt, as I would have been in the same situation when insecurities would have consumed my every thought, he looked confident and optimistic. I felt a surge of attraction to him, submitting to the fact that there was no way I'd ever be able to resist him. Dammit. I knew I had to cut it off before it went any further.

"Look... Andrew..."

"You know, I've always wanted to see the upstairs of Keats House," he said before I could finish in a way that left no room for argument. "Every time I've been there, there's been a renovation or they're rotating an exhibition. Now that I have an insider, I was hoping maybe you could arrange a special tour."

"Oh," I said, thinking about it for a minute before I got excited about the fact that I actually had sometime to offer him. But, then, of course, I kept mulling it over in my head and left another awkward silence. Then, I snapped back and said, "Would you like to see it?" asking a question he had already answered. I was mortified again until he smiled his enchanting smile.

"Why, yes, I would."

We walked strolled down the hill towards the house. I kept catching him glancing over at me and smiling. I spent the whole walk trying to stand up straight, kept fluffing my hair, and rubbing underneath my eyes to make sure my eyeliner hadn't smeared everywhere. We finally reached the house. I used my code to open the green gate, we walked across the front garden, and I used my key to open the front door.

I showed him Keats's bedroom and the room that Fanny Brawne moved into. After he walked around Fanny's room, he entered Keats's bedroom with its charming Georgian décor. He walked over to the window and glanced out into the garden.

"It's amazing to see this view, to see what he saw that inspired him to write those poems."

He put his hand on the wall that separated Keats's room from Fanny's with an air of reverence, taking it in and admiring it for the first time. I smiled at how taken he was that he was standing where they stood, seeing what they saw. Once he looked like he was ready to move on, I asked.

"Would you like to see my office?"

"Yes!"

We walked down the hall and I opened the door. Violet had replaced the flowers on my desk with new ones, as she did every week. I was happy to see how charming it looked, but horrified when I realized what an absolute wreck my desk was. I had had another bought of severe writer's block and had spread my copies all over the desk to try to take in the letters and decide which direction to take with my writing. But, no matter how long I stared at them, I was still stuck.

"What are these?" Andrew asked curiously, walking over to my desk and leaning across the documents.

"Um, sorry it's such a mess," I said, rushing over to organize the papers into piles. But, Andrew picked some up and started flipping through them.

"Are these copies of the originals?" he asked, quite intrigued.

"Yes!" I responded, "I'd love to show you the originals, but they're stored away to keep the lighting levels from damaging them."

"Oh, no, I understand! These are fascinating in themselves. I've never seen his handwriting before."

I beamed again, taking in his fascination.

"What are you studying about them?" he asked, the question I had been dreading.

"Well. To be honest, I don't know. Violet put me in charge of organizing them and I wanted to do something with them to give them some exposure on the website that's not just scanning them and throwing them up there, but I can't seem to think of anything to do with them. It's driving me crazy."

Andrew stood there for a moment with a pensive look on his face.

"You know what I always wish I had in university? I had two books, one of his complete letters to Fanny Brawne and a compilation of his poems. I tried to alternate reading them to get a good sense of how she inspired him, but in all my studies I never really found a good, compiled narrative of them. Maybe you could tell the development of his stories by paralleling the letters to his poems? I think people would be really interested in that and then want to read more of the primary sources."

Well, shit. In thirty seconds, he had managed to come up with what had been stumping me for weeks. Right after he said that, the introductory paragraph popped into my head.

"That's a great idea," I admitted, wishing I had come up with it first and could have actually appeared like some semblance an insightful person.

"I look forward to reading it," he said, smiling.

He walked me back to my house under a beautiful, sunny sky. This time, I kept looking over at him and smiling, taking in how devastatingly gorgeous he was. Before I knew it, we had reached my front door.

"Well, Emma, it was great to see you again," he said, reaching out to take my hand, "Have I earned the privilege to ask for your number yet?"

I laughed, thinking it was only fair. I took his phone and typed it in; sending it into a contact list that I'm sure was a mile long. I handed it back to him, feeling apprehensive and vulnerable all over again, but he drew me in and gave me a long kiss, making my stomach flutter with that beautiful nervousness that comes along with uncontrollable attraction.

"I will be in touch soon."

"I'd like that," I said, submitting to the obvious.

"Good," he said, "If you don't answer, I'll be forced to show up unannounced again."

He gave me another kiss and squeezed my hand. I smiled and gave him a wave as he turned away.

I closed the front door behind me and collapsed my back onto it. I was really in trouble now. Tibbie and Beatrice had left, so I sat there swooning for a moment before I remembered the summary that had popped into my head earlier. I rushed up to my bedroom, pulled out my laptop, and began typing.

Before he began his relationship with Fanny Brawne in the spring of 1819, Keats's early poems from 1816 – 1818 contained little of love. Rather, he focused on nature, mythology, melancholy, and the contemplation of mortality and solitude. He wrote several letters during this period to his family and friends. While he mused on love, there was no indication that he had experienced it himself. Rather, he contemplated his poetry.

In a letter to J.H. Reynolds on 3 February 1818, Keats wrote that "Poetry should be great & unobtrusive, a thing which enters into one's soul, and does not startle it or amaze it with itself but with its subject." Then, on 27 February 1818, he spoke of poetry to John Taylor, writing that, "Its touches of Beauty should never be halfway therby (sic) making the reader breathless instead of content: the rise, the progress, the setting of imagery should like the Sun come natural to him – shine over him and set somberly although in magnificence leaving him in the luxury of twilight – but it is easier to think of what Poetry should be than to write it."

His poems during this period reflected his musings on these subjects. In *On First Looking on Champan's Homer*, he speaks of his experiences in nature, stating "Much have I travell'd in the realms of gold, And many goodly states and kingdoms seen." He goes on to discuss mythology and nature, musing on the beauty of the world

However, during this period, Keats also became more entrenched in his melancholy and fear of his inevitable death. In *When I have Fears that I May Cease to Be*, written in 1818, Keats wrote:

When I have fears that I may cease to be

Before my pen has gleaned my teeming brain...

When I behold, upon the night's starred face,

Huge cloudy symbols of a high romance,

And think that I may never live to trace

Their shadows with the magic hand of chance

This somber tone continued in his poems through the spring of 1819, when he began a relationship with the love of his life.

Well, it was a start.

"Fade far away, dissolve, and quite forget..."

~ Ode to a Nightingale

Now that I had a start with my project, my motivation increased and I spent the next week at work enraptured with keeping up momentum. I continued my work organizing the Keats letters and was starting to write some abstracts and essays about Keats's life and influence. Violet started posting them on the website and she and Dr. Lowell were pleased to see that the public seemed to have a great interest in my writing. Attendance to public programs had even risen twenty-five percent since my columns became a regular fixture on the website, since I linked the blog to the subject of each week's lecture or concert.

I thought back to my idea of a book and thought of ways to expand it. There were many books out there that had their love letters printed verbatim, but as far as I knew there was nothing that put the love affair in context with information about Fanny's interests in sewing and her strengths as an independent woman, as well as Keats's poetic themes and growing literary influence, I thought that it could be a fun story that read like a novel filled with intrigue and romance but still gave people a lot of historical information. I knew it was just a pipe dream, but I thought if nothing else it would be a fun personal project. I kept an outline on my work computer and kept contributing to it, but for now, I had more than enough to do, writing short articles for the museum website.

Violet was so encouraging about my project processing the Keats letters. I thanked her again for putting her faith in me even though when I started I had absolutely no experience. Once, over lunch, she even casually mentioned that if I compiled enough information that I could write a book. She said that the Keats fan base was so big around the world that there would be a lot of interest in it and I could probably get some good funding. I wanted to tell her that I had the exact same thought, but I felt a little stupid and was worried she would say out loud that it was a great idea, when really deep down she thought the romance aspect of it would be too juvenile.

One day, I was sitting at the table in the collections area sifting through Keats's letters so I could write my next column for my blog. I came across a letter he wrote to John Hamilton Reynolds on May 3, 1818. A quotation caught my eye.

> "For axioms in philosophy are not axioms until they are proved upon our pulses."

I reflected on the meaning of Keats's words and thought back to my idea for a book. My dates with Andrew had given me a newfound perspective on all of Keats's love letters to Fanny and I felt like they had taken on new meaning. I understood them a lot more clearly and felt like I could take this newfound knowledge to write a chronological narrative of their growing love for each other that people would really want to read.

I remembered Violet telling me how she had gone to King's College to study romantic poetry. She had raved about her program and professors and I suddenly became intrigued about the possibility of pursing a degree there. Curious, I Googled the college and clicked on its website. As it happened, there was a professor who specialized in Romantic Era poetry. Her name was Dr. Catherine Bateman. Her list of publications was very impressive. I poked around and read her abstracts and thought about how perfect it would be to work with her. I had already written several essays during my research and I had just polished up my resume before sending it to Keats House, so I figured why not apply? I didn't have much going on for the rest of the afternoon, so I spent a few hours compiling all of my information and filling out a lot of forms. Just as the end of the workday was rolling around, I clicked the "submit" button.

I had missed the early deadline and the applications had switched to rolling admission. I knew the chances of me getting picked were next to nothing, but I figured I'd at least get my name out there. Maybe this time next year I would have written more and had a lot more experience and they would recognize my name from when I applied this year.

Meanwhile, I kept thinking about Andrew. So far, I had resisted the urge to search for him on the Internet and scour the hundreds of articles that I would spend hours reading. I had done a little research on his work before the date of course, but I hadn't really delved into his personal life, thinking that no good could come of it and it would do nothing but make me woefully insecure. But, after a few glasses of wine, I broke down and typed 'Andrew Bradford' in my search box. I was instantly greeted by thousands of hits.

There were plenty of articles from serious news sources like the BBC that discussed his positive impact on shedding light on previously neglected world issues, but the vast majority of articles were from gossip magazines. Much to my chagrin, pretty much all of them were stories about him and Amelie, including numerous reports that they were secretly engaged. I knew that a lot of those entertainment magazines and websites sensationalized things, but I felt like there had to be at least some ounce of truth to it if it was so widely reported, and if Andrew had been engaged to Amelie, their relationship was much more serious than I'd previously thought.

I drummed my fingers nervously on my desk, imagining pretty much every worst possible scenario.

"Ask yourself my love if you are not very cruel to have so entrammelled me, so destroyed my freedom."

~ Letter to Fanny Brawne
Shankin, Isle of Wight
3 July 1819

For as long as I'd been living in London, I hadn't done much touring and thought maybe it was time to start taking advantage of the beautiful city and taking in some of its culture. Andrew had contacted me and said he wanted to see me again, something that never ceased to shock me and make me really nervous, but I decided to take advantage of it and use it as an excuse to get out there and take in some of London.

Andrew suggested that I meet him at Hyde Park, which was one of his favorite places to go and relax, to go on a morning bike ride. Of course, out of all the things in the universe, he had to pick a bike ride. For some reason, I'd always been terrible at riding bikes. But, thinking it would be rude to turn down his suggestion, I decided to bite the bullet and hope for the best.

I met him at one of the bike share racks by the park. He was dressed more casually than I was used to seeing him in khaki pants, a checkered shirt, and a navy blue sweater, still looking as handsome as ever. He saw me walking up to him and gave me that devastating smile that made my heart flutter. I smiled back. When I reached him he gave me a quick, yet sweet, kiss that actually seemed so comfortable and routine that it almost felt as though we'd been dating forever.

"Ok, ready for this?" he asked, sounding far more excited than I felt.

"Let's do it!" I said, snapping on the helmet he had brought along for me to borrow and doing my best to feign confidence. He put on his own helmet, gave me a kiss, and mounted his bike. I took a deep breath and climbed onto mine, wobbling already.

I kicked off and started pedaling rapidly, hoping to gain my balance. Andrew pedaled ahead of me, guiding me through his favorite parts of the park. I was still wobbling a bit, but I was finally able to look up and glance around at my surroundings. It was so beautiful. Everything was lush and green as far as the eye could see. Colorful flowers were planted in neat, perfect arrangements and the leaves on the trees blew softly in the wind. People were scattered all over, laying down on the grass and soaking in the sun.

I looked up and followed Andrew around a turn. He looked so adorably preppy, like one of those handsome, well-dressed young men that you see riding across the beautiful Oxford campuses in movies. I smiled as I took in the view that made him even more perfect.

Then, I suddenly realized I had been distracted and gradually slowing down. I started wobbling violently. It was no use. I submitted to the fact that I was going to fall, trying to lean myself over to one side to minimize the damage. Before I knew it, I found myself enveloped in a bush.

I laid there, mortified, for about thirty seconds before I decided that I couldn't delay the inevitable and I'd have to get up and face Andrew eventually. I climbed out of the bush, stood up, and started picking leaves off of myself. Then, I mustered the strength to look up.

Andrew was about ten feet from me, bent over in hysterical laughter. He was laughing so hard at me that he wasn't even making noise. Seeing his reaction, I lightened up and began laughing at myself and the ridiculousness of this situation.

"Well geez, don't ask me if I'm alright or anything!" I said, giggling and continuing to brush the dirt off of my knees.

He came over and gave me a kiss.

"I'm sorry, but that was hilarious. Are you ok, sweetheart?"

I smiled back at his sweet pet name.

"Yeah, I'll live."

"Come on, I'll take it from here. Let's get your bike back to the rack."

We walked our bikes to the nearest bike share rack and I locked mine back in.

"Climb aboard," Andrew said, motioning towards the handlebars."

"What? No. Absolutely not." I said, imagining myself flying off and landing on my face.

"Oh, live a little," he said, offering a challenge I couldn't refuse.

I climbed on anxiously, but once I settled in I felt much steadier than I had imagined. Andrew started pedaling and we were off. I felt instantly exhilarated as I felt the wind start blowing through my hair, the sun beaming down on my face. I looked around at the gorgeous scenery around me. The greenery reminded me of D.C., but the rich history of the old city of London gave it its own unique, magical charm.

After about fifteen minutes, Andrew pulled over and I dismounted the bike. I brushed my shirt off, picking off some little sticks that remained from my little incident earlier. When I looked up, I saw that we were standing in front of Buckingham Palace.

I had seen it in tons of photographs and movies, but seeing it firsthand, I was struck with its grandeur. It was much bigger than I'd been expecting. In front, there was a beautiful garden with red tulips that matched the palace guards in the distance. It was protected by an embellished iron gate with golden wreath statues.

"Wow," I said.

"I thought you'd like that." Andrew said. "So what do you think, should we move in?"

"Hah, sure!" I said, thinking that his parents' house was probably as big, if not bigger.

From there, we walked up more idyllic streets towards the Thames. I saw the London Eye in the background as we made our way up to the houses of Parliament. I don't know why I always had it in my head that Big Ben was red, probably just being an idiot and confusing it with the phone booths, but instead the sun sparkled against the ornate, golden building that rested in front of the glimmering, flowing waters of the Thames.

"So what do you want to do?" Andrew asked.

Now that I had seen my number one, the British Museum, I thought about what was next on my list.

"How about Westminster Abbey? I've always wanted to go there. Is it around here?"

Andrew laughed and pointed to the huge stone church that backed up to the Houses of Parliament.

"Oh. Right." I said, this time laughing internally at myself rather than becoming embarrassed.

213

We walked around to the front of the church with its famous dual turrets, gorgeous stone exterior and grand windows.

"Can we go in?" I asked, growing excited.

"Of course, I actually really love it in there," Andrew agreed.

We paid the fee and entered the interior. The elaborate walls led up to a great pointed, arched ceiling stories and stories above is. It was much more colorful than I was expecting. I took an initial glance around and realized all of the fancy plaques and statues that denoted all of the tombs. I couldn't wait to get started.

Since I knew absolutely nothing about Westminster Abbey, I sprung for the audio tour. After some major fiddling and electronic-ineptness, I finally got the talking stick to work. I put it against my ear to listen to the intro.

"Hello, and welcome to Westminster Abbey. I'm Jeremy Irons."

Scar?! Scar from the Lion King was going to be showing me around Westminster Abbey. This could not be more awesome.

Jeremy Irons went on to detail that the Gothic church in the City of Westminster has been the traditional site of coronation and the burial site for British monarchs since the 11th century A,D. It is the burial site for most kings and queens, Chaucer, Henry Purcell, Isaac Newton, Charles Darwin, William Pitt, and many more. The middle hall led to a gigantic, intricate organ. The inner spires and window decorations made the whole thing so humbling, it was impossible not to feel inspired.

Once the tour was finished, I reluctantly followed Andrew to leave the church. The only thing that pulled me away was how hungry I'd become. Apparently resting on Andrew's handlebars had been hard work.

We walked for a bit along the Thames before we came upon a quaint, intimate Italian spot – my favorite type of restaurant. There was just something about that food, Italian wine, and that dark, intimate atmosphere that made for the perfect romantic evening.

"So, what did you think?" Andrew asked, pouring me a glass of Pinot Noir.

"It was a perfect day," I said, feeling happy and satisfied. "It was so nice to finally see some of London. We should do it again soon."

"Absolutely," he said, lifting his glass in acknowledgement.

"So what are you doing next weekend?" he asked.

"Nothing," I said, excited that he still wanted to make future plans with me.

"Well, it's probably boring, but I rowed crew at Oxford and me and my mate, Harry, are rowing in a race this weekend. I'd love for you to come."

"That sounds great!" I said, excitedly. "Can I bring Tibbie and Beatrice?" I asked, thinking of the ample opportunities a crew race would have for them to meet fit, young men.

"Definitely," he agreed. He lifted his glass one more time. "To the perfect day," He said, smiling widely.

"To the perfect day," I said, clinking my glass softly against his.

Afterward, rather than walking me home, he invited me back to his place. I had a feeling that was a good sign since he was likely considering the fact that unlike me, he didn't have any roommates. I followed him through a neighborhood in Hampstead where the houses grew in size and extravagance with each passing block. So, I was surprised when he stopped in front of a modest, albeit beautiful, row house. We climbed the stairs and he turned the key.

While his place was nice, tastefully minimalist with black and white decor, I was quite surprised how humble it was. I could see us having wine, cooking dinner together, and watching movies, getting cozy on his couch. That night however, I only got a brief glimpse. We were both apparently on the same page of being tired of resisting temptation.

It was so different from that night with Tommy. With Tommy, even though he made sure I was taken care of, it was like he was trying to get it over with so that it would be his turn. Apparently, I was so in love with him at the time that I didn't mind the slight. But, on the contrary, Andrew was so attentive to my needs, so sweet and passionate. It felt so much more intimate, such a loving, affectionate, reciprocal experience, as though we were enraptured with each other, both basking in the pleasure of being that close together.

The next day, I left Andrew's to head back to my place. I felt elated as I walked down the street and felt a gentle breeze flow over my face. I closed my eyes and let the warm sun cascade over my face as I took in the loveliness of last night and this morning. I was so much more secure; so excited about what was to come next.

Then, I stopped in my tracks. Anxiety came flowing back into my stomach. I realized that this was exactly the way I felt after that night with Tommy. Sex changes things. That's the long and the short of it. I had been so blind with Tommy, so stupid. After everything that happened I felt so exposed and vulnerable.

Come to think of it, that almost always happened after I integrated sex into a relationship. Everything would always be so great and the guy would seem so interested in me and so eager to be with me. Then afterward, I would spend every night staring at my phone. The guy wouldn't text, wouldn't call. When I finally mustered up the courage to text and ask what was up, there was never a response.

"Thou art a dreaming thing,

A fever of thyself."

~ *The Fall of Hyperion*

I entered the house and Tibbie and Beatrice were at the table eating breakfast.

"Sooo, how was your night?" Beatrice asked.

"Pretty good," I said, "I had a mild panic attack on the way home though. I just feel like I couldn't handle it if I got screwed over again and he's so famous. He'll get bored with me eventually."

"Oh, don't be daft," Beatrice said, "You didn't call him for three days and he came knocking on your bloody door."

Tibbie nodded in agreement as she picked up a piece of bacon. I really wanted to discuss it further, but I knew that would be super annoying so I decided to change the subject.

"So, what are you guys doing next weekend? Andrew invited me to one of his crew races. You two should come along!"

"Bloody hell, I'm not likely to pass that up," Beatrice answered immediately, "Blokes who row crew are always fit. So, Andrew rows crew, eh?"

"Yeah, why?" I asked, curiously.

"Oh nothing. It just makes him even more bloody perfect doesn't it."

I smiled. It really did.

"Yeah, I've always had a thing for guys who row crew," I said, thinking back to all of my teenage and college fantasies. Whenever I'd go to visit Tommy, even though I was obviously in love with him I would find myself staring at the crew team whenever they practiced and during their races. There was something about them rowing crew and the fact that they went to Harvard that was a perfect combination. Rich, smart, powerful, and oh so lean and muscular. I loved seeing their biceps and thigh muscles as they all moved in rhythm while rowing towards victory. Then there the tight crew uniforms that showed off their often well-endowed packages and then the perfectly tailored crew jacket and khaki pants that they always wore after races to the receptions. I shuttered as I thought of all of the hotness.

"Ugh, I know what you mean," Beatrice agreed. "Those bodies. I shagged half of the Cambridge team. Didn't disappoint – strong arms and thighs. Best bloody sex of my life."

I thought back again to how perfect Andrew seemed. He was quite literally my dream man. It all just seemed way too good to be true. After all, Tommy had been my dream man before him and look how that turned out. There were no perfect guys out there. Every guy has a flaw. Thinking that Andrew had to have one, I felt nervousness rise in my chest.

I thought of Amelie. I pictured her cheering Andrew on at one of these races. She would have been dressed with so much more style and probably would have easily chatted up whoever was sitting next to her because they would have had way more in common than I did with anyone in this crowd, probably including Beatrice and Tibbie with their Cambridge educations.

That weekend, the three of us went to the race and sat down at our seats by the finish line. We chatted as we waited for the teams to reach the end. Before long, I saw two boats round the corner, neck and neck. The three of us stood and cheered for Andrew's team. I held my breath as the two boats alternated the lead until right up to the finish line. Andrew's team pulled ahead at the last minute and won by a nose. Tibbie, Beatrice and I jumped up and down and Tibbie gave me a huge hug.

After the team climbed out of the boat, Andrew picked up a small towel and dabbed his head to cool off. He was wearing the team's uniform of short waterproof shorts with a tight, sleeveless shirt. His arm muscles rippled as he held them up to his forehead and as he started walking towards us, his perfect thigh and calf muscles flexed as he ascended the hill towards us.

Tibbie beat me to Andrew and gave him a huge hug. "Congratulations!" she shouted. "Oh, sorry, he's all yours Emma!"

I laughed and went over to give him a hug. "Congrats!"

One of the teammates emerged from behind him, wiping the sweat off of his brow with a towel.

"Everyone, this is my friend Harry."

A tall, fit guy with light brown hair that looked like he was born in a fancy jacket with an overpriced gin and tonic in his hand sauntered up to us. He held out his hand and smiled the type of smile that makes all girls melt no matter what. He was incredibly charismatic and good-looking, but definitely the kind of guy I could tell what trouble from across the room. Still, I blushed, in spite of myself.

"You must be Emma," he said, grabbing my hand.

"Nice to meet you," I said, returning his handshake.

"Why, hello," Beatrice said, coming up from behind me. Clearly she had her eyes on him already.

"Hi there," Harry said, clearly intrigued.

"The team is having a celebration party over in the clubhouse. Would you care to join?"

"Why yes, I would," said Beatrice. She walked away as Tibbie looked over at me and rolled her eyes. I giggled and followed Andrew towards the clubhouse.

We made our way over and went inside. Apparently, crew rowers have a standard uniform that they wear for post-race parties as well. They all wore khakis with red striped ties underneath a navy blue blazer with white trim. What Beatrice said was true, all crew rowers were hot. It looked like a room full of models. But, Andrew still stood out as the most handsome by far..

"Wow," Tibbie said, taking in the grand room with a beautiful view of the river. Andrew and Harry went to change into their own uniforms.

"Bloody brilliant coming here." Beatrice said, scanning the room and absorbing all of the hotties, "Hard to pick just one."

Still, I had a feeling she was already locked and loaded on Harry.

Andrew and Harry left to go talk to their coach to debrief about the race. When they returned, they came bearing a round of champagne.

"Here you go," said Harry, handing one to each of us. "Cheers to a great win! Feels great to beat the bloody Scottish."

"Here, here," Andrew agreed and we all clinked our glasses together.

Beatrice took a quick sip before immediately sauntering away and walking up to the guy she had her eye on. Tibbie looked back at me and rolled her eyes.

Andrew and Harry took Tibbie around to meet the rest of his teammates.

"This is so fun!" Tibbie said excitedly, "Don't you love these things?"

I laughed, "I wouldn't know, I've haven't exactly been to one of these things before. I feel more out of place here than a parrot in a fishbowl."

Tibbie laughed. "Oh these people are easy. I always had to deal with them when I went to events with my grandmother. All you have to do is let them talk about themselves and stroke their egos a little bit and you're golden. "

I took a mental note.

"So what are you guys up to now? Feel like grabbing something to eat?" Andrew asked the four of us.

"I'm right famished," Harry responded. After watching it first hand and seeing how hard those beautiful muscles had to work to constantly row for that entire distance, it was no wonder they were starving. It made me hungry just watching them.

Tibbie, Beatrice, Andrew, Harry and I exited the clubhouse and got into a limo. The driver took the four of us to one of the famous local wine bars. We sat down and settled in at a high-top table right next to the bar.

"So Harry, what do you do?" Tibbie asked sweetly.

"I'm a wine buyer for Sotheby's," he responded. Just when I thought it couldn't be possible, it always seemed like everyone I'd met in this country had a cooler job then the last one.

"Thus, the choice of venue," Andrew clarified, "Harry says it's one of the best in the world."

Harry smirked back at Andrew. If his smile was charming, that smirk could bring any woman to her knees. Definite trouble.

"That must be so exciting!" Tibbie said, fascinated. "I've always wondered how people figure out all of those hints and flavors and keep track of which ones are the good ones. To be honest, I probably couldn't even tell you the difference between a Cabernet and a Merlot."

"Well, it's really just about practice. I'm sure anyone can do it if they study up. I'm just lucky enough to do it for a living and have the time," he said, shockingly modestly.

"I'm 100% positive that's not true," I said, skeptically.

"Well, let's try a game. We'll order three different wines. I'll try each of them and we'll see if I can guess. Braddy, do the honors."

It was clear from complete 180 of formality that I'd witnessed with anyone who'd associated with Andrew since I knew him that Harry's use of the term "Braddy" indicated that they were definitely on an entirely different level of friendship.

Andrew held the menu up, shielding it from Harry as he smiled and pointed to three different wines. Then, he wrote the list number of each one and said,

"Ok, impress us."

Harry picked up each glass and tilted them to test for legs before smelling the inside of the glass, then taking a small sip and swirling it around in his mouth briefly before swallowing. What followed were in-depth descriptions of things like cherry flavors, hints of sage, and chalky finishes. He correctly guessed the type, year, and region of both correctly. I was really impressed. Finally, he got to the last glass. He looked puzzled as he swirled the liquid, sipping twice this time to reassure himself about the answer. After about five minutes, he presented his guess.

"I'm going to go with the Domaine Fourrier, Morey St. Denis Close Salon Pinot Noir 2010.

Andrew clenched his teeth and breathed in sharply.

"Ooooo I'm afraid you're wrong my friend. It's the Domaine Fourrier, Gevrey- Chamertin Vielles Pinot Noir, 2007."

Harry snapped his fingers, smiled, and leaned back in his seat, picking up the last glass (which was, by far, the most expensive) and taking a sip.

"Don't worry, I'm sure they'll find a job for you in the mailroom," Andrew said with a smirk.

"Yeah, well at least I don't wear bright red lipstick, Braddy."

Tibbie and I snapped our heads around to look at Andrew.

"Um, do clarify," I said, leaning in and putting my hand underneath her chin. I looked over at Andrew and he was shaking his head.

"Bollocks."

It seemed like Andrew knew Harry well enough to know that there was no getting out of it, so he just resigned himself to the fact that this story-telling was going to happen. He sighed and leaned back in his chair.

"In secondary school, Braddy here was confident enough that he could beat me in a one-on-one crew race. So, I accepted the challenge and we made a bet. Whoever lost had to wear bright red lipstick to school for a week. And, of course, I won. And Victor/Victoria here was the bell of the ball."

I thought about Andrew's super posh, all-boys prep school and smiled.

Andrew raised his arm and punched Harry in his bicep.

Harry went on.

"Or the time that Braddy got so drunk at a party at Oxford that I found him passed out on a bench outside the next day in his underpants with his clothes neatly folded next to him."

Tibbie giggled from across the table.

"Not to mention he was found by the Headmaster," he said with a wink. Andrew smacked him hard on the shoulder.

"Do you really want to play this game?" Andrew asked, "Because I think I have stories about you that are about five times more embarrassing."

Harry smiled.

"Oh relax Braddy, I'm just roasting you. Plus, have you ever seen me embarrassed in my life? Bloody waste of time."

Beatrice, Tibbie and I started talking amongst ourselves as the boys caught up with one another. I glanced over at them and saw the level of closeness that comes with years of friendship and the corresponding stories and inside jokes, hoping that one day I'd be close enough to Andrew that we'd be the same way. Plus, it was so cool to meet someone who knew him so well and clearly had enough of his own resources that he wasn't just using Andrew to get ahead.

After a little while, Beatrice changed seats to sit next to Harry. After a few minutes of speaking, she whispered something into his ear. God knows what it was, but about thirty seconds later they were both getting up and putting on their coats.

"Gotta go, mate," Harry said with a wink. The two of them left, arm in arm.

"Well, they don't mess around do they?" Andrew said, flagging down the waiter to order another glass of wine.

The next morning Beatrice, Tibbie and I rendezvoused at Sunday lunch.

"So?" I asked. I was always curious about Beatrice's verdict since she had enough experience to offer an accurate ranking.

"Ten," she said smiling, "bloody sore all over. Give me some of that Pimms." She said, collapsing into her seat before picking up the pitcher and filling her cup up with a glass.

"So do you think you'll see him again?" Tibbie asked.

Beatrice pursed her lips in a 'are you kidding' manner and Tibbie replied with a knowing look.

"Yeah not worth it really. Even if I was madly in love with him, you know the type."

"Oh definitely," Tibbie responded.

"What do you mean?" I asked.

"You know. Oxbridges," Beatrice said casually.

"Oxbridges?" I asked, confused.

"Oxbridges are guys who either went to Oxford or Cambridge," Tibbie clarified.

Beatrice continued, "You know, rich. Good looking. Cocky. Crew. High profile. Entitled. Irresistible. Just bad news all around."

I got worried

"Are they all like that?" I asked nervously.

"No," Tibbie said, "A lot of them are actually really nice."

"Tibbie thinks everyone's nice," Beatrice said, leaning over to take a sip of her Pimm's. "But I know better. I can tell a bloody Oxbridge across the room."

She stole a potato off of Tibbie's plate and popped it into her mouth.

While I'm sure she didn't mean anything by it, it made me pause. I thought about Andrew's Oxford degree hanging next to his desk in his bedroom. My face fell. I had let my guard down with Andrew lately because everything was going so well. But, he was so used to turning on that charm that he probably always came across like that no matter what. Maybe he wasn't treating me special. Maybe he was just treating me the way he treated everyone else. Suddenly, I found myself anxiously slugging back an entire Pimm's cup.

"In spite of all, Some shape of beauty moves away the pall from our dark spirits."

~ *Endymion*

Before I knew it, the holiday season snuck right up. I spent the weeks before Christmas taking in all of the holiday magic that London had to offer. Everything just seemed so much more enchanting and vintage, like Christmas must have resembled in America before corporate giants took over and made everything about standing in line at 3:00 a.m. to get 60-inch flat screens on sale. All of the store windows sparkled against the Victorian style architecture of mom and pop trinket stores, coffee shops, and bakeries. People even dressed more fashionably when they went holiday shopping, wearing knee-length boots, winter-white coats, fancy scarves, and wool hats. It was a stark contrast from the sweatpants and college hoodies I was used to seeing in Maryland malls. They even used real plants for their decorative garlands. The festive smell of evergreen was actually natural, as opposed to the plastic versions sprayed with "Essence of Christmas Tree" air-freshener that I had become accustomed to.

Tibbie and Beatrice took me around to the oldest and most famous annual Christmas market in the city. It was like walking into a Harry Potter novel where they go to the magical alleys and shop for wands, owls, and love potions. Except instead you drank delicious hot cider and mead, stuffed your face with giant deep-fried pastries the size of your head, and bought little handmade trinkets from charming old British ladies.

One week before Christmas Day, I was sitting in my window seat drinking tea and staring out onto the courtyard garden dreamily when I heard a knock at my bedroom door.

"Come in!" I shouted. Tibbie opened the door delicately and came in wearing her housecoat and slippers.

"Morning!" She said cheerily. "Listen, I've been meaning to ask you, I have a bit of time off between jobs and Beatrice has been moaning for weeks now that she needs to get away. We've been thinking of taking a trip and we thought with Christmas coming up, it would be a nice excuse. We're thinking of doing a tour of the Lake District. Somehow, even after living here for our entire lives, neither of us has ever made it there! We'd love it if you could come!"

I had never been to the Lake District, but Andrew had told me just the other day how beautiful it was.

As much as I loved it here, I had a feeling that with the holidays coming up, I might get a bit homesick. Christmas was my favorite time of year. With both my parents' and my busy work schedules throughout the year, it was one of the only times that I got a few guaranteed days in a row to see them.

Plus, all of my family members came in from out of town and we had all of these traditions of playing music, watching movies, and dabbling in charades. It would probably be one of the rare nights when I really missed America and if I didn't go to the Lake District with Tibbie and Beatrice, I'd probably spend the entire night crying nostalgically into my pillow.

"I'd love to," I responded, "When do we leave?"

"This Wednesday, the day before Christmas Eve," she said, "we figured we'd take the bus and go for three nights and come back to relax on Boxing Day. We wanted to make sure we'd be back in time for New Years. One of Beatrice's friends is having a party and inviting all of his single mates, so Beatrice would not be bloody likely to miss out on that opportunity. Will that work for you?"

Ah, of course there was a hitch. I felt guilty asking for time off when I had only been working at Keats House for a few months. It would likely seem unprofessional for me to ask Dr. Lowell when he had been so nice and generous. He would think I was taking advantage of him. But, when I looked back up at Tibbie she looked so excited that I could hardly bear to break her heart.

"I'll figure it out, no worries!" I managed to say with some aspect of confidence. Tibbie smiled wide, turned on her foot happily and left the room. I collapsed back on my bed and sighed anxiously.

———————

The next morning I put my bag down on my desk, put my coat on the back of my chair, and walked straight to Dr. Lowell's office. I wanted to give him as much notice as possible, but I still felt guilty that I was asking so close to when I was supposed to depart for the Lake District. I almost considered turning around just then, but I had a flashback to the look on Tibbie's face, which made me feel even guiltier.

I sighed and knocked on the door to Dr. Lowell's office.

"Come in!" he shouted jollily. How anyone had that much energy in the morning after drinking a mild cup of tea instead of coffee, I will never know.

I entered timidly.

"Good morning Dr. Lowell."

"Ah, Emma!" he responded with a beaming smile, "My rising star! How are you this morning, my dear?"

Ugh he was not going to make this easy, was he?

"Um, Dr. Lowell?" I said, my voice cracking. I put my fist to my mouth and cleared my throat, "Listen, I know that I haven't been working here that long and I probably haven't earned the right to ask you this, but my roommate asked me to go on a holiday with her over Christmas. I'd need to be out of the office on Wednesday. I'm so sorry for the short notice. I can be back straight after Boxing Day. If you need me to stay here though, I completely understand."

Dr. Lowell looked at me for a few seconds without saying anything. Oh God. I knew it. He was going to chuck me out the door right here and now. But instead, he started laughing.

"Of course my dear!" he said with vigor, "You should take these opportunities as they come along! See as much of the world as you can! It's not as though we're paying you. Besides, everyone takes at least a week for Christmas. Please, just take the week and come back on the 3rd of January."

I certainly wasn't expecting that. He went back to sipping his tea and started organizing papers into a pile on his desk. "Can you please gather Violet for our morning meeting? And can you carry this sugar out with you? There are fresh scones and tea waiting on the table."

God, I loved this country

"Much have I traveled in the realms of gold, and many goodly states and kingdoms seen"

~ On First Looking into Chapman's Homer

———————

The day of our departure, Tibbie scurried around merrily gathering all of her belongings to pack and bring along. Andrew had a huge case and had to work for the holidays, so unfortunately he wasn't going to be able to make it. But, it had been a while since I hung out with just Tibbie and Beatrice and I was looking forward to some much needed girl time.

Our bus didn't depart until later that afternoon, but she was already up early in the morning humming happily as she organized everything we would need. While I would have loved to share her enthusiasm, I had no idea how she had so much energy at such an ungodly hour and I, myself, was merely trying to function enough to stay awake and help her.

We finished getting everything together and made our way to Central London to meet Beatrice at King's Cross Station. We found our way to our train terminal. When our call to board came, we climbed aboard, stowed our luggage and were on our way.

I have always had mild narcolepsy upon being a passenger in a moving vehicle. Without fail, I pass out almost instantly after a train, plane, bus, or car starts moving. As such, despite my having drunk two cups of coffee before our departure, I fell asleep on the journey and missed most of the ride there. I was roused out of a deep slumber as we hit a bump in the track that scared me to death. I looked over at Tibbie, who was sitting across the aisle from me happily reading from her copy of *Mansfield Park*. I tapped her and she turned quickly, slightly startled.

"Sorry," I said. "Where are we?"

She smiled back at me, "Oh no worries! We're about twenty minutes out. Should be there soon!"

I stretched and yawned and turned my head to gaze out the window. I didn't know what I expected of the Lake District, but I had no idea it was so beautiful. It was like something out of a Renaissance fairy tale. Gorgeous plains rolled over hills and mountains that seemed to keep gradually climbing up towards the skyline the further they were set out.

Tiny farmhouses were scattered about, inlaid into the hills so perfectly that they almost looked as though they were part of the natural scenery. Old stone bridges sat above stunning streams. Not to mention the water from the lakes, which stretched out as far as the eye could see and sparkled under the mid-day sun.

We pulled into the train station and grabbed a cab. Tibbie had arranged for us to stay at a bed and breakfast. It was a country cottage that stood right on top of one of the local cellar pubs, so we could go downstairs for pub food and drinks and stumble right back up to climb into our beds. Tibbie said that the pub owner had a bedroom off to the back and so each day he would come in and make the beds, restock the bathrooms, and leave tea. It sounded perfect.

Tibbie said she was told to go directly to the pub and check in with the bartender, who was also the owner of the upstairs cottage. We opened the door to the pub and were met with a rather good-looking man who appeared to be in his thirties standing behind the bar, organizing liquor bottles in preparation to open for the evening. This was a welcomed surprise; in my head I was expecting a pub tender to be an aging, short, stocky man with a massive beer belly.

"Hi there!" he said jovially, coming out from behind the bar to meet us, "I'm Hugh. One of you must be Tibbie, welcome to the New Inn! I'm just about to open now, but I can hold off and get you lovely ladies some dinner if you'd like!"

We had eaten a lot of snacks on the train and we were all extremely tired, so we thanked him for his hospitality but said we were just going to head upstairs. The poor guy looked almost heartbroken, so we assured him we'd be back the next day. He handed Tibbie the key and showed us up the stone stairwell that led to the cottage.

We opened the door and stepped into the cozy sitting room complete with plush couches and armchairs and tons of woven blankets. A fire roared in the middle of the far wall. Since it was Christmas-time, the entire interior was decked out with holiday finery. Garland was draped along the walls, wrapped in what seemed like thousands of tiny, twinkling lights. Tiny dove decorations were fastened at each corner. A gorgeous Christmas tree with what looked like hand-blown ornaments on every branch sat snuggly in the corner next to the fireplace.

A quaint, antique table was set up with all of the necessary supplies for serving tea, complete with shortbread, croissants, light cheese and a spread of fruit. They looked so good that I instantly devoured one of the shortbread cookies and it was so delicious that I immediately housed another. We sat down and decompressed with some tea, but as we settled into the comfortable, snuggly couches, we realized that we were in danger of passing out right then and there, so we decided to call it a night.

When we entered, we were met with a room that was just as cozy as the living room area. There were four beds set up in a circle around the room, so we piled all of our suitcases on one and each plopped into one of the three remaining beds. The pillows even had chocolate mint candies, which of course there was no way I could resist until morning. I never wanted to leave.

I woke up the next day feeling rested and refreshed. I looked over to see Tibbie snoozing silently with an eye mask delicately placed over her face. She was lying on her side with her hands rested underneath her cheek, wearing a pink, cotton pajama set. She looked like she was posing for a mattress ad. Beatrice, on the other hand, was sprawled out on her stomach with her face jammed into her pillow. She was wearing a short, black, silk nighty with lace trim. Her mouth hung open slightly and the tiniest bit of drool dribbled from the side of her mouth. Her hair was messy and wild as if she'd been thrashing around most of the night. I smiled. Even when they slept they were so starkly different, yet equally adorably.

I took advantage of the fact that they were still asleep and went outside into the crisp, clean air. The sun was rising, making the lake sparkle with different shades of orange, red, yellow, and violet. I noticed a bench by the water's edge and went and sat down.

I had spent so much time going over Keats's letters to Fanny that I knew most of them by heart. Sitting there with that beautiful view, I got inspired, picked up my journal, and wrote the next section of my paper.

While Keats initially tried to disguise his interest in Fanny, by 1819, he had fallen completely in love and he could deny it no longer. The Brawne family took over the Dilkes' half of the property and Fanny and Keats began living in the same house. During this spring, Keats experienced the great outpouring of his poetic life, his inspiration being his fair love. In the early summer of 1819, Keats left for the Isle of Wight. His longing for her is reflected in the letters he wrote her while he was away, and the theme of love blossomed in his poetry, the beauty of their romance poured all over his words.

Keats first wrote to Fanny on 5 July 1819 from Shanklin, Isle of Wight, expressing, "I do not know how elastic my spirit might be, what pleasure I might have in living here and breathing and wantering as free as a stay about this beautiful coast if the remembrance of you did not weigh so upon me... Ask yourself my love whether you are not very cruel to have so entrammeled me, so destroyed my freedom." On the 10th, he elaborated, "I never knew before, what such a love as you have made me feel." Finally, by 13 October, he declared, "I cannot exist without you. I am forgetful of everything except seeing you again... You have absorb'd me. I have a sensation at the present moment as though I was dissolving."

The poetry he wrote during this time period, famous works such as The Eve of St. Agnes, La Belle Dame Sans Merci, and Ode to Psyche reflect his evolution into the poet that is revered today as the start of a great romantic movement that inspired poets for centuries. His love for Fanny permeated all, most notably in Ode on a Grecian Urn, when he wrote:

More happy love! More happy, happy love!
For ever warm and still to be enjoy'd
For ever panting, and for ever young,
All breathing human passion far above.

The lifting of his melancholy and fear of death was reflected right after they became romantically involved when he wrote Ode to a Nightingale in May 1819. Keats optimistically expressed:

Thou was not born for death, immortal Bird!

The words resonated deeply as I stared onto the magical water and felt a sharp pang of longing for Andrew. I realized that he had indeed enveloped my senses. In that moment, every part of me yearned for him as I longingly craved his embrace. My own thoughts sounded like something out of a tacky romance novel and at one point, I even rolled my eyes at myself, but I couldn't deny that my pining was real. I finally realized what all of these saps have been talking about this whole time. I just couldn't stop thinking about him. He was inspiring me to a whole new level and I knew one of the reasons I could suddenly write about Keats and Fanny with ease was that I was now experiencing it myself.

After a while I figured that Tibbie and Beatrice would probably be awake and I should get back to the cottage. I walked in to see them rubbing their eyes and slowly rising from their beds.

"Morning sunshine!" Beatrice said in a way that I could tell was ironic and what she really meant was that she needed a cup of coffee as soon as humanly possible.

Tibbie, on the other hand, sprung up instantly and started scurrying around the room excitedly, compiling a mound of all of the things she felt we would need for the day. Cameras, snacks, bug spray, umbrellas– Just about anything you could think of, plus the things that would have never even crossed your mind, but Tibbie was bringing it just in case. Beatrice patted her face with some cold water, slung a small purse over her shoulder, and was ready to go.

We headed down to the living room area. Hugh had already set up a breakfast tray with cakes, tea, and orange juice. Since we didn't have a car, Tibbie arranged for a local tour guide to drive us around in a van and take us to the "hot spots". Not sure that's the right phrase for a rustic countryside seemingly untouched by time, but I went with it. We were running a bit late so we ate quickly before hearing a honk. We walked outside and were met with a white eight-passenger van. Standing in front was a tall, portly man with a round face wearing a hand-knit sweater and maroon corduroy pants.

"Hello there, name's Gareth," he said rather monotonously, "climb on in then."

The three of us exchanged a concerned look after hearing the very distinct intonation of a serial killer, but the thin, humble wedding ring and unevenly buttoned woolen sweater set us slightly at ease. Plus, Hugh followed us out of the inn and waved at Gareth as an old friend. So, if we went missing and were murdered, I found some solace in knowing that it was likely a conspiracy that couldn't have been avoided.

We climbed into the back of the van and fastened our seatbelts. Almost immediately, Gareth started talking as he took the van out of park and pulled out of the Inn's driveway onto the main road.

"Welcome to the Lake District. Please buckle your seatbelts. "

He spoke in a tone that left me uncertain he wasn't actually a robot. Beatrice, Tibbie and I exchanged worried glances, hoping that the entire tour wouldn't be filled with dates and statistics. If it continued like this, the narcolepsy would kick back in and I would be a goner for sure.

Gareth – albeit in the same slow drone – continued to tell us all about the history of the Lake District. I'm pretty sure we had all stopped listening to him after about five minutes, but I was too busy staring out on the countryside to notice. One thing I didn't know about the English countryside was how many sheep live there.

As it turns out, I really like sheep. Until that point, I never realized how adorable they are.

We pulled over to get a closer look. We climbed over the fence, and a tiny lamb ran up to me and immediately rubbed his head on my thigh as I crouched down to greet him. I jokingly asked if I could take him back with us but Gareth just stared at me until I put down the lamb and backed away slowly to the van.

On the way back to the inn, Gareth pulled over at the top of a high peak with a steep drop where we could see the beautiful, hilly English countryside spread out before us. Something about standing there in the fresh air made me realize how big and beautiful the world really is.

The next day was Christmas and Hugh invited us down to the pub for a traditional English dinner feast. I felt guilty eating lamb-chops after spending all day yesterday playing with those adorable balls of puffy wool, but Hugh assured me that the lambs they serve for lamb-chops actually almost reached adulthood and were nowhere near as young as the babies I spent the day with. I had no idea if he was just lying to make me feel better, but it was good enough for me to absolve myself from feeling guilty over eating the most delectable, melt-in-your-mouth meat I had ever tasted. The chops were served with roasted potatoes (that I'm pretty sure I overheard Hugh say were cooked in lard, but I chose to remain blissfully ignorant), amazing asparagus, and an entire spread of delicious cakes, scones, biscuits, and chocolates. Not to mention, we had about a gallon of wine each.

It took all of my concentration and will to stand up from the comfortable armchair where I had been gorging myself for hours. It occurred to me that I hadn't talked to my family in forever. I pictured them all cuddled by the fire opening gifts and sipping eggnog as they laughed while reminiscing about all of our famous family stories. I glanced at my clock and saw that it was 12:30 a.m. One of the advantages to being in the U.K. was that I was now five hours ahead of D.C., and being a bit of a night owl, it was nice that I could call my parents during late hours and it would still be their early evening. I decided to try to ring them up.

Even though I bought them a webcam, gave them exhaustive tutorials, and left them a laminated sheet with explicit instructions beside the computer, my parents still could not figure out how to use video chat. They attempted it once, but they just kept repeating loudly that all that they saw was black as I watched them from the other end of the line tap the screen over and over again for five straight minutes. Then, they gave up hope forever and I was resigned to forgoing the free, user-friendly internet service in exchange for an expensive overseas cell phone plan.

Given the fact that we were in the middle of nowhere, my cell phone wasn't even working. I went downstairs to ask Hugh if I could use the pub's phone, offering to pay. He said he would just add it to our bill, making me wince a little, but there was no use worrying about it because I had to talk to my family on Christmas or they'd kill me. Plus, today I was really missing them. Even though I was having an amazing time, it was my first Christmas without them.

I dialed the multi-digit magic formula that allowed me to even access a U.S. line and then dialed my parents' familiar number. It rang three times before my mom answered.

"...YES dear, the package says four hundred degrees, read it yourself if you don't believe me! Hello?" she said in a frazzled voice.

"Hi Mom!" I said, proud that I sounded way more sober than I actually was.

"Emma! How are you my darling?"

"Is this our Emma?" I heard my cousin Olivia ask as she picked up a second line. "So great to hear from you! Why aren't you video chatting with us? We'd love to see your face! Hey everyone, it's Emma! We're putting you on speakerphone."

"THANK you Olivia. See mom? You know this it costing me an obscene amount of money. You're going to have to join the twenty-first century and figure out video chat eventually. Hi everyone!"

I immediately received a response of a jovial, yet incomprehensible, mashing of many voices competing to greet me and wish me a Merry Christmas. That was one thing I loved about my family. There was such an endearing chaos that was indicative of a group of people so comfortable around each other that no one paused to extend the courtesy to let someone else finish their sentence.

It was never in a rude way though, more like we were all so close and familiar with each other that we could have several conversations at once and finish each other's thoughts without having to take turns. But I guess they decided this was a special case, since the phone was passed around and I got to chat one on one with all of the members of my extended family that had gotten together for the holiday. I felt a pang of longing in my heart.

Finally, the phone was passed back to my mom. "I really miss you guys," I said, tearing up.

"Oh Emma, we miss you too!" she responded earnestly, "But don't waste your time worrying about us, you need to focus on yourself right now. You should be out there traveling the world and experiencing new things! If you were here you'd just be stuck with your boring old parents."

I snorted thinking about that last statement.

"Mom, you and dad may be a lot of things, but I have to say boring would be the last word I would use to describe you."

I could almost feel her smiling on the other end of the line, "Oh Emma, you know you are the best daughter we could ask for. Now like I was saying... PHIL! PHIL! Can you get the pies out of the oven? Yes, you, I'm not talking to myself over here! The timer just went off and I can smell something burning. No not the apple pies, the blueberry. No, I told you I was making blueberry. Relax, I made your damn chocolate pie too, it's chilling in the fridge. JUST GET THE FUCKING PIES ALREADY!"

"Okay, I guess I'd better let you go then!" I said, realizing that I had been gone for over an hour and Tibbie and Beatrice were probably wondering where I was.

"Yes, unfortunately I should go before your father burns the house down. But, try not to worry so much my dear, just enjoy the ride! This is a once in a lifetime experience for you. And you know if you ever need anything, we'll always be here. Bye sweetie! NO BRIAN, GET YOUR HANDS AWAY FROM THAT SOCKET! Will you all stop drowning yourselves with eggnog and keep an eye on the children!"

Her voice faded out as she hung up the phone.

I allowed myself one moment to let my eyes well up thinking about my wonderful family and how much I missed them, but then I decided to heed my mom's advice and continue to seize the day.

I wiped my eyes and went back into the pub.

"THERE you are Emma!" Tibbie said enthusiastically, "Come here! Hugh here has made us some amazing mulled wine with homemade chocolate covered pretzels!"

I didn't think I could fit one more single thing in my stomach, but as I walked up to Tibbie and Beatrice sitting at the bar and caught a whiff of the drink that smelled exactly like Christmas and saw the gooey pretzels, I decided to try to make room.

The three of us talked and drank for hours until we realized how late it was. We decided it would probably be smart to get some sleep since we had to get up early to catch the bus and, unlike Tibbie, Beatrice and I were complete mutants in the early morning and needed a bit of time to wake up. We said our goodbyes to Hugh and thanked him for everything, assuring him we would come straight back to the Inn if we ever found ourselves back in the area.

We stumbled up the stairs to our beds. Tibbie and Beatrice immediately passed out in their clothes. Beatrice had face-planted on the bed and was snoring softly while Tibbie curled into a ball. I looked at my new best friends and smiled.

I climbed into bed, but after a half an hour I still couldn't sleep. I went outside for some fresh air. I walked into the courtyard and climbed onto one of the reclining chairs. I laid on my back and stared up at the sky. Then, I started to cry.

Things were so different now. Even though I was so happy with my new life, lying there under the influence of lots of alcohol, all I could think about was how I wished things would go back to the way they were when I felt the comfort of always having my best friends there for me when was certain that they'd always be around no matter what.

The side of my sweatshirt rolled down my body and I felt a hard object graze my arm. I realized it was my cell phone. I pulled it out and unlocked the screen. By some miracle, I had a bar of service. I thought about Scarlett.

I knew her number by heart. I typed in the digits and let my finger hover over her name for a minute before it pushed the "call" button in what felt like an out-of-body experience. I continued to hold the phone out, hearing the outgoing ring in the distance. Then, suddenly, I heard someone pick up.

"Hello?"

Her voice hit me like a knife in the heart. It reminded me how many times we'd called each other over the years to make plans or talk about stupid stuff just to unwind. My eyes stung as tears rose to the top.

"Hello?" she said again, sounding irritated. I tried to say hello but all I could manage was a deep sigh.

"...Emma?" she said after a pause. "Emma? Is that you?" she asked, sounding desperate. I had no idea how she even knew it was me. The only explanation I could think of was that after so many years of sharing just about everything with each other, we were so connected that she could sense me on the other side of the line without me saying anything at all.

"Emma," she repeated. "Emma, if this is you, I'm so, so sorry." It sounded like she was starting to choke up. "I miss you," she said, her voice wavering.

Still, I couldn't speak. I sat there for a moment trying to think of what I could even say to her. Where I would even start.

Finally, I just somehow started to talk.

"Hi," was all I could manage, easing my way into the conversation.

"Hi," she said. Then there was a long pause.

"Emma, I..."

For some reason, at that I felt the anger rising in my chest.

"How could you?" I said, the tears now streaming down my cheeks. "How could you???"

I was met with nothing but silence.

"So you have nothing to say?" I said, my blood starting to boil. I had tried to ignore it for so long that now everything was exploding at once."

"I..."

"Never mind," I decided, "I don't even want to hear what you have to say. You knew I was in love with him. You knew since we were ten for God's sake. How pathetic are you that you couldn't find ANY other guy in the universe to hook up with."

"Look, you're right ok. It was awful. I've felt horrible ever since."

"Why didn't you call me? Why?" I asked desperately.

"I... I didn't know what to say."

"Well anything would have been better than nothing Scarlett."

Then, I thought of what I really wanted to ask her.

"How long did it go on?" I asked, thinking that I might not want to know the answer but I had to know.

"What does it matter?" she asked, starting to sound annoyed herself.

"It matters," I said, wondering how she could be so daft that she wouldn't know why the answer to that question would mean that much to me.

"I don't know, a few years? It wasn't a big deal, Emma. It was only when we were drunk, it never happened when we were sober."

Years? At that, I felt so overwhelmed and I just shut down. All I could do was hang up. I hit the end button. I saw her number flash three times before the screen went black. I hit and held down the power button and shut the phone off, terrified that she would call back. I started at the phone for another minute before my arm collapsed to my side. My grip loosened and it fell out of my hand, plopping on the ground next to me. My eyes dried up as my mind turned numb and I felt my body shutting down into self-preservation mode until I felt nothing at all. Well, another example of a drunken decision that succeeds in nothing but making everything vastly worse.

"—then on the shore of the wide world I stand
alone and think;
Till love and fame to nothingness do sink"

~ When I Have Fears that I May Cease to Be

———————

The next day we headed back to London. It was Boxing Day, which I had never heard of until Tibbie enlightened me. Apparently, on the day following Christmas Day, the servants and tradesmen would receive gifts from their employers. Having started in the Middle Ages, the holiday tradition continued and was now a bank holiday when practically the whole of Britain had off of work. Yet another example of how much better life was in this country. Normally the day after Christmas involved me getting to the law firm at 7:00am and working a twelve hour day with a massive hangover.

We were so exhausted when we got back to the train station that we had pleaded with Beatrice to let us stay at her Central London apartment to avoid having to haul ourselves all the way back up to Primrose Hill. She agreed enthusiastically and we headed back to her giant flat, stopping along the way to pick up a few bottles of wine. We spent the evening watching some horrible chick flick, which we justified to ourselves because the leading actor was so good looking, while eating Chinese food and drinking lots of wine.

When the clock rounded 10:00 p.m., we all admitted defeat and decided to turn in for the night. Tibbie and I were staying on the pull out couch in Beatrice's living room, and she left to go gather us some pillows and blankets. While she was gone, Tibbie and I began climbing into our pajamas, very excited at the prospect of sleep. When Beatrice returned, I was down to my bra and underwear, but we spent the last few days in the same room so it was hardly a new sight for her. Then, she stopped, cocked her head, and a confused look spread across her face.

"What's that on your side?" Beatrice asked as she waltzed over and pulled up the side of my bra to get a closer look. It would seem that we bonded on that trip even more than I thought, since she was now apparently comfortable enough around me to readjust my underwear.

Then, I realized what she was talking about. My tattoo. After the trauma of seeing its identical twin on the worst night of my life, I think I repressed the fact that I even had it.

"Oh," I said, my face reddening, "it's nothing. It's stupid."

"Oh for heaven's sake Emma, don't be such a prude. Let's see it then! I love tattoo stories, I'm fascinated to know what people want to have spackled all over their private bits for the rest of eternity. Come on, it's just us you're talking to."

I hadn't yet gotten into the whole Tommy and Scarlett situation with Beatrice. I'm not sure why exactly, but for some reason it made me feel really stupid. Just another dumb thing we had done in our youth that I let him talk me into. Now I was stuck with this reminder of him forever.

Beatrice must have seen my face fall because she said, "Oh don't worry about it, I'm sure the stories I can imagine in my own head are far more interesting!"

I laughed as I exhaled at the irony.

"Oh I doubt that. This one's a doozie."

I took a deep breath and told her the whole story, how my entire world changed in an instant with one glance at that stupid blob of ink when I suddenly realized that everything I thought I knew about the most important people in my life was a lie. As I finished the story about the trip to Italy with Tommy,

I tried to laugh it off. But the feelings of betrayal flooded back to me and I felt the full force of the sting. I felt tears trickling down my cheek and realized that I was crying. I wiped them away, embarrassed, but my eyes kept welling up involuntarily and I couldn't stop.

I lost sight of everything great that was happening in my life and just dissolved into the solitary focus of that one moment. It wasn't my feelings for Tommy, but rather how stupid and deceived I felt; how I never even saw it coming. I had been living in a state of denial that was bound to catch up with me eventually.

"I know it was a bit cowardly to just run away from them, but I just needed a new life," I summarized.

"Is THAT why you've been so weird about Andrew?" Beatrice said with a look of sudden realization. "Oh, for fuck's sake. Well, I don't think it's cowardly at all," Beatrice countered, "In fact, I think it takes a lot of courage to do what you did. A lot of girls probably would have taken abuse from that heinous toff of a boss, would have forgiven that stupid tart and let her walk all over them, and would have run pathetically back to that selfish, vile wanker. This is why I stay single, flirting is much more fun."

Beatrice snapped up off of the bed she had been sitting on and grabbed me by the wrist, pulling me up.

"Come on then," she said, smirking. "I have an idea. Throw on some clothes!"

As soon as the shirt was over my head Beatrice grabbed me by the arm and pulled me out the door.

By this point, we had been drinking, heavily, for a solid six hours. Before I knew it, Beatrice was dragging me by the arm down Oxford Street. The three of us laughed hysterically as we galloped through the streets trying to keep up with Beatrice's fast pace.

I had absolutely no idea where we were going, but at that point I didn't care. Then, Beatrice halted so suddenly that Tibbie and I almost slammed right into her. I looked up and saw a bright red neon sign that read "tattoo" above a window that looked like it hadn't been cleaned since about the mid-'80s.

"Let's get that dreadful thing covered up!"

We were in such a drunken state that if one of us would have attempted to get a tattoo pretty much anywhere in America, we would be turned away for fear of the sober remorse the next day would cause us to sue the artist for "desecration of the body". However, as we entered the shop, it was clear that we likely would not be signing any affidavits. A few panels with stock images of snakes, skulls, and other trite biker tattoos lined the walls above a "waiting area" of two plastic chairs like the kind you used to sit in during elementary school. We wobbled with drunkenness until a few minutes later when a tall, lean man who looked to be in his mid-thirties came up to the counter.

"Can I help you ladies?" he said in a British accent.

"Hello," Beatrice said sweetly, "We need to alter this lovely lady's tattoo."

She lifted up the side of my shirt before I had a chance to protest and showed him the small letters.

"Ah, a remnant of a wanker, I reckon," he accurately surmised, "Come on then."

He informed me that Tibbie and Beatrice weren't allowed back in the tattoo studio, but as I glanced back at them as they waved me on encouragingly. I must have been drunk because by looking around the waiting area, any ounce of logic should have sent me running in the other direction. However, when we passed through the red velvet curtain, somehow the actual tattoo studio looked immaculately clean. I guess he had to keep a tough profile for his usual clientele. When I stopped to pay attention, he didn't have any tattoos himself and was dressed like he just stepped off the Cambridge campus.

"Let's see then," he said, as I lifted the side of my bra to expose the tattoo. "Ah, yes, I can cover that up, no problem. Would you like a picture? Or perhaps we can add some words to make it a phrase."

Suddenly, I had an epiphany. I knew exactly what I wanted, but I had no idea how to convert it into Latin. I figured, what the hell, I'd give it a shot.

"Do you happen to know Latin?" I couldn't believe I was asking.

"Yes actually," he replied casually, "I studied it for eight years."

I shook my head and ignored the fact that I seemed to have slipped into some parallel universe where tattoo artists were fluent in Latin.

"Alright then, you can help me."

I told him what I wanted and he translated it effortlessly off the top of his head. I lay down on my side as he put the needle to my skin. The entire process tickled slightly and took less than five minutes. Before I knew it, the tattoo guy was taking off his medical gloves and saying, "All done then! You can follow me and pay at the front."

I emerged from behind the curtain to see Tibbie and Beatrice snickering at one of those *Ten New Sex Moves that will Blow his Mind* magazines. When they saw me, they instantly shot up out of their seats.

"So, let's see!" Tibbie squealed excitedly.

I lifted up my shirt in the middle of the tattoo parlor without an ounce of the usual mortification I would have felt upon a complete stranger seeing me in nothing but my bra. I felt instantly empowered with the realization that, even though he would never know, I no longer had the same tattoo as Tommy.

It was like putting a seal on a book I had closed so that there was now no way for the wind to blow the pages back open. Tibbie and Beatrice stumbled over to see my new and improved tattoo that now read *Vivat in aeternum,* Latin for "live ever," the impactful words from the last line of John Keats's final poem.

By the time we made our way back home, it was just past midnight. Given that we were exhausted before we even started this ludicrous adventure, we were now really, really ready to pass the hell out. I went to the bathroom to brush my teeth. I pulled up my shirt to take a look at my new tattoo. I looked at the words and smiled, feeling refreshingly strong.

I brought my purse into the bathroom with me and reached in to pull out my toothbrush. My hand brushed against my cell phone and I realized I hadn't checked it since I'd turned it off after drunkenly dialing Scarlett for fear she would call back and I would have absolutely no idea what to say to her.

I hit the power button and waited for it to load as I began to brush my teeth. I couldn't tell if I was disappointed or relieved that I had no voicemail from Scarlett. No voicemails. Maybe Scarlett had tried to call me back but my phone was off. But still, she didn't leave a message. I felt like she would have if she really wanted to talk to me. I didn't know if I was disappointed or relieved. Suddenly, the little icon lit up to notify me that I had one new email.

I clicked on it to pull up my account. As the message popped up, my stomach dropped as I choked on some toothpaste. I pounded on my chest, spit into the sink, and wiped my face with a towel. Then I picked up my phone again, double-checking that I had seen it right. From Thomas Alcott. The subject line simply read *Please Read.*

I stood there, silently, for what felt like an eternity, contemplating what the message could possibly say. Presumably, he had written to wish me a Merry Christmas. Tommy had always come to my parents' Christmas Eve party, bringing the same bottle of ridiculously expensive cabernet sauvignon and mouth-watering baklava that the Alcott's Greek housekeeper made each year. He was probably stopping to think of me and just wrote a quick note in the spirit of tradition.

Maybe it was more than that though. Despite my better efforts, I couldn't help wondering if it was some kind of apology or if he was begging for me back. Maybe he and Scarlett had gotten together but had since broken up. The probably cheated on each other. She cheated on all of her other boyfriends, after all. Leave it to him to come crawling back just when I was feeling really good about myself.

I looked in the mirror and took a deep breath, wondering what to do next. I stared into my own eyes and had flashbacks to that night and felt my heart breaking all over again. I put my hands on the sink, steadying myself as my eyes filled up with tears.

Then, I caught another glimpse of my new tattoo. I ran my fingers over it gently. I remembered seeing Tommy's tattoo spotlighted on his body as Scarlett covered her face while they both stood there like idiots as my entire world shattered around me. That fucking asshole. Those selfish idiots.

Then, the anger dissipated and I just felt sorry for them. Sorry that their lives were so shallow that they couldn't even care enough about one of their best friends to keep it in their pants. I laughed and rolled my eyes and remembered everything that had happened to me over the past few months and how I had real friends now. How I had a job that I loved. How I had everything I needed.

I picked up my phone and hovered my thumb over the screen directly over Tommy's name. *Please Read,* his desperation oozing through those two words. I hesitated for a moment before clicking on the trashcan icon. The phone paused and asked me if I was sure. Then, I pressed the "OK" button, deleting the email without even reading it.

"At once it struck me what quality went

To form a man of achievement"

~ Letter to George and Thomas Keats
22 December 1817

The next weekend, Andrew took me to a charity event that he had been invited to in the hopes that his presence would lure lots of people to the fundraiser. Not to mention the hope that he would open that big fat wallet. He had invited me as his date. I was a bit nervous because I never seemed to do very well at these high society functions, but I definitely wanted to go, if nothing else just too see what this fancy of an affair was like. Plus, I was really hoping for some tiny crab cakes.

The party was at the Victoria and Albert Museum, which I was excited about because I hadn't gotten a chance to go there yet and had heard really great things. The charity had hired a limo for us, so we got to arrive to the event in style. I wasn't disappointed when I entered the museum. It had beautiful inner corridors lined with classical marble sculptures and gorgeous ironwork. To my great delight, one of the first things I saw was mini crab cakes. Andrew made me feel comfortable enough that I didn't feel bad taking three off of the plate as I normally did back in D.C.

"Come on," he took my free hand that wasn't carrying the precious hors d'oeuvres and led me over to a man who was dressed like a 17th century nobleman, right down to the ascot.

"Hi there Arthur, you're looking fit!"

"Andrew! How lovely to see you. Why thank you, I've been trying out a new tailor and the results have been quite positive, who is this lovely lady?"

"This is my girlfriend, Emma," the novelty of him calling me his girlfriend still hadn't worn off. "Emma, meet Arthur Brumley. Arthur here is one of the Queen's chief advisors."

Arthur puffed up with pride.

Man and I thought Tommy had powerful friends. As we made our way around the room and he introduced me to Britain's elite, I saw for the first time his level of power swag that eclipsed Tommy by far.

"How has work been?" Arthur asked.

"Oh you know, just trying to keep my soul," Andrew answered.

Arthur laughed.

"It's surprisingly difficult isn't it?"

You could definitely tell that Andrew had been doing this his whole life. He was just so effortlessly charming.

"So, my dear, have you visited Paris since you've been here?"

"No," I admitted, hoping that I hadn't offended him for such and unforgivable lack of culture.

"Well, if you two ever want to visit, Andrew, do contact me. I have an absolutely divine flat there but I've been so tied up that it hasn't gotten used in a tragically long time. I'd love for you two to have a nice getaway!"

I blushed. We really hadn't been dating that long and I figured the thought of going away on a romantic holiday would terrify Andrew and send him running. Instead, he put his arm around the small of my back.

"Thank you that would be lovely Arthur."

I looked at him and he smiled before leaning in and giving me a kiss on the forehead.

I'd had so much fun that night. I had expected it to be like the times I went to these things with Tommy, when he just talked the foreign language of politics that I would never understand and just placed me beside him, filling in the obligatory female presence without having to worry about them expecting too much when the night was over. But, it was different with Andrew. He had included me in every conversation and steered things to me, always giving me my chance to talk. He was so sweet and adorable.

I sighed. Well, it was all over now. There was no denying it anymore. I was smitten.

"Pleasure is oft a visitant; but pain
Clings cruelly to us."

~ *Endymion*

———————

Every month, Keats House hosted a tour where they took visitors around Hampstead Heath to give them a better vision of the things that Keats saw when he had his inspiration for his beautiful poems. I had been studying up for weeks and Violet said I was ready to lead my own tour. I had told Andrew, excited I'd be able to start this new responsibility, and he enthusiastically agreed to attend my first tour.

Visitors assembled at the house and prepared to follow me to the Heath. There were more people than I was expecting, around twenty, and I became really nervous I was going to screw it up. I had never been great at public speaking, but everyone was already here and it was goo late to back out now.

I lead the group up the hill along the path shaded by the lush, green trees. Warm rays of sun warmed my face between the shadows cast by the leaves, and the temperature felt perfect against my skin. I smiled, my nervousness fading as I became excited to share the beauty of Keats's experience in this magical setting.

We reached the top of the hill and I turned to see the gorgeous site in front of me. The green hills cascaded down to a lovely view of the town. Brick buildings stood in the distance, looking untouched, as if they were the same as they looked in the 1800s. I started my tour.

"As you can see, the Heath is rich with the scenery that inspired Keats to write his beautiful poems about nature. Sitting by the sparkling lake, he wrote such words as 'I admire lolling on a lawn by the water – lilied pond to eat white currants and see goldfish: and to go to the fair in the evening if I'm good'."

Sitting on the heath and gazing down at the greenery and trees below, he scribed, 'Seasons of mists and mellow fruitfulness, Close bosom-friend of the maturing sun; Conspiring with him how to load and bless, With fruit the vines that round the thatch-eaves run, To bend with apples the mossed cottage-trees, And fill all fruit with ripeness to the core.'

His love for Fanny Brawne enhanced his love of nature. As they took walks along these paths, they would take in the scenery in between staring into each other's eyes and feeling their love for one another. He saw this love all around him, especially in her eyes."

I went on to describe more about their love and the history of the heath. I glanced over at Andrew and he had a smile on his face, tilting his head towards me in reverence. When I was finished, the group made their way back to the house. Afterwards, there was a small reception in the garden. We had hoped to lure people back so that we could continue the dialogue and persuade more people to join the Friends of Keats House organization and increase our donations.

Violet had assembled a picnic of scones, biscuits, and tea, and set up tables and chairs for everyone to relax and process everything they learned on the tour.

Andrew came up to me and gave me a long kiss. Then, he pulled away, smiled, and tucked a lock of hair behind my ear.

"Very impressive," he said.

I smiled. I walked over and picked up a chocolate biscuit. I was just pouring Andrew and I some iced tea when I heard a seductive, French accent speak from behind me. I turned and instantly recognized the poised, posh woman standing in front of me. Amelie L'Amour. In the flesh.

"Hello love," Amelie said walking up to Andrew. He broke his grasp of me and reciprocated her double-cheeked kiss. I scowled internally.

"Um, hi Amelie," Andrew said back, admittedly sounding as surprised as I was.

I glanced her over. She was dressed in all black, a dress that looked like it was custom made for her from an expensive fabric by a famous designer. She was wearing ankle boots that I could never pull off. She ran her hands through her perfectly coiffed hair that was cut just below her chin and angled up towards the back in a super-French fashion. I could tell that under those clothes she had the perfect body. And she smelled like what I pictured the smell of pure romance would be if you captured it in a perfume, which made me picture one of those glamorous French models that walked through the streets effortlessly as men stared and coveted them. Goddammit.

"What are you doing here?" he asked, sounding not too horrified to see her.

"What do you mean? You know I love these programs. I couldn't make the tour, but I decided to come to the reception. Work has just been so busy lately that I haven't had a chance to come to one in ages. All good stuff though, we're making great headway on that analysis and strategic plan for combating the genocide in Serbia."

Great. Now she was saving the world.

"I see you brought a friend," she said, noticing me. I resented her instantly for the use of the word 'friend'. She probably thought I was too plain a commoner to ever be a romantic interest of Andrew's or a threat to her.

"Amelie, this is my girlfriend, Emma."

At Andrew's use of the word 'girlfriend', I could tell she was sizing me up as she lifted her hand to shake mine.

"Pleased to meet you Emma," she said. I swear she gave me a smirk to signify that she wasn't threatened by me at all and was, in fact, accepting some sort of challenge.

"Likewise," I said, using every fiber of my being to be pleasant.

"Well, I must be going now. I have an appointment over at the consulate to present the plan. Thanks again for all of your help, Andrew. I couldn't have done it without you."

She winked as she turned and exited the garden. Her words sunk in. He had helped her with the project? While I'm sure it was long and involved, Andrew and I had been dating long enough that I was sure he had to have worked on it at some point with Amelie while the two of us were together. I felt my confidence shrinking as I wondered why he had never told me about it.

Amelie turned to head over to the refreshments table.

"I'm so sorry, I had no idea she'd be here," Andrew said, staring off into her direction before turning his gaze back at me, looking concerned.

"Oh, it's alright," I said, trying to be cool and sound as confident as humanly possible, as if it hadn't bothered me in the slightest.

He wrapped his arm around me again and gave me a kiss on my cheek. I should have been reassured, but as it happened, I really, really wasn't.

Andrew and I parted ways for the evening and I went home and poured myself a glass of wine to try to calm my nerves. Apparently loving to torture myself, I opened my laptop and Googled 'Amelie L'Amour'.

I first noticed what popped up on the images tab. I clicked onto the page and scrolled down, I was met with tons of gorgeous images of her beautiful face and flawless body. While I knew she worked in fashion, I didn't know until right then that she was a model herself. It showed her in all kinds of designer advertisements, modeling clothes at Paris Fashion Week, and cavorting with celebrities and big-wigs while wearing flawless, stylish dresses with perfect hair and sexy stilettos.

Then, to my horror, I saw that he photos were sprinkled with pictures of her and Andrew. They looked so perfect together, both of them gorgeous. There were tons of paparazzi shots of them walking down the street, sipping coffee at cafes, attending fancy galas, and even some with the two of them alongside members of the royal family.

One that particularly bothered me was one of Andrew with Amelie and her parents. They looked so comfortable together, like he was already their son-in-law. I imagined that it was probably the same for his family; that they had known Amelie for so long that they thought of her as a daughter.

I scrolled through and didn't immediately see any images of the two of them with his parents, so I felt at least a little sigh of relief. But, I wondered what his parents were like. I'd never seen a picture of them. I didn't even know if he had any siblings or not. I began typing to Google the Bradford family when I heard my phone buzz next to me. It was from Andrew.

Hey darling. My family is getting together at my parents' place this weekend and I'd love for them to meet you. Care to join?

I quickly responded yes. Well, I guess I was about to find out.

"I love you more that I believe you have liked me
for my own sake and for nothing else."

~ Letter to Fanny Brawne
8 July 1819

The next weekend, we took the limo the hour ride from London to the Bradfords' palatial mansion out in the countryside. The first sight of it shocked me with awe, and crippling feelings of inferiority. The thing looked like a freaking castle.

We pulled into the driveway, exited the limo, and walked up to the gigantic entry door. Andrew rang the doorbell and I waited in anxious anticipation. Andrew had assured me over and over again that his parents were going to love me, but somehow I thought my comparatively plebian status combined with what would likely be an unforgiveable lack of refinement might be a mild deterrent.

All I could think about at that moment was how many forks would be on their table. Why didn't I think to study up on forks?! Which one was salad again? Great. I was going to go down in infamy as the girl who used the wrong fork. Why were there so many forks anyway?! Oh God, then there were all of the knives and spoons...

As I was trying desperately to draw from memory anything I subconsciously grasped from Victorian literature regarding flatware procedures, the door swung open and I was face-to-face with Andrew Bradford's famous parents. While I had been expecting them to come across as extremely intimidating, they greeted us with kindness and enthusiasm. His mother had on a pressed purple suit, a string of pearls, and perfectly coiffed hair. His father had on a dress shirt with gray pants and polished black shoes.

"Andrew, darling, it's so great to see you!," she leaned in and gave him a huge hug. "And you must be Emma! We've heard such lovely things about you, come on in dear! She greeted me with my own hug, which I wasn't expecting from someone who was so British and proper.

"It's nice to meet you Mrs. Bradford."

"Oh darling, call me Eleanor. This is my husband William."

"Pleasure," he said, approaching me and giving me a kiss on each cheek.

"Come on then, Nanny's made tea in the garden!"

We walked through the house, which I sincerely hoped I would get a detailed tour of later, and out the back door into the divine garden, complete with statues, fountains, and gorgeous, expensive looking flowers. I saw a small elderly woman arranging cucumber sandwiches on a fancy plate.

"Hello Nanny!" Andrew said, going over to give his grandmother a big kiss on the cheek.

"Oh, hello dear, so wonderful to see you. You don't look a day older!"

He laughed. "Nanny, I want you to meet someone special. This is Emma. Emma, this is my dear grandmother. I'm afraid you'll have to get her approval before this can go any further."

I smiled, "Well I'll certainly do my best."

"He makes me sound scarier than I am. Would you like some tea darling?"

"Yes, that would be lovely, thank you," I responded politely.

Just as she was about to hand me my cup, the back door swung open and a petite girl with blonde curly hair ran out, jumping on Andrew and almost tackling him to the ground.

"Happy birthday, wanker," she said, ruffling his hair.

"Thanks," he said, wobbling to recover, "Emma this is my younger sister Charlotte, Charlotte this is Emma."

She came over and gave me a hug just about as hard as she had barreled on Andrew. I struggled to stay standing but succeeded in the end.

"Come on, let's go get some of Nanny's cucumber sandwiches, I'm starving!"

Andrew's parents joined us and we all sat in lawn chairs, taking in the beautiful day. I sat my teacup next to me, quite carefully since I'm sure it cost more than I could ever replace, and picked up a cucumber sandwich.

"Thank you," I said, "So, Charlotte, what do you do?"

"I'm an English literature major at Cambridge, just coming into my third year."

"Yeah, sister here can't help but copy everything I did in my younger days," he said jokingly.

"Oh shut up," she said with a sneer.

Andrew's mother leaned over to me and quietly said, "Charlotte has always worshipped Andrew, they were incredibly close growing up. I'm sure she did copy him. I'm pretty sure if he jumped off of a cliff she would too."

After tea, Eleanor showed us around the mansion. It had seventeen bedrooms and ten bathrooms, not to mention a parlor, a gentleman's lounge, a lady's dressing room, and stables out back with thoroughbred horses.

His mother had an art collection that I would absolutely die to have, with famous paintings that had I seen in any other home I would have assumed them a print, but here I knew they were real.

Andrew's uncles joined us just in time for dinner. We all sat at the grand dining table, eating Beef Wellington prepared by the Bradfords' master chef.

"Andrew, I knew you were coming home so I told Jacques to make your favorite."

"Thank you mum, it's delightful."

After sticky toffee pudding, which was served in lieu of a cake since it was Andrew's favorite dessert, the ladies went into the drawing room while the men went into the gentleman's lounge to smoke cigars and drink what I'm sure was twenty year old scotch. From the drawing room, I could see Andrew relaxing with his father and his uncles, laughing as he puffed his cigar and sipped his whiskey. All of the men were perfectly polished in designer clothes and expensive-looking polished shoes. The lounge was lined with mahogany bookshelves and the men sat in large leather armchairs.

As I glanced in on them, I felt a bit out of place. They were all so comfortable in this world. I was just a normal girl. I didn't know how to do all of their hobbies like horseback riding, croquet, sailing, and rowing crew. I was worried I wouldn't know any of the customs and would say something stupid. I could never golf for God's sake and I would surely go flying off of a sailboat if I ever attempted.

"Emma it's so nice to meet you," Charlotte said from the seat next to me, "You know Andrew's never brought a girl here before to meet Nanny. He must really like you."

I was confused. Surely he had brought Amelie here.

"And no, before you ask, he never brought Amelie here," she said with a smirk.

I was so surprised. It made me feel a lot better to know that he had never brought her around. In all of the time that they dated, I'm sure he could have brought her here if he really wanted to. I suddenly felt a bit more comfortable and thought maybe there was hope in me fitting in with these people after all.

I thanked Andrew's family for everything. They said they hoped to see me again soon. I smiled at how genuine they sounded.

We went back to Andrew's house and we were both completely exhausted, so we climbed into his bed and cuddled. He gave me a kiss on the back of my shoulder. That had always been my favorite spot to be kissed – how it tickled just slightly enough to make me feel a rush of sensation. I quickly drifted off to sleep.

———————

The next morning, I felt really happy about meeting Andrew's parents and thought that since they were all over the internet, it would be easy for me to find out more about them and hopefully have more to talk about with them the next time. My curiosity outweighed my feeling slightly like a creepy stalker and I Googled the Bradfords. I was instantly greeted by hundreds of hits.

The first one was a news article in *The Telegraph* with a picture of Mr. and Mrs. Bradford and Charlotte dressed in fancy morning dress. It was a photo of them walking into the royal wedding of Prince William and Kate Middleton. The title read *The Bradford family attends the Royal Wedding*.

The article read,

> *The Bradford family joined the group of distinguished guests at the Royal Wedding this past Friday. Mr. and Mrs. Bradford were accompanied by daughter Charlotte. Sadly, their son, British heartthrob Andrew Bradford, was unable to attend due to his charity work in Kenya.*

I figured if the Bradfords had attended, that probably meant the L'Amours had been there as well. I Googled "Amelie L'Amour Royal wedding", and sure enough, there was a photo of Mr. and Mrs. L'Amour heading into Westminster Abbey, dressed impeccably and looking very stylish and distinguished.

Distinguished French couple the L'Amours entering Westminster Abbey on the day of the Royal Wedding.

I read on.

> *Business mogul and billionaire Jaques L'Amour enters the church with his gorgeous wife Sandrine by his side. Noticeably absent was the L'Amour's*

gorgeous daughter, Amelie, who was in Kenya on a missionary trip with fellow goodwill ambassador, Andrew Bradford. The two met while attending Oxford University and have been in and on-again off-again relationship ever since. However, with recent pictures of the two getting cozy together at a romantic restaurant in Paris, rumors are flying that the two are back together and more in love than ever.

I sighed, thinking about how fancy they were and how I probably would have tripped down a flight of stairs and had my picture splattered all over the front page of every newspaper in the country. There was a picture of Andrew and Amelie accompanying the article. To be fair, the article was from 2011, but the two of them really did look incredibly in love, smiling at each other as they leaned across the table. I figured that kind of love never really went away, and there was no way in hell I would ever measure up to the glamour that was Amelie L'Amour.

"I never knew before, what such a love as you have made me feel, was; I did not believe in it; my Fancy was afraid of it, lest it should burn me up."

~ Letter to Fanny Brawne
8 July 1819

The next day, I sat down at my computer to keep working on my proposal paper. I had gotten to the part when Keats came down with the case of tuberculosis that ultimately claimed is life and ended their love affair. I put my fingers to the keys and got started.

In February 1920, Keats went into town without his greatcoat and returned late, cold and feverish. After he fell ill, his letters to his friend Brown show that he was tortured by thoughts of Fanny and fearful of death. His letters and notes to Fanny became, rather than playful and loving, cloying and paranoid.

From his sick bed, he wrote, "On the night I was taken ill – when so violent a rush of blood came to my Lungs that I felt nearly suffocated – I assure you I felt possible I might not survive, and at that moment thought of nothing but you."

His illness prevented him from writing much poetry, but during his travels to Rome, where it was hoped that the mild climate would improve his health, he wrote what became the final declaration of his love, stating:

No – yet still steadfast, still unchangeable,

Pillow'd upon my fair love's ripening breast,

To feel forever it's soft fall and swell,

Awake forever in a sweet unrest,

Still, still to hear her tender-taken breath,

And so live ever – or else swoon to death.

These heartbreaking words show how his love had grown strong and true, and how their relationship had blossomed into a fierce reverence. Sadly, it was taken away far too soon, but their love and its inspiration in Keats's words will live on for eternity.

This section was oddly appropriate for how I was feeling. Happy that at least it seemed like a good conclusion, I tried to distract myself and looked forward to seeing Andrew once again.

———————

One day after work, Andrew came over to my place to relax and watch a movie. He walked in with a bottle of red wine and gave me a kiss on the cheek, smiling widely.

"Guess what," he said, wrapping his arms around me."

"What?" I asked curiously, smiling back at him and wondering what was making him so happy."

"One of the charities I'm on the board for is throwing its annual fundraising gala. This year it's in Rome," he said, leaning in for another kiss.

I kissed him back but my stomach clenched with anxiety. Rome? I instantly had flashbacks to the trip Tommy and I took together that I thought was so perfect at the time. I inadvertently rubbed the tattoo on my ribcage and thought back to how much had changed since. I had been so happy lately and I was worried that going back to Rome would bring all of those memories flooding back, and I didn't think I could handle that.

"Did you say next Friday?" I asked, scrambling to think of some sort of excuse, "Oh Gosh! I'm so sorry but Dr. Lowell asked me to help him host the teddy bear tea this weekend! I won't be able to go," I said, feeling a bit guilty that I was lying to him.

"Oh come on, I'm sure he won't mind," he responded, "The gala is for a program that works to instill cultural and educational programs for refugees from North Africa to help them adapt to Roman culture and get the schooling they would never have received in their oppressed countries. It's the one that means the most to me. You have to come. It's such a great cause. Plus, it's at the nicest hotel at the city. I felt bad about it until I was told that the rooms are provided pro bono and all of the profit it would have made is going directly to the charity. I'll show you around to all of my favorite Italian restaurants."

He paused and must have seen that my reaction hadn't changed.

"Haven't you always wanted to see Keats's grave?" he said, pulling out his ace in the hole. Dammit. He had me there. My mind stumbled and failed to think of another excuse.

"Come on, Harry's going too, his company does a lot of business with these donors as well. If they buy wine for distribution, Sotheby's takes a portion of the proceeds and donates it to charity. Of course they picked him with that bloody 'charm' of his," he said, sarcastically."

The thought of Harry there made me feel a bit less pressure. I really had fun with Harry. Plus, Andrew had seemed so reliable lately that I found myself letting my guard down a little bit. He seemed so unlike Tommy. I should give him the benefit of the doubt. Plus, I thought of all of those people less fortunate than me and felt guilty that I was giving up a chance to be wined and dined for a good cause when they were denied the basic education I had clearly taken for granted. And I did miss that food. Ohhh that food.

———————

The next Friday we flew to Rome. We checked into our hotel, which, as Andrew promised, was absolutely gorgeous, undeniably romantic and right in the middle of the city near all of the fabulous things to see and do. I stopped thinking about Tommy and thought about how happy I was to be back in this city that I loved.

We had gotten there two days before the conference to have a day to ourselves before Harry arrived. Once we were finished unpacking, the sun was setting and we decided to go on an evening stroll.

"Why don't we go to Keats's grave first?" Andrew asked affectionately, coming over and putting his arms around me to give me a soft kiss.

"That would be great," I said smiling, giving him another kiss to thank him for being so great.

We made our way to the Protestant Cemetery where Keats was buried after he succumbed to consumption. I looked at the tombstone and saw the famous words of Keats's own epitaph I had read hundreds of times before engraved on the front.

This Grave contains all that was mortal

Of a Young English Poet

Who, on his Death Bed, in the Bitterness of his Heart

At the Malicious Power of his Enemies Desired

These Words to be engraven on his Tomb Stone.

"Here lies One Whose Name was writ in Water."

24 February 1821

Above it was a carved Greek lyre with four of its eight strings broken. It was meant to symbolize his classical genius cut off by death before its maturity.

"Why do you think he wanted that on his gravestone?" Andrew asked, "It seems kind of depressing and morbid doesn't it?"

"It means that everything will pass, nothing is permanent. Keats recognized that in the grand scheme of things, his life might as well have been written in water; that his life, work, and death are fleeting, that his legacy would be swallowed by the passing of time, just as everything will be eventually."

I thought that, while I admired almost everything about him, perhaps Keats was wrong about this one thing. His legacy had lived on. And in that way, he would live forever – just like his nightingale's song.

"Alright, I think that is enough philosophy for now," I said, thinking that Andrew probably wanted to move onto the fun he had spoken of when he was so excited to come to Rome, "Let's get to bed so we can make the most out of tomorrow."

The next night, we headed to the bar to greet Harry and have a drink. While I was getting ready in the gorgeously decorated bathroom, Andrew came in to meet me. He was wearing a perfectly pressed dark gray suit, his flawlessly coiffed, full, shiny dark chocolate colored hair looking effortlessly flawless.

He looked so handsome I thought I would melt on the spot. He came over to the mirror and briefly straightened his black tie before walking up and hugging me from behind. I drew in his soft, yet masculine scent that was now, beyond a doubt, my most cherished sensation in the world. Well, besides the obvious.

"You look gorgeous darling," he whispered in my ear, kissing my neck.

Andrew embraced me as his lips worked his way down my neck, I felt filled with happiness, my insecurities melting away.

"Come on then, Harry will be waiting," I said tentatively, wishing that we could stay there forever. Andrew kissed me once more and went into the room. I looked in the mirror one last time before fluffing my hair to achieve whatever volume I could get and applying one more layer of my favorite dark maroon lipstick.

We headed to the lobby bar. I looked around at the lush, pattered royal blue carpet, custom molded ceilings, the large, incredibly expensive looking Classical vases, and the giant crystal chandelier that hung above a gorgeous winding staircase.

I took in a deep breath and smiled. Andrew put his arm around me as we walked further into the room. He started pointing out all of the famous politicians, distinguished debutantes, and well-dressed millionaires who were there for the gala. We walked up to some of them and he introduced me, proudly. While I was initially scared to death, I remembered Tibbie's advice to just turn the conversation towards them to fluff their egos and I'd be fine.

It turns out it worked. I had a high level executive from Barclay's tell Andrew how special I was and how he should never let me slip away. An elderly woman who was heir to a string of famous high-end British department stores said that I was delightful and she wished that more young women were like me. The French representative for the United Nations gave me a kiss on each cheek and said, with a genuine air, how wonderful it was to meet me. I finally felt like maybe it might be possible fore me to fit into Andrew's world after all.

After making a few rounds, Andrew took my hand.

"Come on, let's go find Harry," he said, "If we find the bar, he won't be far away."

We made our way across the room. Harry was indeed posted up right next to the bar, looking quite debonair in a navy suit and striped tie. He turned and saw us and gave us a wave.

I waved back as we weaved through the crowd to join him.

"Hey mate," Andrew said happily, "Creature of habit. I always know where to find you."

Harry veered his eyes away from me and started nervously rubbing the back of his head.

"Listen, Emma, about your friend Beatrice. I'm sorry, I meant to call her, it's just..." he started, stumbling to make up an excuse.

I laughed. "Trust me, I'm absolutely positive you guys are on the same page. Honestly, I wouldn't be surprised if she's forgotten your name by now."

He smiled with relief before he furrowed his brow, looking confused. Commitment-phobic guys were so predictable. The minute a girl falls disinterested, they are suddenly filled with the challenge of conquest and their attraction to the girl not only returns, but grows ten-fold.

Then, out of the corner of my eye I saw a thin, elegant woman in an immaculately, form-fitting dress and red-soled heels. I recognized the black hair and stylish haircut instantly. It was Amelie. She turned her head, saw us and smiled before sauntering across the room to where we were standing.

"Hello Andrew," she said in that damn, seductive French accent, her eyes focused exclusively on him. She grasped his forearms and leaned over to give him a kiss on both cheeks. I was really hoping that was just a French thing and not a residual habit from their romantic, incredibly publicly adored, relationship.

"Harry dear," she said leaning over and giving him his own set of kisses on the cheek, filling me with relief that she seemed to do it with all men. "How lovely to see you, it's been too long."

Harry gave her a huge hug.

"Bloody right it has. So great to see you my love."

My love? Ugh, she obviously had her spell over him too. I tried to smile at Harry to have him give me the look of reverence he was giving her, but he kept smiling at her and didn't even glance in my direction. I took in Amelie's black dress that hugged her amazing body. While she wore minimal make-up, I could tell she didn't have to with her smooth, flawless skin, high cheekbones, and gorgeous brown eyes. She stood on her designer heels that gave her perfect posture and made her thin legs look incredible. Delicate diamond earrings and a simple white gold necklace gave her a chic sparkle. I felt an overwhelming wave of crippling insecurity as I thought about my plain dress and ordinary black flats.

"And Emma, so nice to see you again," she said politely, in a way that made me wonder if she was covering up feelings of distain.

"Would you excuse us for a moment?" Andrew said, taking my hand, "We need refills of our champagne."

We walked up to the bar casually. Andrew put his hand on the small of my back and whispered,

"Emma, I'm so sorry. I can't believe this happened again. I had no idea Amelie was going to be here or trust me, we definitely wouldn't have come tonight."

I muscled up every once of energy I had to come across as a cool and collected girl who would feel pretty much the opposite as I did then, my confidence now shriveled to the size of a desiccated pea after having Amelie's seemingly effortless model-grade beauty make me feel like a poser frump in comparison.

"It's ok, I don't mind at all!" I said, shocked at how genuine I sounded.

"Ok, great," he said, leaning over and giving me a kiss on my forehead. "Let's get out of here though, I'm tired and we can see Harry tomorrow."

"Sounds good," I said, relief washing over me.

We walked back over to Harry and Amelie, laughing jovially at something and looking effortlessly classy.

"Where are your drinks?" Harry asked.

"Oh, they ran out of the good stuff," Andrew fibbed, "No use getting that vile, sweet type that I hate. Plus, I think we're going to head to bed, I'm knackered."

Harry looked appalled.

"Mate, you can't go to bed at 9:00 p.m. when you're in Rome for God's sake."

"He's right," Amelie chimed in, "Come on, Harry and I were just talking about getting drinks at Cigno Blanco. You remember Cigno Blanco. Last time the three of us met, we agreed it was quite simply the most marvelous place in Rome. You positively must join us," she said, in what even I had to admit was an enchantingly seductive French accent.

I could tell there would be no arguing with her and resigned myself to the fact that I was going to have to deal with her intimidating posh perfection for what would likely be hours longer.

We made our way to Cigno Blanco and entered a dimly lit, private room with plush dark red chairs underneath a sparkling chandelier and delicate Italian instrumental music playing in the background.

After I sat down on what was hands-down the most comfortable chair I had ever sat in in my entire life, Harry ordered what I'm sure was the most expensive red Bordeaux on the menu.

When the waiter returned with the bottle, Amelie picked up her glass and wrapped her hand around the base in what I was sure was the proper way for handling red wine. I attempted to copy her and hoped I wasn't making a complete fool of myself.

"It's lovely to be back here, so many wonderful memories," she said, turning towards Andrew flirtatiously as if I wasn't even in the room. To my horror, he turned back and gave her a warm smile.

"Yeah, had many a success here. French women..." Harry said, shaking his head to denote that not only were French women incredibly beautiful, but also apparently amazing in bed.

"This is positively my favorite fundraiser. It's such a worthy cause."

So now, she was not only a fashion icon, but a brilliant humanitarian who understood and could contribute to the operations of an international charity. Ugh.

She finally tore her eyes off of Andrew and turned in my direction.

"So, Emma, this is your first time to Rome I take it?" she inquired, taking another delicate sip from her glass of fancy wine.

I seethed internally at her snobbish assumption, that there was no way a "commoner" like me had ever been to such a worldly, glamorous city.

"No, I've been here before," I said simply, the only thing I could squeeze out without narrowing my eyes at her and throwing her a look of sheer derision.

She didn't respond. She just took a wine glass that Harry had poured for her.

When the four of us had glasses, we all took sips to evaluate Harry's pick.

"So, what do you think?" he asked.

It was so delicious.

"It's really good!" I said, taking another sip.

Amelie swirled the liquid in her glass before putting her nose into it and delicately breathing in its aroma. "Divine. Lovely cassis and blackberry flavors. And do I detect a hint of coffee bean and vanilla?"

Harry smiled and nodded.

"Right as always."

He turned to me and said, "I swear she's better at this than I am."

She looked at him with sultry eyes before taking another sip. Great. She didn't even work in the industry and had an even better palette than Harry. To be honest, I don't even know if I could tell the difference between a Merlot and a Cabernet.

Amelie turned back to Andrew. "So any new additions to the art collection?"

Andrew shook his head.

"No time lately. I looked up some auctions and saw I missed some good ones."

I thought about whether he had missed out on some fabulous art because he had no time to go to auctions since he had been wasting his time with me.

"Yeah mate, I was surprised when you didn't pick up the newly discovered Degas."

Andrew let out a heavy sigh.

"Found out about it the next day. Bloody tragedy."

I thought about the fact that the three of them went to art auctions where Degas were being bid on. I had no idea that Andrew liked impressionist art, or that he had a collection.

It must have been housed at his parents' house or in storage so I hadn't seen it, but it still seemed like something I should have known about him by then.

"You always did love him after that course at Oxford. Remember?"

"Of course I remember," Andrew responded, "It was the most interesting class I've ever taken. Professor Kiracofe was the one who inspired me to start my collection."

"Remember how he spoke about Renoir? It made me truly appreciate how his strokes and open composition..."

Amelie kept talking but I tuned her out. I was too busy trying to process the scene in front of me. I was fading further and further into the background as their conversation progressed to more and more fancier and worldly topics where I had nothing to contribute to the conversation. I smiled and nodded as I felt smaller and smaller. Even though I was so annoyed with her and I hated to admit it, I could certainly see why Amelie was so entrancing. I hated her, and yet wanted to be her at the same time.

Around 1:00 in the morning, my eyes were shutting beyond my control and I couldn't stop yawning. I was terrified that they would think I was bored since I had absolutely nothing of cultural significance to contribute to the conversation and so I was thinking about unicorns or something. But, I couldn't help it.

"I think I need to get this one to bed," Andrew said sweetly. Although it only made me feel worse for tearing him away from a conversation he was so obviously enjoying with people with whom he had long relationships that I certainly measured up to.

When we went to the hotel room, I changed into my pajamas and collapsed into bed. Andrew got in next to me and gave me a quick kiss on the forehead before rolling away from me on his side. My stomach clenched as the terrible feeling of mortifying inadequateness rose within me.

The next day passed in a flash and before I knew it, we were getting ready for the gala. I put on smoky make-up the way that Tibbie had taught me and applied the dark maroon lipstick to try and plump up my lips.

I curled my hair and put enough hairspray in that if I got too near a heating duct it would catch on fire, but it was my only option. Otherwise, the curls would fall out in less than five minutes. I put on my plumb colored floor-length dress that I had bought because whenever I wore that color purple, everyone commented on how it accentuated my blue eyes.

I put on sparkly "diamond earrings" that I had bought to fit in with the crowd, hoping no one would notice that they were cubic zirconias I'd picked up for $40 at Accessorize. Then, I slipped into some silver heels that I had borrowed from Beatrice and went to evaluate myself in the mirror.

I actually looked really good. The dress did make my eyes pop and the special hairspray I had borrowed from Tibbie made my hair look really shiny. Beatrice's heels forced me to stand with perfect posture, which was pulling my shoulders back and accentuating my boobs.

But, then I thought back to Amelie's chic look from the night before and thought that if that was what she looked like on a normal night, she would unquestionably look model-grade stunning in an evening gown. I sighed as Andrew exited the walk-in closet.

"Ready?" he asked, smiling.

He looked ready to walk the red carpet. He was wearing a tuxedo with a subtle navy blue hue, a black bowtie, and Oxford style black shoes. He looked devastatingly handsome. Even though last night made me think I should keep my guard up a bit, he made me swoon, as always. It wasn't even fair.

"Yes," I responded, feeling star-struck all over again.

We descended the elevator and made our way across the lobby to the grand ballroom.

We walked into a huge open room with shiny marble floors and decorative molded ceilings. In the middle was an enormous sparkling crystal chandelier centered on a medallion upon a detailed fresco ceiling. Two staircases with iron bannisters set on gold embellished balusters cascaded opposite each other forming an oval. They lead up to wrap balcony with plush, red carpets. Priceless sculptures adorned intricately carved wooden high tables and sat in recesses in each wall. I felt like I had stepped back into the grandeur of the Victorian era.

A waiter came over to greet us and handed us glasses of white wine. I looked around at all of the distinguished guests, which only furthered the perception that I had traveled back in time to a nineteenth-century stately affair. Andrew wrapped his arms around me and pulled me in for a soft kiss.

"I'm so happy you're here with me," he said earnestly. I blushed and smiled.

We walked around and Andrew introduced me to the super, fancy, incredibly influential people. I somehow managed to follow the path of conversation of one of Germany's head political correspondents and was able to ask him enough valid questions that he actually talked to me for about twenty minutes before his wife started to look jealous and he had to move on. The lead conductor of the Vienna Philharmonic said we seemed like a lovely couple and he would love to have us visit and he would be happy to secure box seat tickets for us anytime we wanted. One of the British Treasury Ministers even told him I was a 'keeper'. I felt so much better.

"Oh good, Nigel is here. He's the head of the foundation. Come on, I'd love for him to meet you."

He escorted me across the room and stopped in front of a tall, handsome Englishman.

"Andrew my lad, so glad you could make it!" Nigel said, shaking Andrew's hand and pulling him in for a pat on the back."

"It's been too long," he said, pulling me closer to him. "Nigel, this is my girlfriend, Emma."

"Nice to meet you Emma," he said, taking my hand.

"Likewise," I said, delicately flashing my newfound charm.

"What a lovely young lady," he said, looking at me endearingly, "Nice work Mr. Bradford."

I beamed as Andrew pulled me closer and happiness swelled within me.

Then, as if on cue, I looked over to see Amelie at the top of the staircase. Any ounce of confidence I was feeling shattered as soon as I saw her. She was wearing a strapless, emerald green dress that showed off her neck and what was, unlike my earrings, a genuine diamond necklace that rested delicately on her collarbone.

As she descended the staircase, she pulled up the bottom of her dress to reveal yet another pair of shoes that I'm sure cost more than most people spent on six months' worth of rent. She looked at us and waved before descending the staircase. Once she reached the bottom, she walked right over to us, smiled, and leaned in towards Nigel.

"Nigel, darling," she said in that sickeningly sexy French accent. She grasped both his arms, leaning past me as if I wasn't even there, and gave him a kiss on each cheek.

"My dear, so nice to see you," he said, grasping her hand tighter. "Have you two met?" he asked, nodding in my direction.

"Yes, of course. Emma, so lovely to see you again."

She leaned in and it was my turn to receive her signature dual kiss on the cheek. As her neck waved past my nose, I breathed in the delicate floral, vanilla scent of her perfume that just smelled like pure glamour and refinement.

"You too Amelie," I said, smiling and trying to continue to charm. But, Nigel had lost all interest at me and was now chatting with Amelie as she laughed and sipped her champagne. Suddenly, I felt someone come up behind me and pinch my side. I jumped and gasped for breath.

"Whoa, it's just me!" Harry said laughing while holding a scotch on the rocks. "Bit jittery tonight are we? Come on then, they're seating everyone for dinner."

We passed through a set of carved wooden doors and took our seats at our elaborately set table. We were seated at the head table with Nigel and Harry, and of course Amelie, sat at the chairs next to us.

"I have to say, I think we made the right choice when we selected Rome this year," Amelie said to Nigel. "The past years have been phenomenal, but this is such a huge turn-out!"

"It's definitely the biggest so far," Harry agreed, "But I do have to say that selfishly I wouldn't have minded if we did it in Milan again. Fit Italian birds everywhere."

"Ohhh, that was delightful wasn't it?" Amelie said lighting up, "We had such an amazing time! It was so nice to see that the fashion show was such a hit. That's the most we've raised so far, but I have high hopes for this year! I was just speaking with the head of the Uffizi gallery before we sat down and he said we're welcome next year. I think the cultural representation of the art will do a great job of representing our message..."

Blah, blah, blah, BLAGHH! She went on and on. By then, they had served dinner so Andrew and Harry were engrossed in their food. I looked down at my plate of Wagyu tenderloin steak and white truffles and while I knew it would have cost something like $1500 at a restaurant, I just couldn't stomach anything right then. I needed to get out of there.

I leaned over and gave Andrew a kiss on the cheek.

"I'll be right back darling," I said, rubbing my hand across his upper back and trying to act as normal as humanly possible.

"Is everything ok?" he asked, sounding concerned.

"Yes of course" I said, trying to sound reassuring, "I just forgot something in the room. I'll be right back. Please excuse me everyone."

I delicately placed my napkin on the back of my chair. I walked back out into the ballroom and took a seat on the bottom step of the marble staircase, trying to clear my head.

What on earth was I doing here? I didn't belong with these people. I knew nothing about this level of class and refinement. Everyone had been nice to me, but that's just the way it is, isn't it? Of course they're polite, they'd spent their entire lives being trained in etiquette. They would never come right out and say 'by the way, this is cute and everything, but Andrew should really be with someone who is well-versed in romance languages and competes in equestrian dressage, not someone who's favorite food is supermarket bakery birthday cake and honestly cannot taste the difference between Dom Perignon and a $5.99 bottle of champagne.' It was true. Scarlett and Tommy gave me a taste test once.

I thought back to the night they did it. We were out to dinner for Scarlett's birthday and were ordering after-dinner drinks. Tommy got an 18-year scotch and Scarlett ordered a Grey Goose martini. I was in the mood for champagne, so I ordered the cheapest glass on the menu.

Tommy told me to stop being ridiculous, it was his treat and I should get the good stuff. I told him that it would be entirely wasted on me because I could never tell the difference. After some arguing, Tommy ordered the most expensive glass of champagne on the menu and paid the maître d $100 to go to the liquor store up the street and buy a bottle of Cook's. Scarlett blindfolded me with a napkin and I took a sip of each. As predicted, I couldn't tell the difference. In fact, I picked the Cook's. Tommy and Scarlett made so much fun of me that I insisted they take the test too. As it turns out, none of us could tell.

See, THAT was the world I belonged in. My old world with Tommy and Scarlett where everything made sense and no matter what was going on, whenever I went back to them things always seemed to snap into place. Andrew should be with Amelie, someone who he could relate to and who could give him more than I ever could. He was Andrew Bradford and she was Amelie L'Amour for God's sake. Of course he preferred her. How could I have let myself fall for this *again?!*

I needed some air. I made my way out into the lobby and walked towards the front door. Then, I heard a distinctly familiar voice shout from behind me.

"Thorne!"

I turned around. My heart stopped. I thought for sure I was hallucinating until he walked closer to me and I could see who it was for sure. It was Tommy, here, in Rome. In my hotel.

"Hi," he said timidly.

I stood in silence for thirty seconds.

Finally, I managed to ask, "What are you doing here?" Still shocked beyond belief and unable to process what was happening.

"I wrote you an email," he said, walking closer towards me. I backed away from him and he got the hint, halting in his tracks, "You never answered. I had to talk to you."

"How did you know where I was?" I asked, flabbergasted.

"I had a friend of mine at the census bureau call your mom," he admitted. It occurred to me that I had called my mom before I left and given her the name of the hotel where I would be staying in Rome. She always got nervous when I traveled and I knew it made her feel better when she knew exactly where I was. "I told him to tell her he was conducting the census and that he needed your number and this was the last known number listed. She told me you were in Rome and gave the name of the hotel where you were staying."

I had told her my cell phone wouldn't work in Italy, so she must have told him the name of the hotel so they could reach our room number. I scoffed. Of course Tommy would have some sort of connection. He always had one to get him anything he wanted.

"Listen, I understand why you wouldn't respond to my email. But, I want you to know that I've felt terrible about what happened ever since that night. I've thought about you every single day. I can't stand it that I hurt you like that."

That made me even angrier. He couldn't just waltz in here and apologize and expect everything to turn right back to normal. And if he felt so bad about how much he hurt me, then maybe he should have thought about that before his dirty ass hooked up with my best friend. Or sent me more than one email for God's sake.

"Look, I want to explain. Scarlett and I were drunk. She just threw herself at me. I was so shocked, I didn't know what to do."

If I was angry before, my blood was now at full boil.

"Oh, Tommy. I'm not fucking stupid. I was there. You two were all over each other. Plus, she told me this has been going on for years. I know all of those texts you got once we were together were booty calls from her and you went running every time."

Tommy stood in silence. He had no response for that one. Finally, he piped up.

"Look, if you give me a chance I promise, I will never do anything to hurt you ever again. You are the smartest, funniest, prettiest, and most genuine girl I know. I'm so, so sorry."

I closed my eyes as he took my cheek into his hand.

"If you give me another chance, I will never let you down again. We could be so happy together."

With that, I welled up and tears started rolling slowly down by cheek.

"I made a mistake, Thorne. I'll do anything."

I couldn't believe this was happening. The guy I loved for as long as I could remember had just flown across an ocean to beg me to be with him. I had pictured this moment a thousand times in my head (albeit without the backstory of betrayal). So many of my hours and days had been consumed by imagining what it would be like to be the girl who Tommy Alcott chose. I could have everything I'd ever wanted.

But then, I had a sudden moment of clarity. I thought about the person I was when I moved to London. Until that moment, standing there in the lobby looking at Tommy, I hadn't realized how much I'd changed since I'd been there. I wasn't the person I was back when I had wanted Tommy anymore. Since then, I'd learned so much about myself. I had my job and a project I was passionate about. I had Tibbie and Beatrice, who I knew would be there for me to show me a good time and have my back. Most importantly, I had the world at my fingertips.

A year ago, I never would have thought myself capable of quitting my job, dropping everything, and up and moving to a foreign country not knowing another single soul. But, here I was, living abroad, working my dream job, traveling the world, running around and having an awesome time with some of the best friends of my life, who I never would have known if I didn't have the courage to come here in the first place.

Once I was removed from the only microcosm I had known since I was ten, I saw how big the world is and right then I realized how much I had been wasting my time obsessed with Tommy. Let's say we had ended up together and gotten married. He probably would have cheated on me after we were heavily invested in each other's lives, had kids and shared assets, and everything would have been so much more messy and miserable. I was a different person now, and I just knew I deserved better than what Tommy could give me.

I realized how different Andrew was. I'd been being so stupid. I'd had a great guy in front of me this whole time and had been so scared he was like Tommy that I'd been pushing him away. In fact, Andrew and I did have a lot in common. We loved the same things. We bonded over Keats and all of our other shared interest, but our differences complimented each other. I deserved him and he deserved me. I needed to stop being such an insecure moron and get back to the gala and tell Andrew how much I cared about him.

I backed out of Tommy's reach.

"I think you should leave," I said conclusively.

He paused for a moment and looked at the floor.

"Emma, please," he said in such a desperate way that I barely recognized his voice. It was the first time since I'd known him that he had ever called me by my first name. It made my heart sting.

I looked at his desperate face. I had seen him play a hundred different games over the years. He knew every trick in the book to get women. I had personally witnessed him seducing girls in university classes, at bars, at events, at the grocery store. Hell, I had even seen him pick up a girl in the emergency room waiting area while he was waiting to be seen for a broken thumb. He knew exactly what they wanted to hear. But, this was the first time I had seen him at a loss for words. I could tell that he really, truly meant it this time.

I had flashbacks to some of my memories of him over the years. I realized with a newfound clarity that maybe the Tommy I always thought was the perfect guy wasn't exactly as great as my lovesick heart had made him out to be. Like the time we went out on his friend's boat during college and afterwards he ended up slinking off to a girl's apartment while I was left to sleep on the grungy floor of his friend's dorm room with a washcloth as a blanket. Or the time he left me by myself in Chicago to find my way to the apartment of one of his random friends so he could go hook up with a model he met at the bar, even though I told him repeatedly I had no idea where I was or how to get to Midtown.

I did feel sorry for him. People make mistakes; there is no denying that. Everyone has moments of weakness. When I looked back up at him at standing there, I still saw him as my Tommy. No matter what happened, I was who I was partly because of all of the time I spent with him. He would always be the person who had, at one point, mattered the most to me in the world. But, I had nothing for him anymore.

"I'm asking you to leave," I repeated.

He looked up again to stare me straight in the eye. "If that's what you really want."

"That's what I really want," I said, definitively.

He stayed silent for a moment before a look of defeat spread across his face.

"Well, good bye Thorne," he said, quietly.

"Good bye Tommy," I said, the finality of my words sinking in, and yet I didn't feel one ounce of regret.

I turned to head back towards the dining room without looking back. I couldn't wait to see Andrew looking gorgeous in that tux again and tell him how I felt. By the time I got back though, everyone had already withdrawn back to the ballroom to co-mingle once again over after-dinner drinks. I scanned the busy room for Andrew and saw him standing over in the corner by the staircase with a cordial in his hand. I smiled and started working my way towards him through the crowd.

I'd almost reached him when I saw that he was talking to Amelie. She leaned in towards him and took him by the hand. Then, she guided him underneath the stairwell.

The entrance to the kitchen was underneath the stairs, so there was a sheer curtain dividing the main room from the corridor to shield the catering trays and other 'unsightly' serving aspects from the refined guests. I could see them exchanging words behind it. Then, I saw the distinct silhouette of two lips touching. I stood, frozen in place, as the reality sunk in.

Goddammit, COME ON LIFE! This just HAD to happen again, didn't it??? My body filled with anger and I marched over, seeing red, ready to unleash on him the same level of rage I had when I finally lost it and snapped at Penelope and Valerie. I went to pull back the curtain when I heard him start to talk. Curious to hear him express his feelings for her and gather some ammunition before he had time to come up with some bullshit explanation, I stopped, made sure I backed up to the side of the staircase, out of sight, and listened in.

"What the hell are you doing, Amelie?" Andrew asked, sounding disgusted.

"Oh come on, Andrew," Amelie responded. I could hear the ice shift in her glass as she leaned in for another kiss.

"Amelie, don't be ridiculous. I'm with Emma now."

She laughed.

"Oh please Andrew, you can't be serious. I think it's great that you're trying to promote the image of people like us cavorting with poor, boring people. It's great for the charity, really. But no one's here to see you now. You can stop pretending."

"Oh, Amelie, come off it. She has more class in her pinky finger then you have in your entire, vile body. She's the smartest, most interesting, most beautiful person I've ever met. I love her."

I snapped up from my spying position. He loved me? That was the first time I'd ever heard him say that. I felt my heart swell as it started beating heavily in my chest. Shocked, I doubled back on my feet.

Then, I felt a large, hard object slam into my back. I whipped around to see one of the giant bronze vases wavering on its pedestal. I tried to catch it as it began tipping, but it was no use and it fell to the ground, its metal loudly clanking as it bounced around on the marble floor. The entire crowd became silent and stared over in my direction. I didn't know what to say so I just stood there, smiling and gave an awkward wave. Andrew drew back the curtain and looked down at the millions of pieced of the vase casualty before snapping his glance up towards me, looking stunned.

"Emma! Are you alright?"

He rushed over to where I was standing. Amelie emerged from behind the curtain and took in the scene, rolling her eyes as if I just proved her point. Which, I kind of had.

Andrew turned his gaze back towards Amelie before looking back at me.

"Oh my God, Emma, this isn't what it looks like," he said frantically.

Then, I felt the crowd around me disappear as I looked him in the eye and thought about what he had just said.

"I know, I heard everything," I admitted. "I love you too," I said, realizing that no matter how much I had thought I'd felt love in the past, I had never genuinely felt the emotion until right then.

I turned around and gave a nervous laugh.

"Um, sorry about that," I said to one of the hotel employees, meekly. Then, Andrew put his arm around me and we headed out of the fancy ballroom, on to what I knew was going to be the start of something great.

"And so live ever – or else swoon to death"

~ Sonnet by John Keats Written on a Blank Page in
Shakespeare's Poems, facing *'A Lover's Complaint'*

The next morning, Andrew and I headed out to take in some sights. As we walked down the beautiful streets of Rome, I took a deep breath, feeling so relieved. The weight I had felt on my shoulders had finally be lifted. My heart filled with happiness as stopped in the street and pulled him in for a kiss.

"I love you," I said, grinning up at him.

"I love you too," he responded, smiling back.

Then, I felt my phone buzz in my purse. I pulled it out and saw that I had one new email. When I opened it I saw a message with the subject line *Re.: Your Application to the Doctoral Program at Kings' College London.*

My chest clenched. I knew that there was no way it was a yes, but I still got the reflex feeling that had accompanied all of the brief moments before I knew I was about to find out something that could potentially change my life forever. Timidly, I hit the "read" button to pull up the message.

Dear Ms. Thorne,

Thank you for your interest in the English Literature Department at Kings College London. I have reviewed your project proposal and am pleased to offer you a research fellowship to enroll as a doctoral candidate. Should you choose to accept, please contact me via this email address to arrange a brief meeting and orientation.

Sincerely,

Dr. Catherine Bateman

I couldn't believe it. I never thought in a million years that Dr. Bateman would really read my proposal, much less seriously consider it. My mind went blank for a moment as I struggled to digest what had just happened.

"Are you alright Emma?" Andrew asked, sensing that something was off.

I cleared my throat. "Yeah," I replied, "Actually I'm great. I just got an email that Kings' College London accepted a project proposal I sent in. I've been invited to their PhD program." I should have sounded more enthusiastic than it came out, but I think my brain was still trying to catch up.

"That's fantastic!" he said, drawing me in for a huge hug.

This was a dream come true. I could stay living with Tibbie and have more adventures with her and Beatrice. Also, I could stay with Andrew. We could spend a lot more time together and our relationship would have a chance to grow. This would be incredible. I was so lucky.

A thought struck me that dampened my high spirits. What about my parents? I only had so many years with them and I always pictured myself living near them, having my mom's advice and my dad's supportive nature close by. I knew they would be sad that I wasn't coming home. I felt guilty and knew I had to call them right away.

I told Andrew I was going to call them and he said he would give me some privacy and walk around the Pantheon until I was finished. I dialed my parents' number and took a deep breath.

The phone clicked to signal someone had picked up. True to form, it took my mom a solid thirty seconds to acknowledge the fact that there was someone on the other end of the line.

"...Honey, please don't water that plant without adding the nutrient packet. Remember you did the same thing last summer and everything died. No, no, you don't have to spray it yourself... you put it on the end of the hose...yes, exactly. Then unlock the spray mechanism at the top... Hello?"

"Hi mom!" I said, happy to hear her voice.

"Oh, Emma sweetie! It's so lovely to hear from you! How are things? Are you coming home soon? I can't wait to see you!"

My stomach cringed with guilt.

"Well mom, that's why I'm calling. I got into the PhD program at Kings College. But, I'm torn because I'll miss you guys."

My mom didn't even hesitate. "Oh, Emma. That sounds like an amazing opportunity! Things like this don't come along that often. I hope your father and I have taught you that you can't let great things like this pass you by. If you want it, you have to take their offer. It's that simple."

I really was not expecting that.

"But mom..." I started.

"Don't you 'but mom' me lady, my word is final. Plus, you know your father could never live with himself if he thought you'd passed up that opportunity for him. Plus, guess what! Your father and I figured out the video chat! Your cousin wanted to call us from Bangkok, so we read your instructions and logged on. It's really actually super simple."

Were there not so many amazing things happening in this moment, I would have been annoyed that after a year of trying to get my parents to learn video chat, my cousin asked them once and they'd taken the effort to figure it out. Oh well. Focus Emma, focus.

"Thanks mom," I said, tearing up.

"Oh, honey, just take the opportunities as they come. Your father and I are fine. We know you'll keep in touch. We're just a plane ride away!" She faded off again, "...No, not that bush, Phil! You'll kill that bush! Emma, I'm sorry, I have to go. Your father is trying to sabotage the garden. Love you sweetie!"

With that, she hung up. I smiled and headed into the Pantheon to meet Andrew.

"Everything go alright?" he asked.

"Yes, everything is perfect," I said, beaming. He took his cheeks into my hand and gave me another long, soft kiss.

After strolling for some time, we ended up at the Trevi Fountain. I had forgotten how grand it was and how the sun reflecting off the marble making the statues sparkle in a way that seemed almost magical. We stopped in front of it. Andrew reached into his pocket and handed me a one Euro coin.

"Make a wish," he said, smiling.

I thought back to everything that had happened since I'd moved to London. The experience taught me more about myself than I had ever known before. Beatrice and Tibbie showed me what true friends really are and what it feels like to have people who truly care about you as much as you care about them, and you know without words that you are there for each other no matter what. It gave me a newfound perspective on what is real in life and the things that are worth hanging on to.

I learned what it's like to love what you do. I saw what it's like to have meaning in your job and look forward to going to work every morning. It dawned on me how few people really concentrate on doing what they love and how sad that is. Life is too damn short to get trapped in a job that society makes you feel like you're a loser if you walk away from it. Before, I would have always seen a liberal arts profession as either impossible or something that even if you achieved, could never sustain you. But, I had previously underestimated the power of confidence and determination. No matter what you set out to do, tenacity goes a long way. No matter how much other people try to bring you down, if you stick with it, your dreams can take you to some absolutely amazing places.

I learned what it's like to be one hundred percent okay completely by yourself.. I finally understood that you didn't NEED anyone else. You didn't have to wait around to find a day for someone to be able to accompany you to that musical you wanted to see or that museum you wanted to visit, you could just go. When you are completely comfortable conquering things on your own, it's only then that you can truly make room to let someone else in.

And finally, once I learned I would be happy by myself no matter what, it was then that I learned what it's like to truly love someone. When you find the right person, you can be one hundred percent yourself all of the time. Despite all of your quirks, breakdowns, bad hair days, embarrassing family members, etc., nothing can ever change the bond you have, just the two of you.

Even though I probably learned these lessons a lot later in life than most people my age, I wasn't ashamed of that. I realized that even though I felt like I wasted a lot of years in that terrible job, if I hadn't snapped and felt like I needed such a drastic change, I probably never would have come to London in the first place and had such an amazing experience.

You never know what life has in store for you. The best you can do is keep your eyes open, be smart, and don't ignore the signs that are right in front of you guiding you towards where you are meant to be. It dawned on me that this was life, this was growth. Just because you didn't end up exactly where you had pictured doesn't mean that you've failed. It's quite the opposite, really.

It means that you've carved yourself enough roads and learned so much about the surrounding terrain along the way that when you come to a large divergence that will take you to one of two entirely different paths, your heart and gut will be able to guide you far better than any map. D.C. had been my roots, which ultimately allowed me to sprout up into the sun; London was where I finally bloomed.

I took the coin and looked at it in my hand. I had an entirely different feeling than the last time I was here and thought about how far I had come since the last time I stood in this very spot. I grasped my hand around the coin and turned around so the fountain was behind me.

This time, instead of making a wish, I made a vow with myself to never dwell on my past, enjoy the present, and look forward to all of the possibilities of the future. Then, I thanked fate for making all of this happen. It had been a tough road, but it taught me that everything really does happen for a reason, and when you're feeling down, you just have to trust that life has a plan for you that will end up for the best in the end. I felt happy as I thought about all of the possibilities in the power of life and love. Then, I tossed the coin over my shoulder as I smiled, hearing the light splash as it hit the water.

It took some very hard lessons, but I finally realized that I could kill myself striving for perfection day after day, but it would be futile. Standing there in the beauty of Rome, where Keats is laid to rest, I thought of the ending to my paper. The narrative of Keats's letters and the parallel development of his poems are part of his intricately woven love story: pure, special, and beautiful. The letters Fanny wrote to him in Italy were buried with him, unopened. Her words, saved just for him, are a symbol of the incomparable bonds of eternal love and a reminder that if you love someone, tell them, before the chance fades away.

I know now that in fact, poetry isn't perfect at all; it's the exact opposite. There is no one way to interpret the words of a poem, just like there is never one right way of doing anything in life. And just like poetry, life and love are perfectly imperfect, but that's what makes them so profound and beautiful. I certainly don't have it all figured out, but now I know that uncertainty leads to growth. The truth is that life is always perfect in the way one sees it. We make the universe as much as the universe makes us, and we can't wait around for life to bring us all of the things we dream of. We must go out and seize them for ourselves. And so live ever, or else swoon to death.

Acknowledgements

There are so many people without whom this project never could have happened to which I owe a great deal of gratitude. You have all made this project evolve from something I started on a whim to become an actual reality. I can't thank you enough.

First and foremost, I'd like to thank Lydia Shamah, who believed in this project from the very beginning. Thank you for all of the hours you put into making this project better than I ever thought it could be. I learned so much from you and appreciate it more than you'll ever know. I'll carry your guidance and the lessons you taught me for the rest of my life and career.

I'd also like to thank all of my wonderful editors, Mom, Dad, Jill, Tom, Salya, Mandy, Sarah, Susie, Vanessa and everyone else who took the time to read my work. Thank you for all of the tough love and for constantly helping me improve!

Finally, to all of my family and friends for being so supportive and helping me hang in there when I felt like giving up. Thank you for giving me the motivation and belief in myself that I need to continue following my dreams. I love you all!

Made in the USA
Middletown, DE
11 December 2020